The Rise of the Sheildmaidens

DAVID PARKER-ROSS

TAIRIS ANDERS MEDIA, LLC

First Edition 2024

Also by David Parker-Ross

ALL TITLES AVAILABLE ON AUDIO

Perceptions – The Rise of Jenna Plural
Jenna Plural Wants You
That Girl from Wagga
Walking in Her Shadow
Awakening of Hannah Grant
The Angel of Phobos
Memoir of a Martian
Out of the Darkness
The Hand of Jenna
The Rings of Venus
The Cult of Artemis Baily
The Rise of Artemis: The Golden Age Edition

CHAPTER ONE

Last Day - The Lower Orders - Caryn

"Undoubtedly, my new father and mother were responsible for changing my fortunes. However, it was Esselar Rachael Abigail Maine who took it upon herself to fight for justice for all the people who once lived as I did. I wish my father had lived long enough to see the results of her work. He would have been so proud." – Memoir of a Marran Priestess by Emma Roark-Maine

"Hurry it up, Arthur. We have to get out of here now." Madeline Kurdow appeared more irritated than scared as her husband banged in the last planks of wood over the shuttered windows of The Fatted Calf.

"Shut your mouth, woman," Kurdow replied, his mouth holding on to the nails that he was using. There was no way he would leave the only means of income unprotected. He was certain the landlord would not stop charging him rent just because there was a war going on, and he needed to be up and running as soon as they could return to the city.

Caryn Kurdow was not paying attention to her grand-parents' bickering and looked out at the mass of people already on the road. She was surprised to notice that tall, handsome priest who had brought so much trouble to their establishment. He did not seem to notice her watching as he headed towards the north gate and she glanced over at her father banging in the final board. She sighed dejectedly, thinking how much safer it would be if she was with that strong fighting man rather than her pathetic old grandparents.

Her parents abandoned her with them long ago, unable to afford to support her. She had not been received willingly when she had been found on the steps of the Fatted Calf as a fait accompli. Her grandfather was not too happy about the situation and would have tossed her out on the street if he had his way. However, her grandmother, who had just a modicum more sense of responsibility than her grandfather, compelled him to keep her.

However, he insisted that she was to pay her way, and even though she was still a child, barely ten years of age, he began whoring her out to any depraved individual with coin. As she grew older, what he could charge became less since there was more competition for an adult whore. If none of the patrons of the Fatted Calf were interested in her, she was sent out on the street to find a client. She lost count of the number of men who had lain with her. It numbered into the hundreds, but for her, it was all very normal, for that was her life.

Beyond that, her grandparents never paid her any attention. The only time she ever got any sort of kindly affection was from the more compassionate clients. As a result, her low self-esteem was only boosted by what she believed she could do for a man in a bedroom or an alleyway.

She had indeed enjoyed watching that fat slob Bristow start a fight with the preacher. It was all about her, and she relished whatever attention she could get without spreading her knees. However, seeing how easily the handsome Illyan had dispatched Bristow, her heart went all flutter until the subsequent humiliation became what she typically was accustomed to expecting. Maybe if Sebastian had known her history, he would have looked at her less unkindly, but that was history itself now, and as he disappeared into the crowd, she incorrectly believed it would be the last time she ever saw him.

Arthur Kurdow tossed the hammer into the back of the cart and looked at what was loaded up with a sigh. It was the sum of his life, and it wasn't much. "Stop your daydreaming and get into the cart," he snapped at his granddaughter, bringing her immediately out of her thoughts. With a sigh, she climbed into the back as her grandparents climbed into the more comfortable seats at the front. As Kurdow whipped up their half-starved horse, she stared out of the plumes of smoke on the horizon. She did not quite have her far grandfather's confidence that they would be back. She would indeed see the Fatted Calf again, but it would not be for many years, and it would be alongside someone she never imagined she would ever have been friends with.

For now, she said goodbye to the only place she knew as home, as it disappeared when her grandfather turned the horse into another road. She laid back on some sacking and closed her eyes, but it was only momentarily because there was suddenly a jerk of the cart as it bounced down sharply and came back up.

Her eyes shot open, and her grandfather reined in the horse and turned back to look. "Don't stop, you idiot," a man cried, and Caryn found herself staring up into the face of George Bristow as he hissed at her grandfather. She had not seen him since that night in the Fatted Calf when the preacher squarely beat him.

Her grandfather shouted back, "Get out! You brought me nuffing but trouble. The bloody city guard came in every bleedin' night looking for you for two weeks. By the end, I didn't 'ave a single customer in me 'ouse."

"Don't test me, old man," Bristow snarled as he sat next to Caryn. "Those bastards have been 'unting me ever since that night. You're gonna get me out of this city."

"No, I am not," Kurdow snapped back at him. "I ain't gonna do no rope dance for aiding a wanted man."

It occurred to neither of them that no one would have been in the slightest bit interested in Bristow at this moment, what with everything that was going on. Neither Bristow nor Kurdow were particularly educated, and survival instincts ran strong within them. Bristow swiftly drew a blade from his belt and grabbed Caryn by the hair, causing her to cry out. He held her head down onto his lap and placed the knife under her jaw.

"Do as I say, old man or your little 'ore gets it."

Kurdow looked more irritated than afraid and simply shrugged. "Go ahead. One less mouf to feed."

Caryn sobbed silently and closed her eyes, part of her wishing that he would just go ahead and do it. Her grandmother, however, turned on her husband. "Arthur!" she exclaimed indignantly at him.

"No, not this time, Maddy. I am not risking me life for you or 'im or anyone." He looked back at Bristow. "Go on, get out. Take her with you if you must."

Bristow angrily muttered curses and roughly pushed Caryn off him, and she lay in a heap at the bottom of the cart. She closed her eyes and did not see the fat man, who was exceedingly rough with her in the bedroom, jump up to the front of the cart, grab her grandfather by the hair, and pull his head back. The knife made quick work of Kurdow's throat, and he didn't even respond as the life drained from him, and his assailant pushed him out of his seat and onto the dirty road of Jilrir. His body would lie for days until it was burned in one of the mass fires of the enemy.

Madeline screamed hysterically as Bristow took his victim's seat and pulled up the reins. He did not even look at Caryn's grandmother as he roughly shoved her out of the cart, and she fell onto the road. He whipped up the horse, and slowly, it began its way down the road. In the back, Caryn sat up and watched as her grandmother ran, wailing, up to her husband's lifeless body.

She pondered jumping off the back of the cart and going to her, but what would be the point? It would be the last time she ever saw her, and she was unlikely to have survived Last Day.

Caryn turned to look at Bristow's slouched back. It did not really register with her that he had just killed her grandfather and abandoned her grandmother. She was afraid, very afraid, but she certainly did not want to be alone. She had never been alone and without a continuous string of men in her life, albeit for only thirty minutes at a time. To say she felt safe with Bristow would not be quite correct. She felt more unsafe without him. He started to mutter curses, and the cart slowed down as they reached the North, East, West, and South crossroads. People were coming in from all different directions, which caused a massive jam in the city's center.

As he ground to a halt, she looked across the way to a young woman looking quite regal on the top of a horse with a child of around twelve sitting behind her. They were amid the crowd. The child was whacking the people with her riding crop. In front of her was a man who rode with a small, rough-looking boy sitting behind who was looking ahead, most concerned of the crowd. A third and final horse bore an older woman with white hair and a terrified-looking girl clinging to her back. Caryn wondered who they were in their fancy expensive clothes.

She was completely surprised when they dismounted the beasts and disappeared to the crowds as people started the fight over the steeds. She tried to make them out amidst the mass of people, but suddenly, people were clambering onto her cart. She turned about to see that Bristow had jumped down and was now heading north on foot. She pushed a young man out of her way who was climbing in front of her and jumped down, hurrying after him, desperate not to lose him in the crowd. She managed to push her way through and grabbed the back of his coat.

This startled him, and he spun around and growled, "Oh, I forgot about you."

"Please, George, don't leave me here," she said imploringly.

"Bah," he sneered, slapping her hand off him, and he turned away.

"Please, George, don't leave me here," she repeated tearily.

He glanced back over his shoulder and sighed. "Well, you better keep up. I won't wait for you, and I won't be coming back for you if you get lost."

She gripped his coat once more as he pushed through the crowds. After crossing the West to East roads, the crowds began to thin a little bit, giving them more room. She managed to step beside him and hold on to his arm like a lady and a gentleman taking an afternoon stroll after supper. However, it was not long before the crowd began to thicken again. "Marran's beard!" Bristow said angrily, and Caryn was sure she heard a little fear in his voice. "The bloody gate is closed." He joined in the shouts and jeers at the city guard, who, unbeknown to any of them, were following the orders of Ronan Maine, who lay dead back in the Great House.

Suddenly, Caryn felt someone bump into her back, causing her to lurch forward and almost fall down. However, the person who hit her grabbed her to steady her. She looked up into the face of the woman she had seen on the horse. She could not help but notice her delicate features and soft and smooth skin, save for the furrowed brow of concern.

"I'm so sorry," the woman said. "I can get the gates opened if I could just get through."

Caryn moved to one side, closer to Bristow, allowing her to pass. And she watched as the woman continued to push her way through the crowd. Of course, Caryn had no idea who she was, but she had been struck by her beauty and the opulence of her fine handmade riding outfit. Oh, how life could have been different had she been born elsewhere. She did not have a chance to continue looking because upon seeing the woman managing to make her way through the crowds, Bristow became more determined and more violent, shoving people out of his way with both hands as he moved on. She clung to the back of his coat, desperate not to lose him. She saw the woman again when they were near the front talking to the soldiers. She was clearly a woman of power and influence. The guards responded to her every word, and the shout went up, "Open the gate. Open the gate." Cheers of excitement rang out, and Caryn was carried along with the surge as the masses began to head out of the city. Just before she went through the gate, she looked up to the wall and saw the woman standing there on the top, looking back into the city in deep concern. She now had the man with the ragged boy she had seen standing at her side. As she was pushed through the gate, the woman disappeared from her view. However, it would not be the last time she saw Rebecca Maine, First Lady of Jilrir.

Caryn Kurdow, in all her sixteen years in this world, had never once set foot outside the city of Jilrir. She had never been up on the wall and looked out of the city. She had never even seen grass beyond what lay around the graves of the little cemetery on Church Street just outside the Marran Temple. The vast expanse of green fields that now lay before her seemed to go on forever, and the long, straight Nethili Road filled her with dread. She had never seen such an open space before.

She suddenly realized she had let go of Bristow and looking around, she could not see him. Panic started to well up within her as her eyes searched the crowd of people heading north and speeding up as the sounds of the battle behind them grew louder. Finally, her eyes alighted upon him, and her heart skipped with joy as she realized he had stopped going ahead and was looking back toward her. He was trying to find her. She was sure of it. It never occurred to her that he was looking at the rising plumes of smoke in the city in despair. He had had a relatively good life for someone of his class. A nice little criminal syndicate selling untaxed liquor and the occasional bounty of smuggled luxury items. Most of all, he would miss the street whores that would pay him a cut in either cash or services to avoid getting a beating from one of his men. Those little shits had abandoned him once the city guard was out to get his blood.

His little empire fell apart when that bastard preacher came into his life. He longed for the opportunity to be alone with him once more and make him pay for what he had done. He noticed Caryn standing in front of him with a beaming smile. He scowled at her with contempt and slapped her around the head. It hurt, but no more than any of the other past strikes she had received from men. As he turned away, she favored the red mark upon her face, but she smiled once more and followed him as he set off along the Nethili Road with the other refugees. He was a knight in shining armor, and he was going to protect her in this strange new world. She glanced back at the city and the smoking plumes in the distance. Turning away, she trotted up and walked just behind him.

They had escaped Jilrir.

CHAPTER TWO

The Servant of Racknu

"I still find it hard to believe Alannah Maine was related to Rachael, Breanna, and my mother. Her cold, ruthless heart of ice did not bear one ounce of the compassion her sisters carried." – Memoir of a Marran Priestess by Emma Roark-Maine

It was the dead of night over Boddington's Farm when Alannah Maine was abruptly woken with a hand over her mouth. She automatically clawed it with long fingernails and stared up into the darkness. Her attacker gave a stifled cry of pain, and she instantly recognized the voice. She stopped resisting, and the hand was lifted from her, and the woman hissed quietly, "Keep your mouth shut, idiot child. Get up. Get dressed and meet me outside."

And with that, Annabelle Devin disappeared back out of the bedroom door.

Alannah sat up and managed to make out the sleeping forms of her sisters, Rachael and Breanna. Rachael was snoring lightly as the youngest Maine pulled on her clothing very quietly. As she started to make her way to the door, Breanna said something unintelligible, and Alannah froze in place, looking back at her. However, Breanna turned over and was clearly having some sort of vivid dream.

Outside, her aunt stood on the porch, leaning against the rail as she stared out across the fields. "Why on earth are you getting me up at this ungodly hour?" the child said to her curtly.

"Oh, be quiet, you stupid girl," Devin hissed at her. "Sebastian will no doubt have a guard on duty, and I'd rather no one saw us together too much."

"Personally, I don't care what that dumb preacher thinks," Alannah snorted. "He's only alive because I don't have anyone to hang him for the murder of my brother."

Devin spun upon her and grabbed her by her hair, which no longer sported the fine ringlets it had back in Jilrir. Indeed, she looked worse than any of them, having gone through the sewage in their escape from the city. The only one who had any skill in styling hair was Petra, and Alannah would die in hell before she ever asked a favor of the whore's daughter. "Listen to me, you little mental defective," Devin snarled. "The dumb preacher, as you call him, is not as dumb as you think. He is our only hope of getting to safety. If you want to come out of this alive, then you will show him both respect and adoration, just like your sycophantic sisters do. Do you understand me, you little dung beetle?"

If there was one person Alannah hated more than Sebastian Hawk, and it was Aunt Annabelle. However, despite the abuse, she was the only one who appeared to be on her side now. She would tolerate it for now. "I understand, Auntie," she rasped out, wincing under the pain.

Devin released her, and as if nothing had happened, she smiled at the child sweetly. "Come on. We have to go a long way around the house. The menfolk are in the barn, and that's probably where Sebastian has his spy watching out."

However, as the pair slipped around to the back of the house, Devin turned out to be quite wrong.

Sebastian wished that just he and Carter could remain on guard throughout the night, but obviously, both needed sleep. Thus, it was with great reluctance that he compelled Oliver Portkind to at least take a couple of hours of watch duty. Of course, Oliver was most put out at this idea and found it completely unacceptable. Still, his fear of the preacher was such that he did not put up any argument. He begrudgingly got up when Carter woke him in the middle of the night to take over his shift.

However, he decided to walk around the property rather than stand in the barn doorway for two hours, as Sebastian and Carter had done. He really didn't expect to encounter anyone. The whole thing was a complete waste of his time. He had no idea why his mistress put so much faith in that jumped-up priest. Especially since the first family was Marran, and he was a damn Illyan.

It was in a sullen mood that he walked around the grounds, not venturing too far away from the farmhouse. His hands were sunk deep into his pockets, something he would never do if other people were around, as it was most impolite. Of course, that preacher did it all the time. Uncultured swine that he was.

He was at the back of the house and was just coming around the corner as Devin came in the opposite direction. They almost bumped into each other, and although it was dark, they were close enough to see into each other's eyes. He did not have a chance to respond as Devin immediately grabbed him by the collar and pushed him quietly up against the wall.

Oliver had worked with her over the years and found her quite intimidating, especially when Rebecca was not around. She held him in place with her body pushed up against his, and he could even feel her breath upon his face. To say he was shocked would be an understatement. Such close contact was wholly inappropriate, but he found himself unable to speak as he saw the viciousness in her expression.

"Oh dear, dear Oliver." Her voice was soft and quiet yet filled with malice. "I thought your interference with my activities was done."

"I... I... I..," he stammered, unable to get the words out. They had crossed paths before. For all his failings, Rebecca was correct when she told Sebastian what an excellent clerk he was. He was a stickler for detail, and he had come across what he would call 'irregularities' in Lady Devin's accounts. However, before he could take those to his mistress, Devin had found out and made it quite clear that discussing her doings with the First Lady would not be in his best interests. In fact, although she had not said it in as many words, it was clearly implied that his life would be at an end. So, just like Melody, he chose to ignore it. The second thing he was excellent at was self-preservation.

As he looked into those piercing eyes that bore nothing but hatred for him, he wondered if his days were done. "Keep your noise down, Oliver." She hissed and pushed herself harder against him as she became aware of his discomfort at her proximity. A cruel smile crossed her face as she felt him becoming aroused by her body up against his. "Oh, what's this, Oliver?" she reached between his legs and grabbed his crotch. "I wonder what Lady Rebecca would say when I tell her about these sexual advances against me."

He looked horrified at the suggestion but still could not find words to speak as she gently caressed his growing erection through his trousers. She was quite frustrated. Not having that idiot boy Ronan on tap to satiate her whims, desires, and many perversions was most vexing. As she silently continued to caress the terrified Portkind, she found memories of her times with Sebastian. Now, there was a lover and no mistake. He was rough and hard and frequently took her against her will, which she enjoyed more than anything. Oh, how she missed the aptly named Bastard of Jilrir. She stopped moving her hand as she noticed the child at her side looking on in disgust. She had almost forgotten she was there.

She sighed as she looked back at Rebecca's chief clerk. "I'm going to do something, Oliver." Her voice was now syrup. "If you cry out, it will be the last thing you ever do. Do you understand me, Oliver?"

He simply nodded slowly, terrified of what was to come next. Surely, it wasn't worse than the humiliation he was now going through. He was certainly not attracted to this foul woman. But he was a man who did not exactly have great success with the ladies. He did occasionally slip away from the Great House to spend an afternoon in an inn called the Fatted Calf with the young whore that resided there. But apart from that, there was no other woman in his life unless one counted his mistress, Rebecca, who secretly loved and adored. He had requested the hand of Breanna, but that had only been to secure himself a place in a family he felt he deserved to be part of.

No, his reaction to Devin's proximity was nothing more than a natural response to her touch. Devin slowly and carefully ran her hand down his arousal almost lovingly until she cupped his testicles through his garments. His eyes widened momentarily as he realized what she was about to do, and her grin widened. She suddenly squeezed her fist tight, and excruciating pain went through his body. The desire to scream was almost insurmountable, but his fear of her was so great that it even overcame that. He bit down hard on his lip, so hard as he struggled not to cry out at that as he drew blood. As she released him, he fell to his knees and doubled over, clutching at himself with his forehead on the wooden decking that went around the house. He did not know how long he remained in that position, his eyes tightly closed, hearing nothing and feeling nothing but pain. When he was finally able to raise his head, something surprised him. In front of him were Devin's expensive boots neatly tide up and just inches from his face, but it was not all he saw, for at her side was a smaller pair of exquisitely made boots of such a fine design that they could only belong to one person that he knew of. He raised his head higher and looked up into the face of Alannah Maine, who was staring at him with a most amused expression. "Milady." The word came out as more of a rush of air than an audible word.

"Don't talk to her, Oliver," Devin said quietly. "In fact, you can't even see her. You never saw her, and you never saw me. Do you understand me, Oliver?"

He did not respond and just fell onto his side, still clutching himself. Devin sighed. She raised her eyes heavenward and shook her head, then placed her boot on the side of his head, pushing down just enough to be uncomfortable. She had no intention of leaving a mark on his face and raising questions. "When I ask you a question, I expect an answer, Oliver."

"Why don't you just kill him?" Alannah whispered haughtily, impatiently waiting to find out why she was out in the dark when she could be in a nice, warm bed.

Devin sighed and looked at her. "Don't be so mentally deficient, girl. What do you think Rebecca and the preacher will say if he turns up dead or missing."

Alannah was affronted by the way she was spoken to. But she remained silent as her aunt turned her attention back to the man, who was now sobbing quietly. "If the preacher, Rebecca, or anyone finds out that you saw us tonight, you know what I would do, don't you, Oliver?"

He did not, but he could imagine.

Devin lifted her foot from his head and stepped back. "Enjoy the rest of your night, Mr. Portkind."

Portkind let out a sigh of relief as he saw the two sets of boots disappear and walk out of his view. He was certainly never going to speak of this.

"I really do not appreciate the way you talk to me in front of the help, auntie," Alannah said indignantly once they had moved far enough away from the man who still lay motionless behind them.

Devin simply snorted. "Why should you care what that insignificant imbecile thinks of you? Are you truly of such a low value that his opinion matters?"

She had a good point, and at those words, Alannah relaxed, and her anger dissipated. "Why have you brought me out here?" she said as her aunt led her into a small barn.

"If you are to follow in your mother's footsteps, you need to be trained in the ways of Racknu," Devin said as casually as if she was telling Alannah that she was about to teach her to bake scones.

Alannah stopped and stared up at her open mouth. "You are expecting me to follow the God of Death?"

"Your mother did, and that is what she would have wanted from you," Devin said proudly.

"You are expecting me to become a necromancer like you?" Alannah stated indignantly

"And what is wrong with that, may I ask?" Devin glared back at her.

Everything! Thought Alannah, who was raised to believe necromancy was evil, as did most of society. "Necromancy is considered a form of witchcraft. It could get one burnt at the stake. Personally, I like my body to be flame-free."

"Oh, foolish girl," Devin said. She turned away and started to walk around the barn as if looking for something. "What is right and wrong is defined by who's in charge. People maintain power by putting down those who oppose them. I think the true evil is people like Sebastian and his Illyan slut. What could be more evil than judging others and preventing them from reaching their potential? Humanity only progresses when its potential is unleashed, and the most powerful get to rise above the others." She stopped as she saw what she was looking for and bent down behind a bale of hay to grab it. However, there was a sudden hiss at Devin, who pulled her hand back with a cry. She clasped it, and a trickle of blood ran down it. "Alannah, come get this little bastard."

Alannah stepped around the bale and looked down at a small black and white cat that had its hackles up and was glaring at her aunt. She crouched down on her haunches and put her fingers towards the animal, speaking softly. "Here, puss puss, come on." The cat's hackles slowly descended, and it looked at Alannah uneasily. The girl waited patiently and eventually came and sniffed her hand. With her other, she gently reached around it and picked it up, and it settled in her arms as she turned with a smile to her aunt.

Her aunt scowled then suddenly reached out, grabbed the cat by the scruff of the neck, pulled it out of her arms, and with a quick twist, the animal's neck was broken and hung limply dead in her hands. This even startled the ruthless Alannah, who actually had quite a fondness for cats, rabbits, and other fluffy things. "Why did you do that?" She snapped.

"You are worried about a cat?" Devin said, tossed the creature on the floor, and sat down in front of it. "If this is how you react, what will you be like when we kill Rebecca or Rachael?

"That's completely different," Alannah said hotly. "The cat isn't in my way."

Devin rolled her eyes at her and indicated the area on the other side of the cat. "Just sit down over there."

Alannah chose not to sit, but she got down on her knees and sat back on her haunches. She watched as her aunt ran her hand over the space above the dead cat. "Raknu, my Lord," she said in a low, deep voice. "Give me back this beast so that I can show this welp the power and the privilege of following you."

Alannah was expecting some sort of spectacle. A glow or a flash of light, but what happened was the cat simply jumped up and scampered away as fast as it could into the night.

"You brought it back to life!" Alannah stared open-mouthed into the darkness of the barn's entrance, where the cat disappeared.

Devin chuckled, "Oh no, little one, nothing can bring something back to life. Once it's dead, it's dead. I merely reanimated that creature. It has no intelligence and will act purely on instinct programmed into a brain that no longer has any self-awareness. It will appear to be alive. No one will be able to tell the difference because a cat will act like a cat."

"Can you do that to people?" Then she realized something. She said excitedly, "Could you bring back Ronan?"

"Yes, but it would be obvious. As I said, there is no intelligence and no self-awareness. The body would be in a vegetative state. It could walk around and touch things, but there will be no understanding. Of course, I can control it if I were to add that request to my incantation. I could order that cat to catch a mouse, and it would do it and continue trying to do it forever until you told it to stop or it caught the mouse. No, your stupid brother did not have much of a brain to begin with, and if I was to restore him, he'd have none at all."

"Yet, I hear stories that the preacher was risen from the dead."

"Foolishness. I just told you it cannot be done," Devin snapped impatiently.

"So what's the bloody point," Alannah said indignantly. Devin did not like her tone and gave her a quick slap about the head.

"Oh, save me. I thought you had more brains than that brother of yours," she sighed wearily, stretched out her arms behind her, and rested upon the palms of her hands. "Imagine you're in a battle, and you're losing. Imagine being able to bring your dead warriors back with the command to continue to fight. You will have an immortal army that cannot be killed, and the only way to stop it would be to hack the body to pieces. But this is just a taste, young Alannah. In time, I hope to make you as good as me or even as good as your mother, beside whom I freely admit I pale. There is no greater power than the power of life and death. Are you willing to learn? Are you willing to take that road that would make you unstoppable?"

There was a long pause as Alannah stared at her. Then she pointed towards the door to indicate the cat and said softly, "Teach me how to do that, Auntie."

Devin smiled softly and began to teach her new apprentice.

CHAPTER THREE

Boddington's Farm

"I do not recall much about our time at that little farm outside Jilrir. I was around nine at the time, but I do recall I was immensely happy. I was with my beloved father and taken into the Maines' hearts without reservation. It was also when I became close to my own sister Keri." – Memoir of a Marran Priestess by Emma Roark-Maine

"You know, Rachael," Breanna Maine said dreamily, "I could live on a farm like this." It had been several days since they had escaped Jilrir, and the two sisters had come out to escape the constant bickering about what they would do next. Breanna was lying back in the grass, her hands behind her head, eyes closed, and a long grass stalk protruding from her mouth. In contrast, her sister sat beside her, hugging her knees to her chest as she looked out over the fields and the wild plains.

"You will soon get bored," Rachael chuckled. "And it would be a different situation if we were working the farm."

"I want a passel of swine. I'd make a good swine herder," Bree announced casually.

"Ew. No thanks, swinelets are fine, but not the big dirty ones snuffling in mud." Rachael wrinkled her nose, causing her to have to push her spectacles back in place.

Bree was about to reply when the distant sound of a door being slammed made her sit up on her elbows and look around. A hundred or so yards away, Rebecca Maine was storming out of the farmhouse in a fearsome mood. "And there she goes again," Bree sighed. "Wonder what it is this time."

"Rebecca wants to go to Aranar and reestablish the House of Maine. Jenri thinks it's too dangerous to cross the mountains, and Sebastian says we can't go anywhere since 'Becks lost what supplies we had with the horses back in Jilrir.

"How can you know..." Bree started but realized her answer. "Does he tell you everything through that Bond thing?"

"Not really, but as the Bond grows stronger, it's harder to close off his surface thoughts."

"I better start being careful about what I say around you."

"Only if you do not trust Sebastian or me," Rachael said, quite hurt by the idea.

"I was only joking, you mutton head, Marran's beard, can't you take a joke?" Yet Bree knew she had not been joking. The recent reassurances Rachael had given her about their relationship had begun to fade. She had tried to read the Book of Illya to impress Sebastian, but it was filled with words she did not understand, and she was too prideful to ask for help.

"Are you two going to just sit there all day?" Rebecca had seen them and was shouting as she headed toward the pair.

"Hey! Just because you are pissed at the preacher does not mean you can take it out on us." Bree scowled.

Rebecca stopped beside them and, placing her hands on her hips like an aggravated mother, said, "How did you...." She stopped, and her eyes moved from Bree to Rachael, "You can knock that off, Rachael Maine. You should not be listening in to private conversations."

Rachael's eyes widened. "I can't help it," she said, nonplussed.

"Sebastian should never have made you join his church," Rebecca snapped.

Rachael grew angry. It rarely ever happened, but her sister just crossed a line. She stood up and turned to face Rebecca, "First of all, Rebecca Maine, it is not 'his' church. It is Illya's, got that?" She continued, not waiting for a reply, "Secondly, no one made me do anything. Illya called me, and I answered. Thirdly, Rebecca Maine, it is none of your damned business, and, to use Breanna's more colorful vernacular, you can fuck off."

"Woohoo, you tell her, Rach." Bree grinned, but Rachael spun on her.

"You can shut up, too. I am tired of you making me feel guilty for the greatest thing that has ever happened in my entire life. I am Feffer Rachael Maine, and it's finally a title

I earned and can be proud of." With that, she turned upon her heel and stormed off towards the house.

Bree looked at Rebecca, somewhat dazed, and both could not help but grin, "Come out of her shell a bit, has our Rachael," Rebecca said, looking after her sister as she entered the farmhouse.

"Yes," Bree said with a grin. "She is scary."

Rebecca sighed softly, slowly shaking her head, "Come on, breakfast is ready."

Sebastian ate breakfast with the other men in the barn that morning. He heard the altercation between his acolyte and her sisters through their mysterious holy bond. While he was proud of how she stood up for herself, he was mad at Rebecca for what she had said to her. Emma had brought out a small hot cauldron of rabbit stew. He was sullen and spoke very little. Carter knew better than to disturb him. Portkind was clearly afraid of him, and Daniel was simply content to get a hot meal. He looked out of the open door and saw Devin passing by in the distance; it certainly did not improve his mood. There would be a reckoning between him and the necromancer eventually. He regretted his hasty promise not to reveal her true nature when they reunited in Jilrir. He just knew that would come back to haunt him. He had owed her, and he was caught up in his adoption of Emma and had been too hasty.

As she moved from sight, he looked down at his stew and ate silently until there was a knock on the outside wall. The barn had no door, so Rebecca Maine coughed and waited by the front entrance until Sebastian, swallowing the last of his stew, beckoned her in. "Good morning, gentlemen," she said, addressing the others. Automatically, both Carter and Daniel jumped to their feet. Rebecca smiled at them, "I think we can dispense with the formalities, boys." Then, with a knowing smile, she added, "At least for now."

"What can I do for you, milady?" Sebastian asked, tossing his empty bowl down beside him. He did not want to speak with her but knew she would insist until she did.

"We must stop debating and decide what we will do now and where we go from here," she said, sitting on a hay bale beside him.

"It's quite academic, really." He shrugged noncommittally. "The farm supplies Axle left for us will barely last us three more days. We do not have the right clothes for crossing the mountain passes and may need other equipment depending on the weather up there."

"Can you not hunt?" Rebecca asked.

Sebastian laughed at this idea, "No! Can you?"

"But you were in the army." Rebecca frowned, clearly not comprehending this.

"Yes, which was followed by the quartermaster's regiment comprising of supplies, cooks, and washerwomen."

"You have a carbine? If you can shoot a man, you can shoot a deer," she said irritably.

Sebastian snorted, "Those rounds have to be individually handmade. They do not fall off trees. I only have a finite amount, and we will surely need them."

"Well," Carter stepped over to them. "If I had a bow, I could hunt, but I lost mine on that damn...." He paused and looked horrified with himself, "Pardon my language."

She waved his apology away. "Go on, Captain Carter."

"Well, milady, I lost it on the horse, but if I could get another, then we would be quid's in, for I am a dab hand at archery if I do say so myself."

"Could we make one?" she asked him.

It was Sebastian who replied. "No, that is the job of a skilled artisan," he stated.

"So, the only real option is to head for the town of Nethili and purchase provisions?" Rebecca sighed.

"What with? My good looks?" Sebastian said a little more sarcastically than he intended. "I never got paid my last week in Jilrir, and apart from a few sivs, I'm broke."

Displaying equal sarcasm, she shot back, "I am sure you will find many men willing to pay to get those big blue eyes in their bed, Sebastian, but let's leave that as a last resort."

Sebastian laughed and slapped his leg, "Touché, Rebecca. However, we do need money."

"Sebastian, did that rain wash your brains out? Nethili is still within Ithia, and my family has property there. Technically, I am acting Baroness."

"Forgive me for correcting you, my lady," Portkind said uneasily, looking at Sebastian nervously. "Technically, you are not."

She shot him a cold glare. "Explain?"

"You cannot hold that position until the King approves it," Portind stated.

"Nonsense, my father assumed authority immediately upon my grandfather's death." Rebecca glared at him as if he was to blame for any of these issues.

Portkind looked like he was about to back down, but Sebastian interceded, "Spit it out, man."

"Well, with all due respect, milady, there was one major difference between you and your father."

He hesitated, but unlike Rebecca, it clicked in Sebastian's head at once, and the Preacher looked at her. "Your father was a man."

"Precisely so," Portkind backed him up.

"So, the king could choose someone over me?" Rebecca frowned, horrified, "He could hand it to Petra or Rachael?"

"Well, it is more complicated than that. Lady Petra is not in the line of succession. She was when Baron Claudius stated it be so and held the title Second Lady of Jilrir, but the fact she is his ba...." At a start from Sebastian, Portkind rephrased, "She is of a non-legitimate line as in she is not the daughter of Cassandra Maine, the Baron's lawful wife."

"She bares no title now?" Sebastian scowled at the injustice.

"Yes, she is still technically a named heir, but it is up to the king or new baron to continue to recognize her father's intentions. However, with no living male Maine, he may declare it to be a defunct house and award the lands and property of The House of Maine to some cousin or other."

"But they own this land," Sebastian protested.

"We do not," Rebecca said in frustration, "We consider ourselves owners, but we are no more than tenants managing the king's land."

"It is how feudalism works, Kirkman Hawk," Portkind pointed out.

Sebastian brushed it away with a wave of his hand. "This can all be sorted out by the bureaucrats in Aranar. We need to get back to here and now."

"Am I still First Lady of Jilrir?" She looked to Portkind. He nodded. "Until the king rules on this, then yes, you are."

"We are at war, Rebecca," Sebastian said dejectedly. "War stretches loyalty to the limit. Nethili and Ternal are the nearest in line for the next assault. Jilrir and the baron are gone, so as far as many will be concerned, there are no rulers in Ithia now."

"Well, they will not be looking for me, old man," Carter put in. "You can camp outside the town while I go in and get what we need."

"We have no coin, Carter," Sebastian said irritably. "Unless you plan to rob a jewelry merchant while there."

"Jewelry." Rebecca jumped up so fast that everyone was startled. She reached inside her dress and pulled out what looked like a thin, shining chain. She turned away from them and lifted her hair with her other hand. "Would one of you unfasten this, please?" Carter moved in so quickly and eagerly that Sebastian could not hide a grin from his friend, who blushed slightly. The necklace came away in his hand, and he turned and handed it to Sebastian. It was not a chain but a necklace of small, alternating diamonds and emeralds. "That is worth a small fortune." She grinned, not noticing Carter's heavy breathing. "Sell it, and you could buy Nethili." Sebastian noticed Keri and Emma in the doorway, beckoning Daniel to come out. Sebastian smiled and nodded to the Marran priestess as she indicated she did not wish to disturb them. Daniel ran out to her most eagerly.

"You won't get a fair price in Nethili," Sebastian said, handing the necklace to Carter. "That thing needs to be in a fine jeweler's or an auction house. Nothing like that in that town."

Rebecca shrugged, "Enough to get our provisions for the trip should suffice."

Sebastian wasn't sure, "I know Nethili is over a day away, but it is still too close to Jilrir for my liking." He sighed but sat up and decided, "Here is what we should do. We continue north past Ternal, and when we get between the mountain pass and Nethili, we decide then. Though without supplies, I think we will have no alternative than to risk a venture into the town."

Petrana Louise Maine felt her heart racing when she learned from Rachael that Sebastian and Rebecca were considering going to Nethili. She had been born there, and while she lived in poverty for the first nine years, the memories were still happy. Her two older brothers had doted on her, and there was more than one broken heart when Aaron Karl had come in the night and collected her at her father's insistence. She had been Petunia May Greene, but her father did not like the name. So, as she said goodbye to not only the only family she knew but also her very identity. She did not mind being called Petrana. It was the Maine part she could live without. She did not even have an issue with most of her baronial family. Rachael and Breanna truly were sisters to her. Rebecca was more like a starchy maiden aunt.

However, Ronan Claudius Maine and his spiteful bitch sister Alannah had made her life pure hell. She had no good memories of Jilrir. Well, maybe that was not entirely true. Harrison Feyer had been her knight in shining armor for nearly a year. Their secret meetings were wonderful, and she had shared her first kiss with the handsome young guard in his smart uniform. Alas, she felt guilt whenever she thought of him. Not because of his death. After hearing Rachael's full story about their escape from the city, she realized he would have done the same even if she had not been involved with him. He gave his life to save three young girls and kept an oath to a man who had saved him. No, Harrison Feyer died a hero. Her guilt, however, was in realizing how she felt about him. She had convinced herself she was in love with him, but it was only when she met someone else that she knew that she had unknowingly fooled not only him but herself.

Sebastian.

She could barely think of him without her heart skipping a beat. He was strong and powerful yet with a heart so gentle. He risked his life to save hers and never judged or made her feel inadequate or stupid like almost everyone else. She just wanted to be near him all day.

"Hey, Pet." Breanna stomped into the kitchen where Petra was clearing breakfast and interrupted her daydreaming. "Any more food going? I'm still hungry."

Petra placed the pan she was carrying and turned on her, a little irritated, "No, there isn't. I just cleared it up. And take those dirty boots off out outside. I just cleaned the floor."

"Why?" Breanna frowned.

"Because you got mud all over them."

"No. I mean, why clean the floor? We are leaving today."

Petra rolled her eyes. "Well, my spoiled little rich sister, has it occurred to you that this is not our house and that the decent thing to do is to leave it as we found it? War might roll over it, but should its owners survive ...."

Breanna blushed and raised her hand to end her sister's tirade, "Yes, you have made your point. I am sorry." She turned to leave, muttering, "First Rachael, now Pet, maybe the meek will inherit the land after all."

Petra grinned to herself and returned to her chores.

Daniel and Emma stared in amazement at the flower in Kerianna Hawk's hand as it opened and closed and opened and closed. "Do it again," demanded Emma excitedly when it stopped and remained open.

Keri chuckled, "No, I cannot keep calling on Marran just to entertain you."

Emma pouted, and Daniel sighed, sitting back. They were out in the field, not far from where Rachael and Breanna had been earlier. The Marran priestess enjoyed being around the children and had been with them most of the time during their three-day stop. She had been teaching them how the goddess grew things and kept a balance in nature. She had a captivated audience who hung on her every word. However, Emma vocalized what Daniel was also thinking. "Why did you become a Marran priestess when our father is an Illyan."

Keri smiled, let go of the flower, and watched as the breeze lifted it high and took it away. She looked back at the child. "Well, I did not know he was my father until you and I met. My mother was a Marran and raised me as one."

"As a Marran, you cannot fight like Sebastian can, right?" Daniel, who loved the idea of being a knight, asked.

"We look for a peaceful resolution, but we can defend ourselves. We stood alongside the Illyans during the holy wars, and both men and women fought and died to save the churches from destruction."

"My dad wants me to be an Illyan priestess," Emma said but pondered her own words, "But I want to be Marran like you and do stuff with flowers."

Keri stiffened. She was so not going to go down that road and possibly anger her father. "Well, you will know...." She stopped and looked up; she heard the sound of a horse, maybe two, heading towards them. She stood up to see that it was not two but three. They were heading up the track from the Nethili road towards the farmhouse, but seeing her, they turned and headed towards them. She did not need to be a military genius to recognize the grey cloaks of Commech troopers. Her instinct was to run with the kids, but they could easily run them down. "Run," she said firmly, "go tell Sebastian we have company." She could at least try to delay them while the children escaped.

CHAPTER FOUR

Snake-Eyes

"Hate is discouraged in my church, and I am not supposed to share feelings that my father's church permitted him. However, I am his daughter, and emotion is not always something we always have control over, and I can say without hesitation..... I hate the Commech." – Memoir of a Marran Priestess by Emma Roark-Maine

Daniel and Emma ran towards the house, and Keri stepped between the kids and the riders. Keri closed her solid green eyes and said a quick prayer. When she opened them again, they were regular brown. "Can I help you?" She said to the leader as they pulled up in front of her.

"What's your name, lass," he spoke with a northwestern dialect, and to her surprise, he smiled at her.

"Stella," she replied.

"Well, Stella'" He smiled down at her. "I'm sub-inquisitor Balyard. I'm sorry to inconvenience you, but we are looking for some enemies of the state."

"Well, there is no one here. I am here alone with my husband and the kids." She shrugged innocently.

He studied her carefully before saying, "Forgive my bluntness, Stella, but you appear a little young to have kids that age." He indicated the kids up ahead of them. Daniel had stopped to help up Emma, who had fallen over.

"My husband's by his first wife," Keri said, not missing a beat.

"Ah, I see." He smiled again. "Why did you have them run away when we came up?"

"There is a war on if you hadn't noticed." No, don't antagonize them by being sarcastic, she thought as soon as the words came out.

"Ah, well, that makes perfect sense." He nodded, "I do find it strange, however, that you speak like a toff."

"Pardon me?"

"You talk like royalty or a cleric, not a simple farm girl."

"I had affluent parents who fell on hard times," She responded despondently, like it was a sad memory.

"Well," he said cheerily. "That answers all my questions. We will be off," Keri breathed a silent sigh of relief. "Right after we look inside your house."

Ah, it was too good to be true. "Of course." Keri smiled. "I will make you some tea. Follow me."

"That would be most lovely. It has been a long ride from Jilrir." He rode his steed alongside her as she walked back to the farmhouse. His two companions followed behind.

"How are things fairing there?" She was relieved to see the kids had made it into the farmhouse.

"Oh, they put up a nasty resistance, but the city now has stability. You do not seem to be perturbed being in the presence of your enemy."

Keri shrugged, "You are not my enemy. One overlord is the same as the next. We just want to keep our heads down and not get killed."

"Oh, how I wish everyone had your insight, Stella. Everything would go so much easier."

As they reached the porch, she called out, "Carter darling, we have visitors."

A few seconds later, Carter Monroe stepped out the door, "Well, hello there, chaps."

The leader slid from his horse, but he wasn't smiling now, "Carter, did you say? That wouldn't be Carter Monroe?"

"Oh, darn it," Keri sighed, "It didn't occur to me you would know his name." She turned back to him, her green eyes flashing brightly once more.

He went for his sword but was startled when both his companions cried out and fell to the ground, each with an ancient katana blade in his back. "Don't kill him," came Sebastian's voice as he and Jenri walked up from the barn. Balyard raised his hands. "A bit stupid of you not to check the barn directly opposite the farmhouse," The preacher chided.

"What can I say?" Balyard looked at the Marran Priestess, "I'm a sucker for a pretty face." He bowed to her, "Kerianna Mirrir, I presume?"

"I go by Kerianna Hawk these days, but yes."

"Hawk!" He turned to Sebastian, "I assume that must be you." He looked disgusted as he saw Jenri twist her katana in one of his companions several times until he stopped moaning, and she pulled it out.

"That would be correct," said the preacher. "And you are?"

"Obadiah Balyard at your service. Sub-inquisitor for the Church of Commech." He bowed. "Are you to kill me, or will that be Jenri's pleasure?" It did not need a genius to figure out how he knew her. Burakumin were rare in these parts.

"Oh, it will be me who kills you eventually, but we need a chat first," Sebastian replied honestly.

"Is killing him really necessary, father?" Keri asked, biting her lip. "He cannot hurt us now."

"Oh, aren't you a sweetie pie?" Balyard beamed at her. "Alas, yes, he must. I know where you are, see, and even if you run, he can't risk me coming back with death stalkers."

"I see," said Keri. "You do not seem too perturbed by the idea."

Balyard shrugged. "You play the game. You roll the dice. I came up with snake eyes and must pay the debt."

The front door opened, and Rebecca came out, followed by Petra and Rachael. "Oh, I'm to have celebrities at my execution. How marvelous." He clapped his hands. "Now let me see, you must be Rebecca. Oh, and this golden-haired beauty must be the bastard, and the damn ugly one at the end must be Rachael." He hit the ground with a thud as Sebastian punched him in the side of the head.

He shook his head to focus again, laughed, and tried to stand up, but Jenri placed a boot on the side of his head, "I prefer you down there," she said pleasantly.

"Oh, and here comes young Breanna," he said, looking at her walking up from the barn. "All we need is Alannah, and it's a family reunion."

Sebastian looked around. Where was Alannah? Then he frowned. Where was Devin? He looked back down at Balyard. "Start talking. How many scouts are out looking for us?"

"No clue, but we have everywhere in Ithia covered," he said. "Come now, Sebastian. Crotock wants to offer you a deal. A lot of your old men from the war are with us now. He is just looking to legitimize his control of Ithia. He will not harm the Maine girls if you come back with me. He just wants to marry one. The rest can go or stay. You can even keep them as a harem for your entertainment if you have a mind to. In return, he will make you governor of Southern Ithia. Everything south of Jilrir will be yours. If not, he will continue to pursue you, and your deaths will all be slow." Despite the pressure of Jenri's boot pushing the side of his face into the gravel, he managed a smile.

"Turn around, ladies," Sebastian said softly, but only Rachael, Petra, and Keri did. He looked to Jenri, "Esselar, if you please." She nodded, and with a pleasant smile, she slid her boot to his neck, quickly brought it up, stamped it down, and twisted her foot until there was a sharp crack, and the smile slipped away from the sub-inquisitor's smug face.

Keri turned back and looked back at Jenri in disgust. "How can you do that so easily?"

Jenri shrugged. "It's justice, Keri."

"Exactly what crime did he commit?"

Jenri narrowed her eyes at her, clearly not liking the implied judgment. "Treason," said Rebecca sharply.

"Yes," said Jenri, not taking her eyes off the Marran. "That will do."

Keri shook her head slowly in disbelief. "You are not the woman I thought you were."

"What would you do?" Breanna sneered, "Let him go tell his cronies where to find us."

"Death should be the last resort, not the first," Keri retorted sharply.

"Enough," Sebastian shouted, "We will get nowhere with this senseless bickering. Everyone, go get ready to leave. We can't stay here now. Carter and I will hide these bodies."

Breanna looked out across the fields towards Jilrir. "Farewell my city until I return," and, sinking her hands into her pockets, she stepped into the farmhouse.

The tension between Kerianna Hawk and Jenri O'Fere spread among the group as it gathered in the yard to begin the trek north. At some point during the preparations to leave, Alannah and Devin reappeared. When Sebastian enquired of the youngest Maine where she had been, she sweetly told him, "Oh, just out walking with Aunt Annabelle." The preacher was none too happy. He didn't want anyone near the necromancer, especially the impressionable twelve-year-old Maine. However, Devin appeared to be very careful about ensuring she was never alone with him, so he could not pursue the subject without drawing Rebecca's attention.

"Maybe we should say a prayer before we depart." To the preacher's surprise, the suggestion came from Breanna.

"Maybe we should." He looked at his daughter. "Keri, would you do the honors?"

All bowed their heads and closed their eyes as Keri began. "Merciful Marran and Illya, watch over us as we undertake this journey. Guide us and lead us to peace and prosperity and help our enemies see the error of their ways." Jenri gave a soft snort, and Sebastian elbowed her. "Keep us safe. In your names, we remain your servants." As their eyes opened, Sebastian sighed as Keri and Jenri stared daggers at each other. Slowly, the group moved out. Sebastian and Carter took the lead, with Emma holding on to the preacher's hand and skipping alongside him. Breanna walked with Rachael and Jenri until Sebastian asked her to walk with Portkind and push him on. The officious clerk was lagging so far behind that they had to keep stopping for him to catch up, seriously delaying any progress.

Judging from the weather, Sebastian thought they could easily be fooled into thinking all was right in the world. The sun shone down, and a cool breeze saved them from overtiring too quickly. For women raised in the leisurely opulence of Jilrir, he could not help but be amazed how they had adapted so quickly and never said a word of complaint about any hardships they had to endure. Just ahead of him, Keri now walked with Daniel. She seemed to have quite a rapport with him. Her arm rested caringly around his shoulders like an image of mother and son, even though she was just fifteen. "Which way are we heading?" Rebecca called from behind him.

"You want an honest answer or a good answer?" Sebastian called back with a smile.

"Honesty is the best policy, is it not said?" She laughed.

"Well, I am not entirely sure," he replied. "I had no time to plan a route and did not bring any kind of map. However, the plan at best is that we head north, creating as much distance as we can from Jilrir, then at some time head east to Nethili."

"How long do you think it will take us?" Petra called back. She was ahead of him now and turned around, walking backward. She suddenly stumbled back and fell flat on her backside, injuring her dignity more than her rear.

"Many weeks if you break a leg," Sebastian called as they all found much humor in her plight. "But a day at most if you don't."

"Very funny, everyone," Petra said good-naturedly as Jenri stopped to help her up. "I am glad I am entertaining you all."

Regrettably, the journey got harder as they left the cultivated lands and entered the wilds. As dusk reached them once more, the preacher called a halt near a small, picturesque brook at the edge of some woods. He only knew this land from maps seen long ago, and with clouds now overhead and no sun to gauge direction, neither Carter nor Sebastian could be certain they would not stray from the right direction.

"I will see if I can find us some forage, old man," Carter said.

"Use my carbine. We are far from anywhere, so the noise should not be heard." Sebastian handed over the weapon. "I wanted to save the rounds, but my stomach says otherwise." They had not eaten since the morning stew.

"Right on, old man. Should be fun." He grinned.

"Why do you not take Bree?" Sebastian suggested. "She might enjoy learning her way around the carbine."

Rebecca clearly did not like this idea and looked at him reprovingly.

Breanna beamed at Carter as he said, "What you say, old girl, want to learn to shoot like a man?"

"Yes, sir," she replied as if it were the most exciting suggestion she had ever heard, and the preacher watched the two wandering off towards the trees.

"Do you think that is an appropriate activity for a woman?" Rebecca said curtly as she made Emma and Daniel wash their hands and faces at the brook's edge. "Breanna is a handful enough without you giving her ideas,"

"Well, these days, it is better to shoot a carbine than read a book," Sebastian said with irony. Rachael frowned at him halfheartedly. She was already sitting on the floor reading a book. "And if you are going to read a book, it should be scripture," he admonished.

"Sebastian, I have it virtually memorized," Rachael said, catching an apple Devin threw to her from the bag she was handing them out from.

"Well, that's encouraging." Jenri smiled.

"Hey now, you already got one Maine in your order. Don't go recruiting anymore," Rebecca said as the two kids ran off to see what Keri was doing.

"Yes, well," Sebastian looked away. He was not going to make a promise he knew he could not keep. "Now, which of you will help me find firewood?" He called out, walking away from her.

Jenri and Emma volunteered, much to Rebecca's chagrin. "Oh, Sebastian, we just washed Emma's face. She will get dirty again." Rebecca looked at him with exasperation.

"Ahh, but getting dirty is much more fun than getting clean, right Emma?" he chuckled. She smiled in return but clearly did not agree. His daughter was fastidious about her cleanliness and hygiene.

As Rebecca watched them go, she wondered where Devin and Alannah had gotten to. She was curious about how they frequently went off together. However, it was one thing less for her to worry about. She saw Keri reading with Daniel and realized this was the first time she had Rachael alone since they had been in the Great House. Petra was unpacking the things they needed for the camp. So, she sat beside the young Feffer, who looked up at her sister curiously. "Hey, Becks."

"Hey, Rachael," Rebecca leaned back on her palms and crossed her ankles. "We have not spoken since we left Jilrir. I just thought we might catch up."

Rachael sighed and closed her book. "You pretty much made it clear how you felt this morning."

"I'm sorry. I didn't mean it," Rebecca responded, trying to sound as apologetic as possible.

Rachael smiled dryly, "But you did mean it, Becks. You called it 'Sebastian's church.'" She frowned. "Do you have even the vaguest concept of how insulting that is in so many different ways?"

"You know what I meant," Rebecca said defensively.

"Yes, I do. You think either Sebastian took advantage of your naïve little sister or I am so besotted with him I wasn't thinking."

"Well, don't you have feelings for him?" Rebecca said irritably.

Rachael looked bemused, "Yes, I do, but not how you are thinking. He is like family to me."

"You have known him just weeks, though," The First Lady snorted.

"Yes, and in that time, he has been more caring than anyone except maybe Breanna."

This stung Rebecca. "You know how I feel about you, Rachael."

"Do I?" Rachael's eyes narrowed. "Do you know this is the first time we have talked, one-on-one since you lectured me in the parlor?"

"A lot was going on."

"There always is." Rachael then gave a weary sigh. "Look, Rebecca, I am not trying to make you feel bad. I am trying to say that you can't suddenly become the interested sister when you haven't ever shown interest before just because I made a decision for myself for once. Right now, I am happier than I have ever been, and it is thanks to Illya, not you and not Sebastian."

"I will try to understand. That is all I can say," Rebecca said softly.

Rachael smiled, "That is good enough for now, Becks."

Rebecca leaned over, and they hugged, "I love you, baby sis. Never forget that."

"I won't, and I love you too, big sis."

As they both sat back, Rebecca looked over at Petra. "Come on, let's go help our sister."

They had roast venison that night. Breanna looked immensely proud of herself for having made the kill herself with Sebastian's carbine.

They all lay around the fire on the bedrolls Rebecca and Petra had made back at the farm out of blankets sown together and stuffed with hay. Sebastian took a seat between Rachael and Alannah, and, much to the disgust of Breanna, the youngest Maine slid closer to him and hugged his arm. Sebastian pondered about the girl and her time with Annabelle Devin. What was the manipulative bitch up to? He noticed Devin watching them again, but she quickly looked away. He let Alannah stay on his arm long enough so she would not think he was trying to escape her when he moved. His excuse was to help Rebecca hand out more venison-filled tin plates they had liberated from the farmhouse. As he approached Rebecca, he caught her eye and whispered, "When you were fleeing Jilrir, how long were you separated from Devin and Alannah?"

"For several hours. Why, what is the matter?"

"Nothing important," but he studied them closely, wondering what happened to make them so close.

CHAPTER FIVE

Rite of Passage

"The Invigoration is a Marran Rite only beaten by ordination. To commune with nature as one is an experience that is beyond description. I only wish my father had lived long enough to see me ordained." – Memoir of a Marran Priestess by Emma Roark-Maine

"I intend to do my share of the night watch, Sebastian," Jenri said firmly as she stepped up to the preacher. She knew he was going to object, and she was ready for it.

"Oh, that's not necessary, Esselar. Carter and I have it covered," he replied as if that ended the subject.

"Oh, don't be silly, Sebastian. You and Carter are hardly going to function on half a night's sleep each. There is no practical reason I cannot keep watch. Indeed, you cannot deny my race has better night vision than you."

"It is my responsibility to take the role of the protector," he said casually.

"Oh, Sebastian, I plan to keep watch with my eyes, not my genitalia. While I agree there are many physical differences between a man and a woman, I do believe our senses are the same. If you cannot come up with a better reason, consider the matter resolved, and I will take the watch."

A thin smile crossed Sebastian's face as he looked at the determined expression on the young priestess. "Actually, mistress, my reluctance is not because you are a woman. It is because you are the Esselar of our church. Keeping watch is unbecoming of your station."

"Oh," Jenri flushed slightly. She had been ready to attack Sebastian for his misogynistic attitude towards their roles, and this took her by surprise, but she recovered quickly. "Well, given our circumstances, that is utterly ridiculous, too." She waited for his next argument.

To her surprise, he simply shrugged. "By your will, Esselar. You can take the last watch. Carter will wake you two hours before dawn."

When Carter did wake her, she found herself quite annoyed. She was having a particularly nice dream where she was in a room full of her favorite desserts. She was polite with the young officer, at least in words, although her tone was irritable. As he went to lay down on his bed roll, she settled herself up against the tree. There was a slight chill in the air, and she pulled her cloak around her and her knees up to her chest, hugging them for extra warmth. It was silent except for the faint distant sounds of the nocturnal creatures that lay within the forest behind her.

She fought the urge to go back to sleep, and although she succeeded, she found herself in that twilight of not quite asleep and not quite awake. She did almost drift off, but then she was suddenly startled by two green glowing orbs floating in the air by the fireplace that had long gone out. She was about to cry out, and her hand was already down by her blade when a voice hushed her. "It's only me," came Kerianna's voice as the two orbs rose and headed towards her.

"I don't think I'm ever going to get used to those eyes of yours, sister," Jenri responded in a whisper as if it were the Marran's fault.

"Well, I humbly beg your pardon for being a Marran," Keri said with humorous scorn.

Jenri just harrumphed quietly, saying, "Why aren't you asleep.?"

"It's starting to happen," Keri said cryptically, and when she only saw a blank stare come back from the Illyan, she elucidated. "The Invigoration. It has started."

"Forgive me, Keri. As I'm sure Sebastian can attest to, the study of other faiths was not one where I excelled. What are you talking about?"

"We Marrans have an empathic connection to nature. Even as a Feffer, we connect with the beasts. Upon ordination, this becomes stronger and more powerful, and we call it the 'Invigoration.' It usually happens quite quickly, but for some reason, it has taken some time for it to happen to me. I must admit I had been growing concerned."

"And I assume you're telling me this for a reason for something that would involve me?"

Keri looked uncomfortable. They had not resolved their differences over the incident at Boddington's farm, and it was not easy approaching the Illyan about this most personal matter.

"Had things not happened the way they did, I would be doing this with my mother. There is a right I must perform, and while I can do it alone, I would rather not. I need to go into that forest and commune with nature, and I believe my father would have a heart attack if he was aware I went alone."

At that, Jenri smiled. "Indeed, he would," she said, slowly getting up to her feet and stretching out her aching joints. "How long will this take?"

"It needs to take place at dawn, which, by my guess, is not far off."

"Very well, let's go do this."

But Jenri's eyes narrowed as the Marran hesitated. "There's a catch, isn't there?" Jenri rolled her eyes.

Keri hesitated before saying, "You have to remove your boots."

"By all that's holy!" Jenri retorted. Huffing and puffing with irritation, the Illyan Esselar sat back down and began to unlace her boots.

"What is going on?" the whispered voice in the darkness was that of Rachael, who had been woken by Jenri's irritation.

"Don't worry about it. Better you go back to sleep," Jenri responded irritably.

However, the young woman stepped over to them out of the darkness, quickly putting on her glasses.

"It's the time of the Invigoration," Keri explained to her.

Rachael's look of concern turned into a huge smile. "Oh, how exciting for you," she said. Jenri glared up at her as she continued the laborious task of undoing how long boots annoyed at the fact the young Feffer apparently knew more about this than she did. "May I join you?"

Keri smiled, "I would be honored," she said, although in reality, in Marran culture, it would be considered that Rachael was the honored one for being permitted to attend.

"No," Jenri said firmly. "Sebastian would have a fit if he found out I took you into those woods."

Rachael looked most disappointed but quickly said, "But surely he couldn't be, for not only will it be a good part of my education, but as my Esselar, he could hardly argue with you."

Keri grinned and looked down at Jenri. "She does have a point there."

Jenri frowned at Keri, and then, turning to Rachael, she lifted her boot in the air towards her. "If you don't mind." Rachael took the boot by the heel and pulled. It took quite a tug, and the young feffer almost fell back as it came away suddenly. Jenri placed her bare foot up on the ground and began to work on the laces of the other boot. "Fine! You can come," Jenri said begrudgingly but could not maintain her sullen mood as the young feffer pushed her glasses up her nose and grinned widely. It took about another ten minutes before Jenri finally stood up barefoot and looked severely disgusted by the situation. Rachael had removed her own shoes long before her mistress had removed the second boot.

Keri led the way into the forest. It was slow going. For the Marran years of going barefoot had hardened her feet to the extremities of nature. Jenri was a little better than Rachael. Although never barefoot, the Esselar had been raised as a hunter and forager and had frequently spent

many hours walking. But for Rachael, closeted in her gilded cage of opulence, her feet were used to soft, padded
handmade shoes and walking on the plush carpets of the
great house. However, she bore the discomfort in silence
and watched ever more carefully where she stepped. They
ventured further and further into the forest. She ignored
the scratches and the cuts, but her body could not, and she
slowed the further they went. Keri didn't seem to care, but
Jenri grew less and less patient, although she did not say
anything.

Eventually, Keri stopped, and Rachael flushed bright
pink as the Marran slipped off her robes and stood naked
in the forest. She closed her eyes and held her head back,
facing up to the sky, and she stretched out her arms. She
stood there silently as the two Illyans watched her and
occasionally glanced at each other. Slowly, through the
roof of the trees, a dim light of dawn started to appear, and
the sounds of the forest began to change.

Jenri started to look quite bored and began examin-
ing her fingernails. Rachael, on the other hand, watched
the motionless Marran with fascination, then suddenly
gasped as a small bird flew down and settled on the top
of Keri's head. More birds began to fly down until they
covered her head and arms.

Rachael looked down, startled, as something started to
tickle her feet. She saw little mice running along toward the
Baron with No Fear or concern. She covered her mouth as
she giggled, for she had the most ticklish of toes. However,
she quickly stopped as, from the corner of her eyes, she
saw Jenri turn around with a look of concern. Slowly, the
Illyan Esselar's eyes widened, and with her own concern,
the Feffer turned around to look where her companion

was looking. Then she heard it. Jenri had keener hearing than hers and had heard it long before she had, but now she heard the low, ominous growl. In the blink of an eye, the priestesses' blades were out and at the ready. "Have no fear. The beast shall not harm you as long as I am here," Keri said in a light tone as if half asleep. Rachael looked back to Jenri, who had not relaxed her stance, but before she could say anything, a cold chill ran down her spine. A large grey wolf snarling stepped into the clearing, eyeing each of them in turn. "Jenri, please lower your weapons. The beast is here because it trusts me. Would you have me faithless before it should you bring it harm?"

"Oh, trust me, it's perfectly safe if it stays where it is, but if it does come closer...." She did not finish her sentence, for the meaning was clear.

Rachael trusted Keri, but it did not reduce the fear that came naturally when facing such a predator.

Keri sighed and gently lowered her arms, and as the birds took off, she turned slowly. "Would you at least let it pass you by and come to me."

Jenri hesitated but, with great reluctance, lowered her weapons, but she still did not sheath them. Slowly, the wild creature began to move between the two Illyans looking at each of them as it passed. Then it seemed to relax and stopped growling as it stepped up to Keri and sat down at her feet, looking up at her. "You're a fine fellow." she reached out and stroked the back of its neck, lowering herself to its height. The wolf nuzzled its face against hers. "Mind you don't get fleas," Jenri muttered. She had no fondness for animals unless they were cooked and on a serving plate. Rachael, on the other hand, had very little experience with them. The family had once had a dog in the house, which she had grown fond of, but the palace guard killed it after it bit Ronan. Alannah had frequently had pet rabbits, but that was the limit of Rachael's experience of the natural world, and she now stood in awe as the Marran priestess rested her forehead against the wolf.

Jenri tensed once more as more noises of the forest came towards them. Several more wolves came out and made their way to the Marran priestess. She was surrounded by them and petted each in turn. Rachael could almost feel Jenri's tension. Then, with a single wave of her hand in the air, the beasts gave a howl, turned, and ran off back into the forest just as another low rumble came from the undergrowth. Rachael almost expected a bodragel to come out, but she knew full well that even a Marran priestess could not tame one of those beasts. What came out next was just as terrifying. A large golden cat with two large saber teeth stepped forward, looking uneasily at Keri. Even on all fours, it came up to her shoulder. Its lack of a mane told the educated Rachael that it was female, and more reluctantly than the wolves, it came forward as Keri reached out an upturned palm towards it. Finally, it sat down before her, looking at Jenri and Rachael before relaxing. Again, the Marran priestess stroked it, smiled at it, and lay her forehead upon it. Then, with a wave of her hand, it turned and ran back into the undergrowth.

Keri turned back to her companions with a beaming smile on her face. "We are done. Come on, let's go back."

***

"I do not know what you were thinking," Sebastian growled. He sat cross-legged by the fire with Rachaels barefoot upon his lap as he healed each of the small abrasions on her feet. Petra was making breakfast, and Rebecca stood over Sebastian's shoulder, looking as angry as he was. "Positively idiotic taking my Feffer in there."

At first, Jenri was willing to put up with the dressing down that she was expecting from the preacher, but he had not shut up for half an hour, and she was getting tired of it. "Have a care, Sebastian," she said quite sharply, fixing him with her eyes. "Try to remember who it is you're talking to."

It was the first time the new Esselar had pulled rank on him, and it took him by surprise. He felt uncomfortable as all eyes fell upon him, awaiting his response to the sudden dressing down. Only Devon appeared amused by it. He hesitated, then swallowed his pride and responded. "My apologies, mistress," he said softly.

"I will not be that easy to silence, Jenri," Rebecca said, taking over where the preacher had left off. "You not only took my sister into the forest, but you also left us unguarded."

"Yes, well," Jenri now looked as embarrassed as Sebastian, "I must admit that was a mistake on my part and that I was distracted. For that, I apologize."

"You know Rebecca, I am an adult and can't take responsibility for my own decisions," said Rachael as she swapped her foot for the other for her master to start working on.

"I'm still responsible for you, Rachael," Rebecca snapped at her.

Actually, she was not. Sebastian was. But Rachael decided to keep her mouth shut and not escalate Rebecca's already irrational temper.

CHAPTER SIX

Nethili

"Breanna was the beating heart of the family that emerged from the ashes of Jilrir and the House of Maine. Her spirit is that of pure light, and I do not think she even comprehends the concept of darkness." – Memoir of a Marran Priestess by Emma Roark-Maine

As the party ate, no one paid heed to Rachael's comments that a diet of just meat would soon affect their health. Sebastian noticed Keri was with Daniel again, and she appeared to be teaching him to read by drawing letters in the dirt with a stick. He knew he should talk to her, get to know her; she was his daughter, after all. However, the subject of Lillan would come up, and the pain was still fresh. He pushed the thoughts from his head. No, things were already complicated enough, and there would be time later to try father-daughter bonding.

"Sebastian, why don't you read to us from your Book?" Rebecca asked as they finished, and Jenri took Emma to wash the plates in the brook.

"Breanna has a copy." Rachael looked over to her, "Why don't you read us some?"

Bree colored slightly, "No, you do it," she said curtly, surprising Rachael by getting up, shoving her hands in her pockets, and walking off in the dark. Carter got up and followed her.

"What was that about?" asked Alannah stiffly.

"Don't worry about it," Sebastian smiled, guessing that her reaction was that she found it hard to read the complicated text. He would have to talk to her about it sometime. "Go on, Rachael."

"Maybe Keri would like to read to us from The Book of Marran?" Rachael asked hopefully, looking at the Marran Priestess.

Keri smiled back, "Alas, I left it in the Temple in Jilrir. Anyway, I am looking forward to hearing you." She was seated cross-legged; Daniel was now curled up asleep with his head snuggled into her lap, and she gently stroked his hair.

Nervously, Rachael opened the Book of Illya to the first page. She coughed and began. She read it so sweetly that it felt like when Sebastian had first read the words fifteen years before.

Slowly, one by one, everyone started to lie on their bedrolls and drift off to sleep. Carter and Bree returned sometime later, just as Rachael closed the book. Bree didn't say anything and threw herself on a bedroll beside

Rachael. Soon, the only sound was deep snores coming from Petra.

"Shame we don't have any salt; we could make this venison last some time," Sebastian said, thinking only he and Carter were still awake.

Carter pondered this before saying, "Well, the village of Nethili is half a day from here out west. If I set out now, I could be back by noon. I can move faster alone."

"Do you think it wise to go alone?"

"What choice do we have, old man?" He looked around. "One of us needs to stay with the women folk."

"Portkind can go with you," Sebastian suggested.

"Be serious, old man." Carter frowned.

"I can go with him." Bree sat up and looked eagerly at the Preacher.

He was about to protest when Carter said, "Can't keep a hellcat on a chain all its life, old man. We will be in and out before you know it."

Again, Sebastian was about to protest, but the beseeching look on Bree's face smashed down his resolve. "Fine," he said after a lengthy pause. "Have her back by noon tomorrow, or I'll disembowel you." Carter laughed, but Sebastian gripped his arm. "It wasn't a joke."

Carter, still smiling, nodded. Bree jumped up and kissed Sebastian's cheek, "Thanks, Dad," she said cheekily, and he just managed to clip her around the ear before she could jump out of the way.

Breanna Maine glanced back at Sebastian as he stood in the light of the dying fire, watching her leave with Carter. He was fussy and overprotective, and she loved every minute of it. She did not understand her affection for this man who had come suddenly into her life. Was it simply that he was the only man ever to be interested in her and her opinions? She had joked about calling him Dad, but she wondered if this was what it felt like to have a father, a real father, and not just a man who palmed her off on nannies and tutors.

It concerned her that she felt no grief over her real father's death, but Claudius Maine had never really been a part of her life. To him, she was just another jigsaw piece that made up The House of Maine. She regretted and was saddened by the demise of Jilrir and the suffering it had brought, but this new life was exciting and free. She wanted to feel guilty at the joy she felt, but she simply couldn't. She knew it was possible that Sebastian would take her to Aranar and return her to that Maine way of life, but perhaps she could persuade him to let her stay with him. She was sure that idea was hopeless. After all, why would he want her tagging along?

So, she intended to enjoy every last minute of this grand adventure. This was no game. This was no firing rocks at dumb guards. She had killed men, and she knew, she just knew, she would get the chance to fight and kill again. Was it so wrong to enjoy it so much? Had she not saved her sisters? Did those men not deserve to perish? All these thoughts went through her mind as she turned away from Sebastian and ran to catch up with Captain Carter.

He glanced at her, "Hope you can keep up, milady." He grinned and increased his pace a step.

She had to trot until she got in step with him. "Do not worry about me, sir." She grinned back. "I'm here to back you up, not hold you back."

"Good show, milady." He chuckled.

"I ask just one concession, though," she said, trying to tighten her sword belt, which had begun to slip with the jerky movements of her pace.

"And what would that be, milady?" He asked, glancing down at her with a raised eyebrow.

"I prefer it if you would call me Bree," she said, having to trot again since the tightening of the belt had made her lose her step with the royal guard.

"Ha. Is that all? Well, I most certainly will do that then, Miss Bree." He patted her on the shoulder. She thought it to be patronizing, but she let it go.

"Just Bree," She replied.

"Ah. That I cannot do, Miss Bree. I am an officer and a gentleman. You must concede that to me."

Bree grinned, "I suppose I could live with that. It beats milady."

"Good show, Miss Bree, good show." He patted her again, and she returned his smile through gritted teeth.

They kept up the pace for several hours, and the journey became much easier back upon the Nethili Road. Breanna found herself getting tired but determined to neither slow down nor complain.

Finally, it was Carter who stopped them, "I don't know about you, old girl, but I need a rest."

Bree shrugged. "If you need one, that's fine with me," she said, wanting to cry out with relief. They sat on the roadside, and Carter pulled out a small silver hip flask and took a swig. He wiped the spout and offered it to Bree, who took a swig. The liquid burned her mouth and throat, and she spat it out, wiping her mouth with her sleeve.

"Steady on, old girl. That is the last of Jilrir's finest Ambrosia Brandy." He chuckled, taking the flask back. "Never shall we see the like again."

"Amen to that, Captain." Breanna looked at him in disgust. "If you put that in a medicine bottle, people would throw it out."

He laughed and took another mouthful, "The finest medicine money can buy." He shoved the cork back in the top and pocketed it. Then he pulled a small water skin from his belt and handed it to her. It was warm, but she did not care, anything to quench her thirst and get that foul taste from her mouth.

They set off again, and as dawn approached, she saw the familiar sight of Nethili. She had only been there a few times but was too young to recall much about it now. "Our best bet, Miss Bree," Carter said. "Will be to hit the market. As soon as we can palm off Lady Rebecca's jewelry, the faster we can stock up and head back."

She had no idea what he meant about the jewelry, but she merely nodded, not because of a lack of interest but because she was distracted by how quiet it was for this time of day as they approached the town. "Something is not quite right here, Mr. Carter. I cannot hear the sounds of a community waking up. I hear no traders or merchants. None of the normal sounds of a new dawn."

"Oh, this isn't Jilrir, old girl," Carter reassured her. "This is a small provincial town. Things are a lot quieter out here."

She accepted this argument but still felt uneasy.

Nethili was one of those towns that sprung up by accident. Originally, it was a small illegal outpost where traders would barter their wares to avoid excessive Jilrian taxes. Soon, it became a boom town and grew even more over the last few centuries. However, town officials stopped its expansion to avoid drawing the attention of modern tax collectors. The more successful the town, the more the levees would come down upon them.

Sixteen years ago, Breanna's grandfather had dismissed the officials and replaced them with a single man. Kalvin Fenris was a rather curious choice. He had been a Jilrian Royal guard of no noteworthiness, and his appointment as Mayor of Nethili had raised many eyebrows and was the subject of quiet gossip for many years.

Breanna knew none of this as she stood on the outskirts of the town. She noticed how much cleaner and more orderly its design was than Jilrir. Jilrir was a mesh of randomly constructed streets with no order. It was easy to lose one's way in Jilrir, but there had been more thought to the layout here, and most roads seemed to run north to south and east to west. Another major difference was no building seemed to have more than a single story. There was no wall, yet its newness and cleanliness made Bree feel more secure here than in Jilrir. Of course, she was not foolish and knew this was about as secure as a fishing net with a great big hole.

Carter confidently strode up the cobbled street with Breanna just behind him. She was looking at the neat and uniform square houses with colorful shutters and empty window boxes waiting for spring to return. "Have you been here before, Captain Carter?" She asked.

"Oh, many times, Miss Bree, many times," he replied.

They finally saw signs of life as they approached the marketplace. Women were hanging laundry on lines between their houses, and their children stopped and stared at the two scruffy and armed characters. Bree still found it bizarre that no one spoke, and it was even more strange as they stepped out into the market. The stalls were lined up in a large horseshoe configuration, but only about a third were in use. Those who had set up did so sedately and without the usual banging, crashing, and shouting. There were barrows of fruit and vegetables, but they were old and on the turn. There were textile merchants, but their clothes looked hastily put together with bad stitching. A gnarled trader in his late forties noticed them and eyed them curiously. "Refugees?" he asked with a hint of contempt.

Carter frowned slightly. "Well, sir, not a term I would use to describe us, but probably accurate."

"Well, unless you have kin in Nethili, you won't be welcome. And we can't trade you nothing unless your coin is gold and you have a ration card."

"Ration card?" Carter asked curiously.

"There is a war going on. The mayor is saving our goods for our people. No ration card, no trade.

"We are all the same people," said Breanna indignantly, "We are all Ithians."

The man snorted, "Haven't you heard? The Maine's are all dead, no government. No army, and therefore no Ithia."

Breanna started to correct this statement, but Carter pushed her roughly aside and interrupted. "Quite understandable, old man. Forgive my sister's impertinence." He looked at Breanna. "Apologize to the gentleman, Betsy."

She looked at him as if he was mad, but moments later, it clicked. "Sorry, sir," She muttered, looking down at her feet like a scolded schoolgirl.

The man snorted but appeared less confrontational. "My advice would be that you hot foot it out of here. Go to Ternal or Rankson. I hear they have camps for Jilrian survivors."

"I thank you for your advice, sir." Taking Breanna's hand, Carter bowed and led her out of the market.

Once out of sight of the man, he let go of her hand and said quietly, "I think it would be wise not to advertise your illustrious origins, old girl."

"Yeah, I got that," She replied, glancing back up the street and wondering about the odd behavior. "But 'Betsy'?" she screwed her nose up.

"My sister's name."

"Oh!" Bree responded meekly. "Sorry."

Carter led her up another street, and they came out in a much more exclusive neighborhood. They found a row of upmarket stores, one of which was a jeweler. Carter grinned at Breanna. "We just need to hock this, and then we will return to the market."

"But they said they wouldn't sell us anything?" Breanna said, perplexed.

"Oh, you would be surprised what can and cannot be done if you have enough brass in your money bag." He chuckled and opened the door for her. A small bell rang, and they stepped into a dark shop. The shelves were mostly bare, which was not a good sign. Bree never wore jewelry unless she had to, but she had been around a lot, and the stuff on display behind the glass cases was not even on par with the cheapest item her family had owned.

A tall, gaunt man with a rosy complexion and a well-trained customer smile stepped out from behind a dark red curtain covering the back doorway. He stood behind a counter and assessed their attire. His smile faded, "I do not deal in trinkets. Whatever you have to sell, I am not interested. I do not run a charity for Jilrian refugees."

"What the fu...." Bree started to say but stopped as she felt Carter surreptitiously pinch her arm.

Carter slapped the necklace on the counter, and the man's eyes lit up. "What do you think that is worth on the Jilrian market?"

Composure returned to the man's face. "Well, maybe it would be worth something if there *was* a Jilrian market."

Carter smiled ruefully, "What do you say, old man? Seven fifty?"

"Oh, be realistic, sir. There is a war on, after all." He picked up the necklace and ran it through his fingers. "Thirty-five is my best offer."

"It's worth a hundred times that," Bree protested.

"Was, maybe," The jeweler replied.

"You have a deal, sir." Carter offered his hand, but the man shook his head.

"I need to check its authenticity first, sir." He pulled a small black loupe from his pocket and screwed it into his eye. He examined the necklace carefully. "Yes, very nice," then paused. "Why, there is even a hallmark it's..." Suddenly, he tensed, lay the necklace down on the counter, and gave Carter and Bree a hard, cold, and edgy look. "May I ask from where you obtained this item?"

"It was our mother's," Carter replied without hesitation. "Sadly, she did not make it out of Jilrir."

"I see." He looked unsure but smiled, "Wait here while I get your cash."

As he stepped back behind the curtain, Carter smiled at Breanna, "See, a piece of cake."

"Something is wrong, very wrong," Breanna said through gritted teeth as she stared at the curtain.

"Stuff and nonsense," Carter replied. "You're being paranoid."

She looked at him with a scowl. "Did you not see his reaction when he looked at the hallmark?"

"Yes, I saw him realize he just made the deal of a lifetime."

Breanna snapped her fingers as it dawned on her. "The hallmark bares the baron's seal. The seal of The House of Maine." She spun to face him. "Carter, I have a bad feeling about this."

Carter pondered a moment, then nodded. Breanna slipped the necklace back into her pocket and turned to the door. As they stepped outside, Breanna looked up and down the street and saw the jeweler heading their way with two armed men who were clearly city guards judging from their matching tan tunics. He must have gone out of a back door.

She and Carter headed up the street briskly in the opposite direction, ignoring shouts for them to stop. As they turned a corner, they broke into a run. Breanna glanced back and realized they were gaining on them. Just as one was about to grab her, she spun around and brought her knee into his groin. He cried in agony but did not go down. She was tempted to pull her knife on him but knew this was not an enemy. This was simply a man in her father's service who was only doing his job. He grabbed her cloak and copied how she had seen the Preacher do it. She head-butted him as hard as she could, and he let go. She turned to see Carter had been forced to the ground and pinned there. He cried as she went to his aid, "Run, girl, run."

CHAPTER SEVEN

The Rowe Street Posse

"Katherine Longfellow became Breanna's lifelong friend, but rumors that they were in an intimate relationship continue to live on even though Bree is now married with two fine sons." – Memoir of a Marran Priestess by Emma Hawk-Maine

B ree hesitated with her hand upon her sword but only for a hint of a second. Turning on her heel, she sprinted down a back alley. A guard was in hot pursuit, blowing hard on a whistle. Her heart pounded up into her throat as the muscles in her legs strained to give her more speed. Then, ahead of her, another guard appeared; she was trapped, but no, Breanna Maine did not give up. Ever! She kept running to this new opponent and slid to the ground and into his legs at the last moment. As he toppled over her, she rolled out of the way and was back up and running.

She had come out, once more, into the marketplace, and at the sound of the whistles, more guards came and blocked the exits. With a flying leap and profane cries of the tradesmen, she landed on a stall. The guards kept pace at each side of her as she ran across each stall, knocking the trader's wares flying and leaping from one stall to the next.

Now, the merchants themselves were trying to grab her. One merchant ahead of her had the smarts to tip his stall and leave her nowhere to go. She spun around fast, catching the guards unaware, and they were a few paces past her before they could stop. She turned towards a drainpipe on the wall and jumped to it, only just managing to get a grip. In seconds, she was up on the roof and out of sight.

She jumped to another building and climbed down, cursing as she heard the guards getting nearer again. She leaned against the wall, resting her hands on her knees and panting. She was spent. They would now catch her. Resigned to this, she slid down to sit on the ground and wait.

Breanna slowly tried to regain her breath so she would be composed when arrested. She looked down at her hands and smiled. Small cuts surrounded her knuckles, and hardened skin formed around her palm. She smiled softly as she rested her forearms upon her raised knees. So much for the soft and pampered Honorable Lady Breanna Maine, she thought. She glanced up the alleyway as the sound of the guard's whistles and shouts grew nearer.

"Pssst." Breanna looked around nervously, wondering from where the voice had emanated. "Down here, idiot." At the end of the alley was a small door set into the ground, the sort that led into a cellar. It was raised slightly, and a pair of child's eyes were looking out at her. "Come on, hurry up."

Although she did not know if she was jumping out from the frying pan and into the fire, she scrabbled to her feet, ran low as the boy raised the trapdoor, and slid into the darkness.

Breanna fell about seven feet and landed awkwardly on her ankle. She cried out in pain, but someone grabbed her from behind and smothered her mouth with a hand. "Shut up, shut up, damn you," Came a young girl's hoarse whisper just at her shoulder. She placed her hand firmly over Bree's mouth as the boy held her in place. "You wants the peelers to put us all in the clink?"

Breanna had tears in her eyes from the pain in her ankle but clenched her teeth to stop the urge to scream. The boy had closed the trap, and the muffled sound of pounding feet and shouts could be heard from overhead. It slowly died away, and the girl with the common working-class accent said in a less muted tone, "If I lets you go, yous gonna be quiet?" Breanna nodded, and she was released. However, now bearing her full weight, the pain doubled and shot through her ankle, and she fell to her knees with a squeal.

"I told you we shouldn't have gone got her," The boy said aggressively. Breanna could see nothing in the almost total darkness. As she slid back onto her backside and favored her ankle, she cared about little else than this excruciating pain. From the sound of it, the boy was now on one side of her while the girl was on the other.

"Leave her to Fenris's Freaks? No way, Chip, we said...no, we pledged... we would help any kid in trouble."

"Is she a kid, though?" Chip replied, "She looks eighteen or nineteen or sommink like that."

"I'm fifteen," Breanna growled through waves of pain.

"See, I told you, she ain't no kid," Chip stated with that 'I told you so' tone.

"She's younger than me, you moron. 'ere lass. 'Ow long you bin fifteen?" the girl asked.

"For Marran's sake, why does that matter?" Breanna spat.

"I guess it don't," the girl replied.

Breanna's eyes started to become accustomed to the exceptionally dim light, and she could just make out a girl with wavy reddish hair that hung down to her shoulders. She was a year or two younger than Breanna and was skinny, which the long knitted grey cardigan that hung down to her knees did not hide. She stood facing Chip with her arms folded and a grim expression. Chip was even younger in tattered pants and a grimy blue shirt several times too big for him. He stared at Breanna, and while still rubbing her ankle, she stared back. "She ain't one of us," he said sneeringly. "Look at her clothes, Kitty."

Breanna looked down at her battered and bloodstained attire. What was he going on about? "They need a good scrub, is all I can see, Chip," Kitty replied.

"Bodragel shit." He pointed to her cape. "Ever seen material of that quality on any of us? And look at those pants, hand-stitched by bloody arty zans. Made to measure."

"If you have quite finished discussing me, can you have the decency to tell me who you are?" Bree asked haughtily.

"Illya blimey," Chip exclaimed with a cold, hard laugh. "She even talks like a crust."

"A what?" Breanna exclaimed, starting to get irritated beyond distraction.

"Crust. You know," Kitty said, looking down at her. "Upper crust. A toff. A nob."

"And that's a problem because?" Breanna snapped.

"You're one of Fenris's lot. That's why," Chip said with equal aggression.

"I don't even know who this Fenris is, you dumb fuck." Breanna wished she could get up and slap him.

Kitty laughed. "Now she sounds likes one of us."

"I still don't trust her," Chip said, but his tone lowered.

"And I don't know what the hell is going on," Breanna snapped.

Kitty stuck out her hand to her, "I'm Kaferine Longfella, but they calls me Kitty. "I'm the 'ed of the Remington Street Posse, and I fink I trusts ya."

Chip muttered under his breath.

Breanna was about to make up a name as she shook her hand, but those simple words 'I trust you' filled her with guilt at the idea, "I will tell you my name if I have your word that it will not be repeated to anyone?"

Kitty studied her with curiosity at these words but then shrugged it off and said, "You got it. You trusts me, and I trusts you. Can't make a fairer deal than that." Breanna looked at Chip suspiciously. Kitty spoke for him, "I'm elected leader. 'e won't go against me whatever 'e finks."

"Very well," Bree said after a long pause. "I am Breanna Maine."

Her companions tensed and stared dumfounded at her, "Did you say Maine?" Chip said softly.

"Yes, and yes, I am one of the Maines you are thinking of," Breanna replied.

"Is there uvver Maines?" Kitty asked grimly.

Breanna shrugged, "I assume the name is not unique to my family."

"Well, you'd be wrong," The young girl responded. "No one can use that name."

"I didn't know that." Breanna shrugged again.

Chip stepped up to Kitty and, looking her in the eye, said sharply, "This is bodragel shit, Kitty. If she is a freaking Maine, then why were Fenris' Freaks chasing her around the market?"

Kitty placed the splayed tips of her fingers on his chest and pushed him back. "Personal space, Chip, personal space."

Breanna was surprised at how nervous he was as he stepped back. "I is sorry, Kitty. I forgot meself."

"No problem, love." Kitty smiled, and he relaxed but only a little. "Maybe Fenris has taken sides with the invaders. Fatboy got the news that there is a five 'undred siv reward fer any Maine caught."

This was not good news, and Breanna felt in imminent danger. Five hundred sivs was a fortune that only the wealthiest possessed at any one time. Avarice seemed to light up in Chip's eyes. "That is a ton of bread, Kitty. We could do a lot of good with that."

Breanna was startled as Kitty suddenly slapped him hard around the face with a force that made him stumble. "Get that outta your 'ed now." She approached him, and he flinched, clutching his reddened cheek. "We made a pact, she and I. We is going to trusts each other. We may 'ate the Maines, but not this one. Not now, not ever."

"Yes, Kitty, of course. Whatever you say."

"All righty," said Breanna. "Now you are freaking me out. Who are you, why did you help me, and how do I get the hell out of here?"

A warm smile returned to Kitty's face. "Remington Street Posse, work'ouse kids oo don't like the work'ouse. We lives underground, and we takes what we needs. We fight against Fenris and the 'ole bloody system." She then laughed. "We fight against the likes of you. What did you say your first name was?"

"It's Breanna, but I prefer Bree."

Kitty smiled, "Then Bree, it is." She then seemed to remember something, "You don't know Petunia Greene, does you."

Breanna frowned. "No."

Kitty's smile widened into a grin, "Yeah, I always thought it was just a story. She was s'posed to go live with the Maines. She is apparently The Honorable Lady Petra Maine now." Kitty pronounced the "H" clearly.

"Now that name I do know. She's my sister. Do you know her?"

Kitty shook her head, "Nah. But I knew her brothers."

Breanna vaguely recalled knowing Petra shared two half-brothers with her mother. "Where are they now?" she asked.

"Well, they 'anged Russell four years back," Kitty said as if he had simply gone on vacation. She looked at Chip, "Cattle rustlin', weren't it?"

Chip shrugged. "Dunno, Kitty."

Kitty looked back at Breanna, "Yeah, I fink it was that."

"That makes no sense." Breanna looked at her quizzically. "People don't get hanged for that!"

Kitty and Chip chuckled at this, and Kitty smiled at her a little patronizingly, "Aww, they 'ave kept you all snug in your big 'ouse in Jilrir, ain't they?" she patted Breanna on the head, "This is Nefili, sweetheart. Fenris will execute you for any crime."

"*Any* crime?" Breanna scowled, "You don't mean that literally?"

Chip looked at her grimly, "Roger Bell was hanged for not keeping his dog on a lead."

"Tis true." Kitty shrugged, "Fenris is a right bastard, and there ain't no mistaking that. Excuse me language, me'lady." She giggled and curtsied.

Breanna just stared in disbelief. No, this must be wrong. No such injustice could possibly be allowed under her father's rule. She knew he could be a 'right bastard' too, but not this. She thought about Captain Carter and the trouble he may be in. "A friend of mine, he was caught by the guards..."

"We call them the freaks," Kitty corrected her.

"Fine, he got caught by the freaks. What will happen to him?"

"'Anging," The pair said in unison.

"Just like that? No trial?" Breanna tried to stand but could not bear the weight on her right leg. Kitty glanced at Chip, then nodded towards Breanna. He moved in and placed her arm about his shoulders.

"Yeah, like, when was there a trial 'ere?" Chip snorted.

Kitty picked up a lamp and, striking a match, lit it. Bree winced from the sudden light but could now see she was in what had once been a beer cellar for the racks where the barrels once hung were still against the walls collecting mold. "I have to get back to the others," Bree said urgently, wincing in pain as she put her foot down.

"You ain't going nowhere on that foot, girlfriend." Kitty smiled, shaking her head. "Come on. We'll take yous back 'ome with us. Guess you could do with an 'ot meal."

She had not thought about it, but as if her body suddenly reacted to the suggestion, she became famished. "But I got to get to Carter," she said, tears of pain and frustration filling her eyes.

Kitty looked at her like a stern mother, placing her fists on her hips. "Now you just chill there, missy. I'll send out Fatboy, and he'll find out what is going on. Don't worry. They won't 'ang the blighter for several days." She took the other side of Breanna, and they led her to a hole in the wall that had been smashed out. This led to another cellar and then into a dark tunnel.

"How come no one uses these cellars?" Bree asked as she hopped between them.

"No one knows they're 'ere. They were built to 'ide goods from the tax guys," Kitty told her. "They run all under the town."

"And you live down here?" Breanna could not hide the disgust in her voice.

"Yeah, but only while our castle is renovated," Chip sneered.

"Now, now, Chip, we 'as compnee," Kitty chided. "And when we 'as compnee, we 'as good manners, right?"

"Yes, Kitty, sorry, Kitty."

As they led her on, Breanna wondered at the fear Kitty could inflict on Chip with just a single look or word. Finally, she saw a badly fitting door over a badly made arch, and another kid stood outside leaning against the wall, holding a small toy crossbow. However, the pointed quarrel resting in it was certainly no toy.

"Hey, pretzel," Kitty smiled, and the boy stood up and opened the door.

"Odd name," Breanna commented as they turned to fit through sideways.

Kitty laughed. "His name is Charlie. Pretzel is the password."

"But he must know you?" Breanna questioned.

"Yeah, but what ifs I was bein' forced to get Fenris' Freaks in 'ere? Then I would tell 'im another password to warn him, and they would 'ave a surprise in 'ere waiting for them."

They stepped out into a large open area. Carpet remnants had been laid, old mismatched furniture from armchairs to sofas were scattered about, and mattresses with holes were makeshift beds. Candles lit the room, giving it an eerie flickering of shadows. Two more boys and a girl jumped up as they entered, and the girl, who was no more than eight or nine, helped Breanna into a lumpy armchair. "Thanks, Midge." Kitty patted her on the shoulder.

"Yeah, thanks." Breanna gave a forced smile, for her pain was too much for a genuine one.

Midge just smiled and nodded, "She can't talk, bless her," sighed Kitty.

"How come?" Breanna asked.

Midge pulled down the neck of her moth-eaten jumper and showed a jagged scar. Bree winced. "Some bastard cut 'er throat," Kitty said as casually as if she were discussing the mild weather. "We dunno what 'appened 'coz she can't tell us."

"Why doesn't she write it down," Breanna was surprised when everyone laughed at what she believed to be a reasonable question.

"The likes of us don't read and write, sweet'art." Kitty smiled as she slipped into the chair adjacent to her.

"Oh right, I didn't think." Breanna flushed; the truth was that apart from servants who rarely even spoke to her, she had not encountered anyone below the middle class before. Well, not unless one counted Emma.

"I fink we need some introductions." Kitty clapped her hands for complete attention. "Everyone, this is Bree." The boys bowed, and Midge curtsied. "Nice manners, now that's good. You know Chip and Midge, but this is 'ank." She indicated a tall, chunky lad with tousled brown hair. Breanna nodded to him. "And this is Fatboy." She indicated the other, who was short and skinny with shoulder-length brown hair.

"Fatboy?" Bree raised an eyebrow.

Fatboy looked at Kitty before he responded, and she smiled and nodded. He then looked at Breanna, "Dunno my real name. It's what they called me in the work'ouse. I was a bit bigger then."

"He was a big tub of lard when he came to us," Grinned Hank, but it faded fast from a glare from Kitty.

"Make yourself useful and go gets some supper for our guest," she ordered, and he sloped off.

"Why not choose a name for yourself?" Breanna sat back as Midge ran over to a table.

"I never fort of it." Fatboy shrugged.

"I needs you to go to the sheriff's office," Kitty instructed, and then, looking at Bree, she asked, "Carter? Was that the geezer's name?"

"Yeah, but I don't know his first name," Breanna said, unaware that this was, in fact, his first name.

"Go find this, Carter."

Fatboy nodded and was gone in a flash. Hank brought her a plate of moldy cheese, dry bread, and a glass of water with things floating in it. The idea of eating it made her nauseous, but she ate so as not to offend. Midge returned with a small pot and sat before her as she ate. She started unfastening Bree's boots, and Kitty explained the girl would put a special salve on her ankle. The smell of was embarrassing as the boot came off, but Breanna seemed to be the only one bothered by it. As Midge applied a greasy substance to her ankle, it was like magic. The pain just disappeared.

"You look shagged out, love," Kitty said. "Get some kip. I'll wakes you if we 'ave any news of your mate."

Breanna could not argue with that. She was exhausted. They led her to a mattress, and Midge covered her in old blankets. She was asleep in only moments.

CHAPTER EIGHT

The Preacher and His Maiden

*"My father and mother may not have been
related to me by blood but they were more
parents to me than the woman who birthed
me and the man who supplied his seed."
Memoir of a Marran Priestess by Emma
Roark-Maine*

S ebastian woke as the early morning sun hit his eyes. He
had finally fallen asleep sitting up against a tree. He
smiled as he looked down to see that Emma had crawled
on his lap at some time during the night and was snoring
softly against his chest. He tried to work out how to get
up without waking her. He saw Rebecca grinning at him.

She was the only one awake and was busy boiling oats for breakfast. "You make a good father, Sebastian."

Sebastian shrugged, "I try my best." He looked back down and gently stroked Emma's hair. "She reminds me of my own daughter, though she is much older."

Rebecca looked confused, "Keri?"

"No, I had another daughter, Eadala. She died when she was three, along with her mother."

"I'm sorry, I had no idea you had been married."

"No reason you should. It was about twelve years ago, and I do not talk of it." He looked once more at the child on his lap. "But I thank Illya daily for bringing Emma into my life and giving me another chance."

"Will you ever marry again?"

"To be honest, I have never thought about it."

He saw Rebecca glance over to where Petra lay asleep, then back to the preacher, and she said, "The two of you seem to have become very close these past few days."

"I feel very close to all of you," He replied, deliberately misinterpreting her comment and checking the dirt under his nails.

"Don't be a smart-arse, Sebastian." Her voice was cold, and she fixed him with a hard stare. "Have you lain with her?"

"That is hardly your busi...," Sebastian started to protest.

"Just answer the question," Rebecca growled.

"No, I have not." The preacher glared with indignation at her. "I am a priest and have not broken my vows."

"That's a relief. It would be hard to find her a husband were she not intact." The First Lady relaxed.

"Really? Is that all she is to you?" The preacher sneered.

"What do you mean?"

"All that matters to you is restoring your House. If she can help you achieve that, you will use her just like Ronan tried to do with you."

"Now, just a minute," Rebecca desperately tried to keep her voice low. "Do not dare to presume how I think about my sister. She has been through hell with my brother, and I am just looking out for her. I do not want her getting hurt again."

"You think I would hurt her?" Sebastian felt affronted as he responded now.

"Yes, not deliberately, but in the long run, you know you two cannot possibly work out. You are like family to us, but not in that way."

"I am not good enough. Is that what you are saying?" Sebastian laughed sarcastically.

"No, you are just too different," she responded defensively. "You are a priest. She is the Second Lady of Jilrir, and if the king recognizes her legitimacy, she will be third in line for the throne. You would make her a preacher's wife. Whatever Portkind says, she is of a royal house. Can you see her following you around in a pretty frock, making tea for your acolytes?"

"Cannot say I have given it any thought." Sebastian sighed. "My feelings for Petra are very confusing. I care greatly for her, but I also see your point."

"I do not know what will happen when we get to Aranar." She looked away towards the still distant mountains as if she were trying to see the future come racing down the snowy peaks. She then looked back at the preacher with the authority of the Lady of Jilrir. "But now things have changed. My father and brother have gone. Rachael has denounced her heritage. Petra..." She paused once more to look at her sister. "Well, she wants to run far away from politics and nobility. Now they can do what they dreamed of, and I won't stand in their way, but I will fight to restore the House of Maine." She then looked back to the preacher, "However, I will die before I let either come to hurt, be it body, mind, or even heart."

"I must disagree with that and with you. You and your sisters were born into privilege, which comes at a price. You can't expect the rights you have without the duty. As individuals, you Maines are not important. As members of The House of Maine, you are."

"With all I know of you, Sebastian, I never considered you a royalist." Rebecca chuckled.

He laughed back, "I'm not really, but what is the alternative?"

"Rachael lectures us that democracy is the way of the future."

He laughed even harder. "She is young and idealistic."

Rebecca smiled, but it was polite, not amused. "Government for the people by the people sounds much fairer."

"Fairer, maybe, but it would be anarchy. You cannot have ordinary people with the lowest basic education, if any, choose who decides their laws and makes economic policy. You would end up with a government where no one agrees, and laws will be based on public popularity, not common sense. It would be like giving the keys to a lunatic asylum to an inmate and saying, 'Don't forget to lock yourself in at night.'"

"Instead, having one man decide for everyone else is better?" Rebecca mused.

"Of course, it is. It may seem unfair, and he may sometimes make the wrong choices, but that is better than anarchy. People like you are raised to rule; you are educated from birth to decide what is best. If you all wake up one day and decide, 'Oh well, I want to be a scientist' or 'I want to run off and have adventures,' the system would collapse."

"But that does not include us; we are women we will never rule, not directly," Rebecca said. "Even if I were Baroness, I would be expected to remarry and have my husband rule in my name."

"Who raises the children? Who teaches them right from wrong?" he argued. "I agree with Petra that it is not fair for her to be expected to marry and just be a wife, but then I step back and look at the big picture. You may not become ruling barons or kings, but you *make* ruling Barons and Kings." This was indeed his view on how things should work, yet it also conflicted strongly with his personal feelings, and he looked over to where Rachael slept curled in a ball. "So ultimately, whatever I feel for Petra, her duty comes first."

Rebecca smiled. "I can't wait until I see you talk politics with Rachael. She thinks everything you say is some sacred truth. I'd love to see her face when you tell her this."

I smiled back and said, "I have indeed discussed this, and we almost had a fight, but politics is not a game I play, and whilst I believe in our current system, it is as far as my interest goes. No, I'll do my best to get you to Aranar. Then it's best that I will be on my way. I have much work to do with Jenri restoring the ministry."

There was a pause as the First Lady of Jilrir studied him carefully. She reached out and placed a gentle hand upon his arm. "Sebastian, you will always have a home with us," Rebecca said softly, "You do not have to leave us."

Emma stirred, stretched, and yawned.

"As soon as Carter gets back, we will get going," The preacher said softly.

Rebecca, clearly unaware he was missing, looked around before asking, "Where is he?"

"He headed into Nethili with Bree to save us time."

"Was that wise?" Rebecca frowned.

"Wise or not, we need provisions." Sebastian shrugged.

"No, I mean about selling that necklace."

"Well, I'm sorry, but heirlooms are rather meaningless now," he said, surprised at the apparent pettiness.

"I don't care about the damn necklace Sebastian," she cursed. "But the authorities will if I am not there with it,"

"I don't understand you." The preacher felt a cold chill run through him.

"It bears the hallmark of my family crest, the seal of the Baron of Jilrir. And trust me, we don't generally hock the family silver," Rebecca snapped sarcastically as she rose with great concern in her eyes. "The moment he tries to sell them, he could be arrested as a thief."

"Are you serious?" Sebastian cried urgently, jumping up.

"Well, unless he has black market connections, which, considering it is Carter, I find that most unlikely," Rebecca spat out.

Sebastian stared off into the direction Carter had headed off.

Could he do nothing right?

As time passed and the sun arced overhead, Sebastian watched, hoped, and prayed for Carter and Breanna to return without incident. As the golden globe passed noon and started its descent, and afternoon drew in, he knew things had probably gone as Rebecca had predicted. "Sebastian," Rebecca said, finally approaching where he stood just outside the camp, staring out toward Nethili. "We cannot stay here forever."

The preacher sighed and reluctantly agreed. "Very well, I will go after them."

"But you cannot go alone," Rebecca stated, clearly concerned at losing him too. "They will not believe you anymore than Carter. You need a member of the First Family to go with you."

"How will that help? Correct me if I am wrong, but Breanna Maine is a part of this family and is now missing."

"Don't get sarcastic with me, Sebastian. Breanna was not going to the authorities."

"Well, unless you happened to pick up your father's seal, you could be anyone saying they are from the first family," He replied haughtily.

"Yes, but 'anyone' does not have their portrait hanging in the town hall," Petra said, coming up to join them. "At least anyone in authority would recognize us. I can go with Sebastian," She added a little too hastily.

Rebecca shook her head. "No, it will be better if I do."

"Beck's, be honest. Does that really make any sense?" Petra smiled. "If we don't get back for some reason, the others need you."

"Well, that makes sense," Sebastian stated. "And she is right. We need you here for the others. With Carter and I gone, there are no men here."

Rebecca raised her eyebrows, "Then what is Oliver Portkind?"

Sebastian glanced at the man sitting by the fire, hugging his knees and mumbling. "To be honest, I am not sure, but I do know this." He looked back to Rebecca. "You're more a man than he is."

"Oh, thank you very much," She replied curtly.

"Oh, come on, Rebecca," Petra looked imploringly at her sister, "I would so like to see Nethili again, please."

"Fine," Rebecca snapped at Sebastian. "You go with her then." She turned and stormed off back to the fireplace.

"Wait for me here," The Preacher muttered to Petra and went up to Rebecca, who was almost white with rage. "Hey, what's with the tantrum?" Sebastian asked quietly.

She turned to him and, in an aggressive whisper, asked, "Do you think it's wise to go with Petra? She is looking for excuses to be alone with you, and if it is truly your intent to leave us at Aranar, then is it not leading her on?"

"I intend to find Carter. That's my sole aim, and she can help," Sebastian replied, though he was not sure it was the truth. "Look, I will talk to her and make everything clear."

She sighed and relaxed a little. "Just be sure you do, Sebastian."

As the pair headed off toward Nethili, Petra looked up at him and asked. "What was all that about?"

"She's a good woman," he replied. "She is just concerned about you."

"Yes, she is," Petra replied, but her voice was cold.

"Now, what's the matter with you?" The preacher asked with a long sigh.

The heart-melting smile returned to her face, and she gripped his hand tightly. "Hey, don't worry about it."

"If something is wrong, I would like to know." To be honest, he was not sure he did.

"Are you attracted to Rebecca?" She asked after a short silence.

He smiled. "Your sister is even more off-limits than you are."

"Don't avoid the question," she said, turning in front of him and walking backward while still holding his hand.

"Your sister is a little too austere for my liking."

"Good." Petra grinned, wondering what austere meant. She fell in step beside him again. "And now, why is she more off-limits than me?"

"Your sister is now head of the family. Whoever marries her becomes the acting baron until their first son arrives. That is not a destiny I would choose, even if such a union would be permitted." He laughed.

"Oh yeah, I forgot that," and she chuckled. "You would also be the direct heir to the throne if you wed her."

"Oh, sweet Illya." He felt his draw drop and cursed his lack of political interest. "Do you realize what that means?"

"That you can't bonk my sister?" Petra raised an eyebrow.

"That is why the Commech want one of you alive, don't you see?"

"No clue?" she said.

"The king may well be pressured to recognize the husband of a Maine as ruler." He stopped walking as the weight of the world descended upon him. "This is not real. It can't be." The multitude of thoughts whirled around inside him. "I tried to keep a few girls from dying."

"And you're doing a pretty good job." Petra shrugged, a little bewildered by his rambling.

"But I now have the fate of the line of kings in my hands." He looked into her eyes.

"Yeah, but you get to hang out with the prettiest sister." She grinned.

"Sweetheart," he said as, now more than ever, he realized that socially and politically, they were a thousand miles apart. "It's not going to happen. You and me, I mean."

"Can you really deny that you have feelings for me, as I do you?" Her optimism seemed undeflated.

"I care about you after all we have been through. However, the king has a son, but he has no children. Whoever marries the eldest surviving Maine woman is third in line to the Kingdom. It will be undisputable."

"I don't count in this, Sebastian." Frustration filled her voice, "I am a bastard. Why does any of this affect us?"

"Your position is not established, my dear. You are still blood kin to the king." Before he could stop himself, he ran a hand gently through her hair. "Come, let's get going."

They continued in silence for a while. "I have never been in love before," Petra said suddenly.

"You still have a year or two to find a husband."

"Ronan was raised to rule; Rebecca was raised as First Daughter, the rest of us just decorations or bargaining chips to wed off in diplomatic games. I have been expected to do nothing all my life, just look pretty as my father tried to marry me off like some concubine. Rebecca sat in council; Rebecca was in charge of this and that. I hate that I have no future. I don't believe I am here to be just a wife."

"I understand this, but I cannot lead you anywhere else." Sebastian sighed. "I cannot keep you safe."

Petra gazed ahead in the deepest thought. "I'm as good as Rebecca. I'm just never allowed to prove it. I keep being told how beautiful I am, but no one wants to look beyond that."

"Do you really want to be like your sister? She has her fate preordained more than you. If she is to be the mother of a Baron or king whose husband will rule until the child is of age, she will never get to choose her own destiny, either. The king's courtiers will most likely choose a new husband for her, maybe the king himself. As soon as she does marry, her job is over. All she will do is produce heirs, and the moment her first son is born, you are moved down the line of succession as that line moves in a new direction."

"I never thought of it like that," Petra mused.

"Being born into a ruling family forces duty upon you from birth. The good of the people comes before your needs and those of your sisters. That does not mean you should stop respecting yourself. You are a good person, Petra. You just don't see it in yourself, and you can do good things from your position. Be a guide to your important spouse. Raise your children to be good, kind rulers." Was he convincing her or himself? The idea of another man touching her, defiling her, even impregnating his sweet, precious Petra brought bile into his heart. They walked on, and their conversation turned to lighter matters. Then, a darker thought slipped into his mind. Was he the new Feyer? Was her interest in him just another ploy to escape the Maine legacy? He tried to push the thoughts from his mind, but they lingered and grew.

CHAPTER NINE

The Mayor of Nethili

"It could hardly be said that Petra's return to the town of her birth and childhood was one of fanfare. On the contrary, it would be a time of torment that made her life in Jilrir look like a summer holiday." Memoir of a Marran Priestess by Emma Roark-Maine

It was almost dusk when they arrived in Nethili. People went about their business with a casual air. He asked for directions toward the marketplace, and they headed in the directions given. His carbine attracted a lot of interest, and it was only heightened when he asked around about a man and girl matching the description of Carter and Breanna.

"Aye, there was a thief here," said an old, gnarled woman at a cheap pottery stall. "Stole the king's silver or sommink

they did. The militiamen came an' took him away. Why?
You friends of theirs?" She looked suspiciously at them.
"'Praps, we should call them back for you?"

"You said 'him'?" Sebastian narrowed his eyes. "What
about the girl?"

"Got away she did." She pointed to an old drainpipe.
"Climbed up there like a feral monkey she did."

"Thank you for your help." Sebastian offered her a silver
coin, but she waved it away.

"Get art ovit. I am an honest woman. I don't want
no messing with thieves." So, they bade her farewell and
moved on, somewhat bewildered.

"What an unpleasant woman," Petra sneered as the
Preacher led her away through and out of the market.

"And strange, too," he said.

"In what way do you mean?" Petra queried, her eyes
narrowed in thought.

"Have you ever seen the lower classes turn down good
money?" He asked. "Regardless of the source."

"No, but to be honest, I have not exactly been around
them much in recent years," Petra admitted.

"Well, trust me, they do not." They were not heading in
any particular direction, but he thought it unwise to stand
around talking while drawing so much attention.

"How do you know? You're not exactly from humble
stock yourself these days," Petra chuckled.

"I am a Priest, and we don't just Minister to the idle
rich," he replied in mockery.

"Well, she thinks your coin is stolen. She said as much."
Petra pointed out as they wandered aimlessly up the street.

"Sweet Petra, you truly have led a sheltered life. Most of these folk live near starvation. In Jilrir or even Heron Bay, you would get your throat cut for less than this."

"Seriously?" The girl looked shocked.

"That woman did not seem so much as honest as afraid," he pondered.

"Afraid of what? You?"

"No, she was clearly not afraid of me." He stopped walking, and so did Petra. He folded his arms and tapped his lower lip with his knuckle as he stared at a nonexistent place over Petra's shoulder. Then he looked at her. "Being afraid of being seen associating with me maybe, but not of me."

"Perhaps we should simply head down the town hall and ask about Carter," She suggested, not as concerned about the old lady's response as he was.

"Yes, but not yet. She has piqued my curiosity. I would like to find out what exactly is going on here first. I think it is the authorities she is mostly concerned about."

"What about Carter? We hang thieves, you know?" Petra reminded me.

"Not without a trial, and considering the size of this town, I assume they would normally get a judge from Jilrir," He reminded her.

Petra grinned. "Perhaps they do not give folk trials here, and that's why she was scared."

"Is that possible?"

"I was joking, Sebastian. If they did that, my father would throw a fit." She tried to reassure him but failed.

"I think you are right, but we should get to that town hall." Without thinking, he took her hand in his and went in search of the town's seat of government.

As in all cities, villages, and towns in the region, the seat of government was at the heart of the community and always easy to find. The town hall turned out to be more of a grand house in a street of grand terraced houses. The only difference to the town hall was the sign stating that that was what it was. There was no front yard, and the four or five steps led straight down to the pavement. Almost immediately, Sebastian could see something was distinctly not right. Rather than neat, uniformed guards, three scruffy-looking men lounged about on the steps, smoking long pipes and idling slovenly. The buttons on their tunics were undone, and they seemed more interested in chatting and laughing than in any duty. They ignored the couple completely as they approached, but as soon as he set his foot upon the first step, one rose to his feet and was obviously very annoyed at being disturbed. He hitched up his trousers, then folded his arms and barred my way but said nothing. His head hung to the left as he looked him up and down contemptuously. Then he looked to Petra, and his demeanor changed. He stood up straight and ran his hand ineffectually through his matted, unwashed hair. "'Ello darling." He gave her a lewd grin.

Petra raised an eyebrow and looked at him, then at Sebastian, who was fighting to keep his temper in check. "Good evening," Petra replied with a cool air.

The thug looked her up and down lecherously but said nothing more. His companion had not moved from where he leaned cross-legged against the side of the open doorway. He was looking down at his fingernails, which he was cleaning with the tip of a hunting knife.

Sebastian made to step in, but the first man just looked at him and made no attempt to stand aside, "Do we have a problem?" Sebastian asked, raising a questioning eyebrow. His tone was one Petra would come to recognize as potentially dangerous to the person on the receiving end.

"No." The man gave a feigned, surprised look. "No problem here, mate," He glanced over his shoulder at his companion. "You got a problem, George?"

"Nope." George did not even look up. "No problem 'ere Jack."

Jack looked back at the Preacher and smiled. "No, no problems."

"Then would you mind letting us through?" Sebastian said with an enforced calm, not at all interested in this lout's attempts to be amusing.

The man raised his hand to his lower lip, gazing up and down in mock pondering. Lowering his hand, he folded his arms again and hung his head to the right. "Yes. I would mind letting you through." He waved his finger towards the street to indicate the direction they should go. "Goodbye."

"We wish to enter."

"No, thank you. Goodbye," The man said mildly.

"Well, let me rephrase myself. We *are* going to enter," Sebastian said coldly. Petra, at his side, tensed, and she gently slipped her arm through his.

Jack stepped down to the Preacher until their noses were a hair's breadth apart. "Listen, you lanky streak of piss. The mayor don't want no pimps or their whores in 'is 'ouse." Then he grinned at Petra. "Well, not unless he sends out fer one." He looked her up and down again. "Though I must say that's a right nice bit of crackling you have there. I'm off in an hour. If she goes down fer me, I might not run you in for carrying an illegal weapon." He indicated Sebastian's carbine.

"Now there is an offer you can't refuse, eh Petra?" Sebastian grinned at his companion.

"Well, as delightfully romantic that proposal is, I think I will decline it," she replied with her own amused grin, and Sebastian could not help but like that. She could show humor similar to his own in a tense situation.

"You have disappointed young Jack here." He smiled at her.

"My apologies for that." She smiled and gave him a half curtsy.

"Oh, by the way, Lady Petra, please accept my apologies for the needless violence you must now witness, milady."

"No apology required, Kirkman Hawk. I look forward to it," she said in her most delicately feminine voice, taking two steps back as Sebastian rammed his knee into the idiot's groin. He doubled over towards the Preacher, who slammed his fist down onto the back of his neck, hastening his drop to the ground. Before his startled comrade could rise, Sebastian's sword was out, pointing at his terrified throat. "Don't even think it, boy," he snarled. The one he hit tried to rise, but a boot to the head persuaded him he was better off lying face down. "Kindly inform the mayor that the Lady Petra requires an audience."

"'E ain't seein' no one guv," The man spluttered, his eyes crossing as he tried to focus on the point of the blade.

"Do I need to carve an invitation into your skull and throw it through the window?" The Preacher said, pushing the blade just enough to draw the faintest trickle of blood.

"I'm a-goin' guv. Just be careful with that thing." He scrambled inside as Sebastian drew the sword back and sheathed it. Taking Petra's hand, he helped her step over the man on the floor, and they followed him in. The hallway was more like the lobby of a domestic residence with carpet and furnishings. A portrait of the elderly king stared at them from the wall in front, and an ornate hand-drawn map of the region hung to their left. In the center, a grand staircase wound upwards. The thug had entered a second door to the right, and they heard him speaking, "Sir, there is some bastard outside. Says 'is bitch is Lady Petra. 'E dun in Jack proper like."

They entered the room without waiting for an invite, and a sudden look of recognition crossed Petra's face as she saw the fat, balding, bespectacled man behind the desk. He rose from his seat quickly and, with a look of alarm, backed away from them against the wall. Sebastian was surprised to see a look of hatred and contempt on his young companion's face. However, as the mayor appeared to recognize her, he seemed to relax immediately. He returned to his chair, baring a wide patronizing grin. "Well, well, well, my dear Petra, how good to see you again." The man, who was in his late fifties, arched his fingers.

"Fenris? Since when have you been a mayor?" Petra growled.

"You means she is Lady Petra?" The thug looked horrified, and his jaw dropped.

"Indeed, she is. You can go, Parkes. I'll deal with this." He smiled, rising from his chair again.

"I think you need to deal with them first," Sebastian stated coldly, nodding towards the departing 'guard,' "A re-education in basic manners, dress code, and drill."

"Who is this man, Petra, your latest conquest?" The mayor sneered, waving his spectacles at the Preacher.

"You will address me as My Lady or Lady Petra, and I asked you a question?" Petra almost spat in contempt.

"After you refused my marriage proposal, which your father kindly went to a lot of trouble to arrange, he appointed me here. A matter of appeasement for the humiliation you caused me, I assume." The mayor looked him up and down. "I must say this one is much cleaner than your usual tastes."

"He is Sebastian Hawk, a Priest from Heron Bay, and you will show him due respect." Petra sounded almost like her sister as she spoke with authority.

"Petra, Petra, Petra," The odious man twirled his glasses back and forth between thumb and forefinger before replacing them upon his nose. "Whilst I must show respect for the daughter of My Lord, I have never really felt the desire to respect her multitude of lovers. As for claiming he is a Priest, well, that only adds to the charges."

"Charges? Lovers?" Sebastian made to move forward, but at a sudden loud call from Fenris, two side doors burst open, revealing several armed guards who came running in brandishing sabers.

"You obviously do not know Lady Petra as I do. You are not the first upstart to run away with her, but you are the first to be caught stealing family jewels, for I assume you're with the thief we picked up earlier in the market?"

"Listen, you fat obnoxious bastard," Petra ranted at him. "You have no right..."

"Oh, still sweet of tongue with dulcet manners, my dear Petra." The mayor smiled. "My orders on you are very clear. The last time you ran away, your father left instructions in every town that were it to happen again, we were to charge the man with kidnapping and return you to the baron. We can charge your lover with theft and impersonating a church minister this time."

I pulled the Illyan symbol from under my cloak and tossed it on the table. "Impersonate that." Sebastian snapped.

"And theft from an Illyan temple." He smiled up at me.

"Jilrir has fallen to the Commech," Petra shouted. "My father is dead, you big tub of pig fat."

The mayor actually laughed. "I did not say I'd return you to your father, Petra. I meant the new baron who has made it quite clear that any ruler will have his town spared if they turn over just one of the daughters of Maine. And, praise Commech, you walk right into my office. How thoughtful of you."

"You're a son of Commech?" Sebastian glared contemptuously at the man who had invoked the name of the god he so loathed. "That, sir, explains a lot."

"You will be returned to him today." Fenris ignored him. "Whilst your lover here will be hanged in the market square as an example to all who defy my law."

"You know full well you cannot hang me," Sebastian growled. "The Treaty of Massir..."

"Oh, the new baron has dispensed with that, and your faith is now heresy," he said, looking immensely proud of this achievement. "Take this filth and his slut away." He ordered the guard.

The idea of this fool returning Petra to Jilrir made Sebastian's actions very clear to him. His own demise was secondary in his thoughts. Some malice obviously guided Fenris's decision.

The moment a guard placed a hand on Petra's shoulder, he spun and backhanded him with his fist. "Keep your hands off of her." Then all hell let loose in his brain as something hard slammed down on the back of his neck, and he went down. Petra screamed, and that fear that goes through you when you know you are defeated and there is nothing he can do ran through him. "Please don't kill him. I'll come with you. Just don't kill him."

"No, Petra," Sebastian gasped, trying to regain his feet, but was pushed down again, and with a knee in his back, the guards bound his hands.

"Listen, Fenris. I'll do whatever you want. Just don't kill him." Petra pleaded. "I'll marry you even if that is what you want,"

"My lady." Sebastian heard the syrupy voice chuckle. "Do you really think I'd marry you after the public humiliation I suffered at your hands?"

"I'm begging you, Kalvin, and that is something no one has ever got from me. Sebastian is an honorable man, and I love him," Petra implored.

Despite all that was going on, this drew Sebastian's attention. "Fenris, listen to me," He managed to say. "If you send this girl back, she will be married to the baron, and trust me, she will ask for your head on a silver plate as her bridal gift."

The mayor just sighed. "Get them out of my sight."

The Preacher was hauled up, and Petra flung her arms around him. "No," She cried out, but she was dragged from him. "Sebastian."

He could not answer as he was pulled from her and led out by the guards. Was this how it was to end? Escape the Commech but die at the hands of their own people just because Petra had not married a fat bureaucrat. Sebastian had to warn the others. "Rachael, Rachael," he called out with his mind.

The town jail was a small, compact building of just three rooms: the sheriff's office, a reception, and a room containing three cells. Two of the cells were connected and shared a common grilled wall. They stood seven feet high, and the only ventilation was a tiny glassless grille near the ceiling. There were no furnishings of any kind, just straw covering the floor. The only adornment was a cheap ceramic chamber pot that had barely enough links on its chain to move it from the wall. The concept was that the contents could not be thrown at anyone. Sebastian was remorselessly thrown into one by two of Fenris's thugs. Jack, who had already beaten him constantly as he was dragged down the street, took a final opportunity to inflict one last humiliation on the Preacher. Sebastian, unmoving, face down upon the floor. His face was a swollen mass of blue and black bruises. Jack bent over him, thrust his hand between his legs, and squeezed. The Preacher gave a barely audible cry. "I'll make earrings out of these when we is done hanging you, Josser."

Sebastian opened a swollen, bloody eye. He said in little more than a whisper, "If Petra is safe, I promise I will kill you fast. If she has so much as a mark on her, then I will make you beg for your death." The last thing he saw was Jack's fist before oblivion overcame him.

CHAPTER TEN

Logan

"Logan Braithwaite may have been a hulking brute of a man whose appearance positively terrified me, but in truth, he was a man of considerable kindness." – Memoir of a Marran Priestess by Emma Roark-Maine

Rachael Maine had spent the day meditating and reading the Book. As dusk approached, she was sitting talking to Emma by the campfire when suddenly she felt a hard whack to the back of her head. She lurched forward, and then the pain came hard and fast. Watching her, Emma looked startled and scared as she lurched back and forth for no apparent reason.

"Lady Rebecca," she called out but was unable to take her eyes off this strange dance Sebastian's new acolyte seemed to be performing. "Somefing seems to be wrong with Lady Rachael."

However, Jenri made it to her first, and skidding down to her knees, she grabbed the acolyte from the back and wrapped her arms about her to hold tightly and stop her from hurting herself. "Shut it out, Feffer. Whatever it is, shut it out."

Rebecca was next at her sister's side, "What is going on?" she asked, her voice trembling with fear as she fell beside them.

"Someone is beating Sebastian." Tears streamed down Rachael's face as her glasses fell, landing in the grass in front of her.

"Shut it out," Jenri said soothingly.

"I can't. I mustn't. I have to know what is happening." Rachael tensed. "He is trying to tell me something." Then, as fast as it started, it stopped. Rachael's eyes widened. "Oh my goddess, I think he is dead." Gasps and murmurs erupted all around the camp until Rebecca shouted for them to shut up.

"It is all right," Jenri said softly. "If he were dead, you would know it. He must be simply unconscious. Did he manage to tell you anything?"

Rachael took the handkerchief proffered by Alannah and wiped her eyes. "It all came as a rush. Give me a moment to sort it out in my head." She closed her eyes and began to relate things, "The Mayor of Nethili has made some sort of deal with the Commech not to invade Nethili." An angry gasp came from Rebecca. "Sebastian has been arrested, taken to the city jail, and separated from Petra. Oh, sweet mercy, the mayor intends to send her back to Jilrir and turn her over to the enemy."

"Why that ...." Rebecca started but was quickly hushed by Jenri.

"Sebastian has learned that Carter is imprisoned but that Breanna escaped." Rachael continued.

"So why did she not come back?" The First Lady asked.

"Let her finish," Jenri snapped. "She can lose these memories if distracted."

"He does not know where Breanna is." The Feffer said. "He is scared for them and feels he has let them down. That's it. He then went silent."

"It's all right, honey," Jenri hugged her tightly, letting her lie back against her chest. She looked up at Rebecca. "Give us some time. We need to relax her mind."

Rebecca nodded but was frustrated that this relative stranger cared for her sister and not herself. Not for the first time, Rebecca thought she was losing her sister. She rose and turned to the others who were now all gathered around. "Looks like it is down to us," she said solemnly.

"With all due respect, milady," put in Portkind. "What are we supposed to do? If the Hawk is taken down, we are not exactly going to do better."

"You certainly are not," Rebecca snapped. "You can stay here with the children until we send for you."

"Out here? Alone! In the wilds? With children? Milady, I must protest."

"If you do not start pulling your weight, we will leave you behind altogether," Rebecca growled at the clerk.

"He does have a point, though," Devin stated. "What are we to do?"

"We unleash hell upon Nethili, and by the time we get there, hopefully, we will have had enough time to formulate a plan on how to do it."

Breanna Marie Maine woke in total darkness. She could hear faint snores from different people around the room. She sat up and waited a minute or two for her eyes to adjust, but no amount of waiting could compensate for the total darkness of the Remington Street Posse's cellar lair. "Anyone awake?" She asked softly, not wanting to wake anyone.

"Wassup, Bree?" Came back an equally soft-toned voice of a boy.

"Who is that?"

"Fatboy," Fatboy replied.

"I need to get out of here." Bree felt around her surroundings and climbed to her feet.

"Why the urgency?" Bree was startled when the voice moved right next to her.

"My sisters are expecting me back," she hissed, "They will be shitting blocks with worry right now."

"Ain't safe, babe. You best off here."

"If you twos wants to natter, take it outside," Kitty Longfellow's sleepy, irritated voice said from the other side of the room. "Somes of us needs our beauty sleep."

Bree felt a hand on her arm, and it slid down to find her hand. Fatboy led her carefully out of the door, and finding their way to the trap door, they headed outside. Breanna headed to the end of the alley with Fatboy right behind. She stopped at the corner of the street and leaned against the brickwork wall. It was a beautiful cloudless night, and she looked up at the myriad of stars that twinkled down at them. The town sat in total silence. It was so different out here than in Jilrir, with its cramped streets, foul smells, and tall buildings and towers. "It is so beautiful here."

Fatboy raised an eyebrow, "Never 'erd Neflee called that before." He stood close, just by her left shoulder, and as she looked back at him, she felt a funny little tingle in her tummy. He was a few inches taller than her and had a fair complexion, smooth skin, and no sign of facial hair. His high cheekbones gave him a gaunt appeal. His light brown, almost blonde hair was longer than was typical for a man and touched his collar. The front of it stuck out over his forehead as if he used some feminine hair styling product. She averted her eyes, not understanding his effect on her, "I rarely left Jilrir before last week and have never been this far north."

"I growed up 'ere in Neflee.' He shrugged. "Ain't seen nuffink else."

"You lived in the workhouse here?"

"Yup, born in there." He stared out into the street at the empty market stalls with the vacant expression of someone with unpleasant memories. "Didn't stay long. Got out 'n' met up with Kat."

"Kat?" Bree frowned.

"Kitty."

"Oh, right, of course." Bree felt silly at not realizing this and then annoyed at why what Fatboy thought of her bothered her. "How come you don't know your name?"

He looked at her and chuckled lightly. "I does have a name, Anna. Everyone called me Fatboy, so's Fatboy is me name."

"Anna?" Bree raised an eyebrow.

Fatboy shrugged, "Short for Breanna,"

"Everyone calls me Bree."

Fatboy grinned. "Well, I ain't everyone, Anna. Brie is a type of cheese. You ain't a piece of cheese, is you, darlin'?" Had anyone else referred to her as darling, they would have got a slap, but that weird tummy sensation did a flip as he said it.

"Well, you are not a fat boy, Fatboy. So, you call me Anna, and I'll call you Fred."

He grinned. "Yous gots yourself a deal, Anna."

"What?" She had only been joking.

Fatboy offered her his hand to shake on it. "A deal. You do do deals up there in your golden palace tower, don't ya?"

Bree rolled her eyes and shook her head, but then she shook his hand. "You are incorrigible, Fred." She said with a chuckle.

"Dunno what incorrigible means, but yous is prolly right." He winked at her, and her knees wobbled imperceptibly.

She turned away, wondering about these new sensations. She had grown up closeted with sisters and had no experience with boys, and whilst pleasant, she found the feelings distracting. "I must let my sisters know what is happening to Carter. We need to get him out of here."

"You can't just walk out in the streets, babe."

Bree scowled at him. "You are not calling me that," she advised forcefully.

Fatboy just grinned. "You got it, blossom."

Bree rolled her eyes but turned her attention to the matter at hand. "Why can't I just walk out there?"

"Curfew, Freak's got his bovver boys patrolling. Shoot on sight policy."

"I can avoid them." She said, but as she stepped out into the street, Fatboy grabbed her by the shoulder and pulled her back.

Breanna spun about to give him what for, but she stopped as she saw a look of genuine concern on that handsome face. "Please, Anna, don't risk it. Let me 'elp. We can go talk to Logan."

"Who is Logan?"

"'e was the captain of the rozzers." At her blank look, he elucidated. "The militia, but he, like, hads this fallin' out wiv Fenris, right. Fenris fires 'im. But, Logan ain't going away like. 'E watches Fenris, and 'e works out all the bad stuff 'e's doing, and 'e is preparin' for when 'e can take out Fenris and 'is cronies. 'E 'elps the posse with food n 'iding us out and the like."

"You mean he is operating as a resistance movement."

"Kinda, 'e is loyal to the state, see, and your pappy." Another blank look from the girl. "Your Pa, ya Dad." Bree nodded, "Well, 'e put Fenris there, and Logan is like all a tiz about going 'gainst the Maines."

Breanna grinned, "well, I am a Maine."

"That's what me is finking." Fatboy grinned. "'E may be able to 'elp."

"Let us go see him."

"Nah, likes I said, too dangerous. We best be going at first light." Reluctantly, she agreed. "Come on, let's go get some more kip." He slipped an arm about her shoulder and led her back to the hideout, and she let him, much to her surprise.

"Kip? You need to learn to talk properly."

"Oh, look at you with all your hairs and graces."

"That's airs, not hairs." Bree giggled as she slipped down through the trap door.

"Whatevs!" He shrugged and followed her down.

Alannah, Emma, and Daniel were less than impressed by the idea of being left with the whiney Oliver Portkind. However, they said their reluctant goodbyes and watched the party head off toward Nethili.

About half an hour into their journey, Rachael said brightly, "Sebastian is awake," but her face fell. "He is telling us not to come. That we are to flee the area."

"Like that is going to happen," Jenri growled, and Rebecca agreed.

"Does he remember the town's layout or anything that can help us?" Keri asked.

"He says there is militia on the streets, but they are not Ithian regulars and basically untrained thugs."

"Well, that should help us," Rebecca stated. "However, we would do better with some muscle of our own.

"Yous told 'er 'bout Logan?" Kitty slapped Fatboy hard around the face.

"Knock it off, Kat," Fatboy glared as he nursed his reddened cheek. "Yous the one who done the deal to trust her."

"Yeah, but it wasn't our secret to share now, was it?"

"Look, if it's a problem, I can just leave," Breanna said uneasily.

"Oh, darlin' yous is just fine." Kitty smiled at her, then glared once more at Fatboy. "Yous got dumbstruck by a pretty face?"

"Don't you gets it, Kat," Fatboy said earnestly. "She's a Maine, and Logan won't go against Fenris 'less he knows the Maines don't wants him no more."

Kitty bit down on her knuckle, pondering, "I guess it's werf a try." She looked at Bree. "Yous sure we gots Maine support 'ere? I mean not just you like, but the nobs up there."

"If anyone is going to hurt Carter, then trust me, they ain't going to ..." She stopped with a frown and backed up. "They *are not* going to be any friend of the Maines. I can't promise you what my sister Becca will do about the mayor, but I can promise you that if she comes to town, none of you will ever have to fear going back to the workhouse again. I give you my word on that as Fourth Lady of Jilrir." Technically, she was now Third, but old habits...

Kitty sighed. "Alrights, you gots me convinced. Let's go see Logan."

Dawn rose with a grey, cloudy sky. Kitty, Midge, Hank, Charlie, Fatboy, and Breanna emerged from the secret home of the Remington Street Posse in that order. Kitty made her way to the end of the alley, signaling to the others to stay back as she peered around the corner and assessed the situation. She then looked back to them, saying softly, "Alright, posse, let's go two at a time, all casual-like. Don't you go being all sp'icous!"

Hank and Charlie went first, then Bree and Fatboy. As Bree strolled down the street, she glanced over her shoulder and saw Kitty and Midge following someway behind. "How far is it to this Logan's house?"

Fatboy shrugged. "About ten min...."

"Shit in a cradle," Bree interrupted as they passed a stall she had knocked over the previous day. The merchant was there preparing to start his day. "Cross the street, quick, in case that guy recognizes me." They dipped in and out between the carts that trundled up and down the street. Fatboy quickly led them off the main road, and they wound their way through the back alleys until they came to the poorer district of the town. It was nowhere near as bad as the Jilrian tenements, with Bree only thinking it poorer because the residential single-story buildings became much smaller. They stopped outside, one where Hank and Charlie were waiting. They then waited for Kitty and Midge to catch up.

Kitty went up the pathway and knocked at the door. A plain-looking woman in a patterned dress and apron opened the door. She looked at each in turn before saying, "Well, you can't all come in. I don't have the room. Two of you only. The rest of you can skedaddle."

Kitty looked back at Bree. "Come on."

Bree glanced up at Fatboy, and both looked disappointed at separating. Kitty noticed this and grinned to herself but said nothing as the workhouse girl and the noblewoman entered the house.

Logan Braithwaite was short but powerfully built. His black beard made him kind of intimidating to Breanna. "Katherine, this better be important. I really don't want my neighbors to see me fraternize with outlaws. Fenris does not need the excuse to have me do the rope dance, but one would make it easier for him. He looked at Bree.

"Who's this?" He noticed that although they were the worst for wear, her clothes were not cheap.

"You isn't gonna believe it, guv," Kitty said with a grin.

"Try me," Logan replied suspiciously.

"I have the honor," Kitty emphasized the 'H' in honor. "Of introducing yous to the Lady Breanna Maine of Jilrir."

There was a pause, and then a grin started to appear, barely noticeable under the beard. It quickly turned into a laugh. "Either you take me for a fool, or you have been taken for a fool yourself, Katherine. You would have me believe this dirty little urchin is the Fourth Lady of Jilrir."

"I'd like to see you look better if you were chased out of a burning city," Bree snapped indignantly. "Then, walked all the way to this town to be chased again by the town guard. All without a change of clothes in a week."

Logan stopped laughing and studied her. "You talk like a Maine."

"I am a Maine," Breanna said with indignation.

"Let's say this is true. What brings Breanna Maine to Nethili?"

"We are on the run, of course. The Commech are hunting for us."

"So, the Baron has fled Jilrir?" Logan frowned.

"No, the baron is dead, as is his son Ronan. My sisters Rebecca, Rachael, Alannah, and Petra travel with the last of the Illyans. They are camped a few hours east of here but will no doubt be coming to look for me since I have been unable to return to them. The guard has detained my companion Carter, and I fear my sisters may get a similar welcome."

"So, the House of Maine is no more. That is a shame." Logan sighed.

"It is not dead yet. It lives on in us and under the leadership of Rebecca Maine, First Lady of Jilrir."

"A woman cannot rule a province." Logan shook his head.

"Why not? How does having a penis aid in governing?" Breanna tilted her head to one side.

"It is the brain, tis smaller than a man's," Logan responded with conviction.

"Well, you clearly need more room for your ego," Bree muttered under her breath.

"You sound truthful, but I'm not ready to bend the knee just yet." The man rubbed his beard thoughtfully.

"I don't want you to bend your knee, just your sword arm." Bree frowned.

Logan laughed, "I like you, Lady Maybe. Tell you what. I will ride out to see if I can find your sisters. However, I have a condition."

"Name it."

"If I find them, you will have my sword and the swords of the last honest men in Nethili. If, however, you prove false and a traitor to our cause, Katherine gives me her word she will cut your throat."

"Oh, I cants agree to that," Kitty said, most perturbed at such a suggestion.

"Yes, you can," said Breanna coldly, "I am true in my words, and it shall be shown."

"If I agrees, Bree, I'll do it. Make no bones about it. Me word is me bond."

"I understand."

Kitty shrugged, "Yous gots me word, Logan."

CHAPTER ELEVEN

Desperate Plans

"Lady Rebecca was fastidiously dedicated to restoring the House of Maine. I honestly think she would have given her life if it meant the family's power was restored." Memoir of a Marran Priestess by Emma Roark-Maine

J enri grew impatient at the speed the group of women made as they headed across the plains towards the Nethili Road. The pace was slow and laborious as she strode ahead with Kerianna.

It was Annabelle Devin who saw the rider first. "We have company coming," she said, pointing to the horizon at the horse heading their way.

"Oh great, just what we need when we have no fighters here," muttered Rebecca, only to receive an offended look from the Illyan Esselar.

"You have your sword," Devin stated.

"Indeed, but barely a basic understanding of its use." Rebecca snorted.

"You did fine on the road to Ternal," said Rachael encouragingly.

"I was lucky and desperate." Rebecca drew her blade all the same, and Jenri crossed her wrists and rested her hands upon her blades.

As the grim-looking man drew nearer, Rebecca pointed her weapon at him and cried, "Halt. What is it you want?"

He reined in his horse and called over to them. "I seek Rebecca, First Lady of Jilrir of the House of Maine."

Jenri narrowed her eyes and slipped her slender fingers around the grips of her weapons. "Why do you seek her?"

"That is the business of mine and hers," the man replied.

"Are you of the Commech?" Jenri continued.

The tall bearded man looked offended at the suggestion. "No. Do not think that, and do not speak that accursed name in my presence. I worship none other than Illya, Goddess of Justice. I am come as a friend to the Maines. Rightful rulers of this province."

"How can we know you speak the truth of this?" Rebecca narrowed her eyes.

"I bring a message from one who she trusts," he replied.

"We trust few these days. Who sends this message?"

"She claims to be Breanna Maine, Fourth Lady of Jilrir. Though I have my doubts."

Rebecca gasped, "How fairs she?"

"She is well and as safe as one can be in Nethili these days. That is why I seek the Lady Rebecca, who I assume you are. You are walking into danger. And I am here to assist you."

"What is the message from Breanna?" Keri asked.

He looked at the Marran and seemed to relax somewhat at the sight of her green eyes. He pulled out the paper and looked back at Rebecca. "Forgive the informality, milady, but I'll read it as she wrote it."

"Go ahead," Rebecca commanded.

"'Becks, this guy is on our side. He is a former town guard. I am safe, but Carter is in jail. If you have doubts that I wrote this or am being coerced, here is proof. Inside the Book that Rachael has is an inscription to Sebastian from a person called Meri. Only one who has seen it would know, love B."

Rebecca looked to Rachael, who nodded. She lowered her sword, "I am Lady Rebecca Maine. You may join us."

Logan rode up to them, and as soon as he slid off his horse, he hand went to drew out his sword. In a swift, barely visible move, Jenri's blade was at his throat. "Oh, that is not wise, sir." She said softly. The man reached out his arms in a gesture of peace. Without stepping closer, not that Jenri would let him, he lowered himself to one knee and offered Rebecca the hilt of his sword. "My service, milady." As fast as Jenri had drawn her blade, she returned it to its sheath.

Rebecca's eyes widened, but she said, "Accepted, sir. Does a name go with that service?"

"Logan Ruel Braithwaite, milady. Former Captain of the Nethili Guard." Logan responded with his head still bowed.

"You may rise, Braithwaite." The First Lady was in her element. He did, returning the sword to its sheath.

"May I introduce my sister? Lady Rachael." Rebecca indicated her sister, and he bowed to her.

"Feffer Rachael, actually." Rachael corrected with a smile.

"Sorry, a force of habit." Rebecca shrugged.

This drew his attention. "A Feffer, you say, which of the gods do you honor with your testimony?"

"Illya."

"Praise be! Aren't you precious? I am honored to meet a supplicant of my church." He bowed again and even lower this time, and Rachael had to stifle a chuckle as she pushed her glasses up her nose.

Rebecca grinned, "Well if that gets you going, I can't imagine how you are going to react to the Esselar of Illya."

He frowned as Rebecca nodded to Jenri and turned to look at the young woman who, moments before, was ready to slit his throat. "Esselar?" The word barely escaped his mouth.

"That's me." Jenri chuckled at his open-mouthed expression.

He fell to his knees and lowered his head towards her feet. "Oh, holy one, you are Kara Adair?"

The amusement fell from her face. "I am afraid not. The Commech slew her. I am Jenri, her successor."

"Commech bastards," Logan growled.

"Come, let's make a fire, and you can tell us of both Nethili and, more importantly, Breanna." Rebecca invited. She introduced him to Devin and Keri, and soon, the group was seated around a small fire heating leftover venison.

Logan took his place between Rebecca and Rachael. "Her Ladyship Breanna is relatively safe. She resides with an outlaw group of workhouse children known as the Remington Street Posse."

"What?" balked Rebecca, almost choking on a piece of meat.

Logan raised a reassuring hand. "Have no fear, milady. You will not find a more daring, cunning group of young people this side of the mountains. They are just classed outlaws as they hid from Fenris' slavers."

"Forgive me here, Logan, but I am out of touch with Nethili politics." Rebecca frowned. "Start at the beginning."

"Well, the beginning is years ago when old Mayor Mc-Fillion was put out to pasture by your father. He replaced the mayor with a most unlikely candidate. Kalvin Fenris was a royal guard up in Jilrir. Did you know him?" Rebecca shook her head. "Well, at first, nothing much changed, but my guard discovered untaxed goods were being stored in town warehouses. When I raised the matter, I was ordered to ignore it. When I refused, I and those loyal to me were dismissed. Gradually, members of a crime syndicate replaced the guard. Fenris started raising taxes, and when the people protested, he had the ring leaders hanged."

"That's terrible." Rachael looked appalled.

"Aye, well, everyone now lives in fear as almost any crime, other than the ones his cronies perpetrate, ends on the gallows."

"Of course, this is only your side of things," said Rebecca coolly.

"Oh, that's not even the worst of it. Messengers came from Jilrir and the Commech scum. There is a price on your heads, and he agreed to post it publicly."

"That is aiding the enemy," Rebecca said sharply.

"Rumor is, he has done a deal that if he can bring in a Maine, he will be left alone in Nethili."

"What can we do?" Rachael asked.

"Well, if your brother or your father still lived, we could depose him, but alas, we have no one to rally behind."

"You won't rally behind Rebecca?" Jenri argued, unable to hide her irritation.

Logan snorted, "I have already had this argument with Lady Breanna." He looked at Rebecca, "No offense, milady, but you understand it's just not right that a woman should do a man's job."

"Offense is taken, Mr. Braithwaite." Rebecca responded with growing inpatince. "You offer me your service, then withdraw it."

"Wait, what? I did no such thing." He looked most perturbed at the suggestion.

"Well, I intend to take Nethili with or without your help. You offered me your service, and I'm calling on that service. Will you rally those loyal to my banner?"

He looked at her for a long moment. "You're serious, aren't you, my lady? Do you really think that you have what it takes to become the new leader of Nethili?"

"My dear Mr. Braithwaite, I have what it takes to move the province. Do not ever express your doubts about my abilities again. I am not here as a woman. I am here as a Maine."

"Say what you will. They will never accept you." He shook his head.

"Do you accept me?" Jenri said softly but with authority. "As Esselar, head of the church?"

"Aye, milady, of course." He said without reservation.

"What if I were to tell you it is the will of Illya that Rebecca rules Ithia." Jenri fixed her eyes upon him.

"Then I will lay down my life and the lives of all men to see that come to be," he stated.

"Now you're making sense, Mr. Braithwaite." Jenri smiled.

"Fine. By tonight, I can muster about fifteen guards. We will rally behind your banner."

"Just fifteen?" Rebecca looked disappointed.

"All we need. We will keep the bloodshed to a minimum," he said, getting up. "Wait till dusk, then meet me at the edge of town near McCaffery Street."

As he rode off, Rebecca turned to Jenri, "It is Illya's will that I rule?"

Jenri snorted. "Of course not. Illya does not concern herself with politics unless it directly relates to her church."

"But you said...."

"I said 'what if' not that you do." Jenri shrugged and smiled.

Breanna woke with a start. Kitty was shaking her. "Your friend, Captain Carter Monroe. They is gonna hang 'im in an hour."

Breanna jumped up, "Are you sure about this?"

"As sure as sure can be, love." Kitty stated, "Fatboy is never wrong."

"You said it wouldn't be for days."

"Yeah, well, I was wrong on that. They got some other guy that Fenris wants strung up urgent like. Sebastian 'Awk."

Breanna's eyes widened. "They have Sebastian, too?" her voice faltered. "You have to help me get them out."

"No chance, love," Kitty said softly. "They is done for."

"Sebastian is my Guardian; they can't kill him. It's illegal. He is an Illyan priest, damn it."

This had an odd effect on Kitty. She went white, "Illyan priest, did you say?"

"Yes." Breanna wondered if she had said something wrong.

"I'm an Illyan. Praise be her name," Kitty said through gritted teeth. "Now that changes evryfing." She stood up and turned into the room. "Listen up, Posse. Fenris's gone too far. "E is gonna kill a priest of our blessed lady. I fink we need to get him out and kill anyone who tries to stop us."

The image of Rachael entered his head, followed by Breanna, Petra, Keri, and Emma. Dear sweet Emma. He realized he loved them all, especially Emma, beautiful, spirited Emma. She needed him; she was the only one who *truly* needed him. Everyone else would get by, and they had each other. "Get up for Emma." He heard a voice say angrily at him. Then he realized it was his own. No, not just Emma; the others may not need him, but they wanted him. They were all his family in every way, save blood. "Get up for Breanna." He said louder, but still, his muscles would not obey. "Get up for Petra," He raised himself a few inches and cried out, "Rachael Abigail Maine." A sudden strength propelled him up to his knees. He turned himself over, and the pain shot through him, but he did not give it a second thought.

A familiar voice greeted him from the adjacent cell. "I say, old man, is it visiting day already?"

Carter sat on the straw-covered floor in the ajajent, smiling at him. He looked none too good, himself, with a large gash upon his forehead. He was pale and looked a little bleary. "Sweet Illya, what happened to you?" Sebastian said, moving over to the bars that separated them.

"I believe the term they used was 'a damn good kicking.'" Carter actually grinned. "I managed to break the nose of one of the bastards, though. You don't look any better."

"This place is certainly a mad house." Sebastian shook his head in disbelief. "Come closer."

Carter got to his feet and probably thinking the Preacher wanted to speak quietly, he put his ear towards him. "No, face me." The Preacher said.

Sebastian wiped some of his own blood from a cut on his chin. "I say, old man, what are you doing?" Carter looked bewildered and stepped back as Sebastian tried to smear the blood on the man.

"Stay still." He reached through the cell, placed his hand upon Carter's forehead, closed his eyes, and muttered the prayer. It was a mild wound, and apart from a little nausea, he was fine.

"I say, old man," Said Carter, amazed as he felt his healed forehead. "I knew you religious chaps did some weird stuff, but wow."

"Religious chaps?" Sebastian raised an amused eyebrow. "If we ever get out of this mess, remind me to discuss your spiritual well-being with you."

"When we get out, old man," Carter said assuredly. "I don't suppose you can do any hocus-pocus on the old locks?"

"Not unless, by some amazing bad luck, I convert to Rinki, the God of Thieves." Sebastian replied, "I understand their high priests can unlock anything."

"Well, do you have any ideas?"

"Plenty, but they all involve being on the other side of the locked door." The Preacher sighed, kicking the bars of his cell door in a futile gesture.

"I barely had the necklace out of my pack when these militia bastards came up. Sorry, old man, I really got us in a bit of a mess."

"Where is Bree?"

"She got away, but I have no idea where she went. Sorry, old man."

"Don't fret. I have done as bad, if not worse. At least Bree was free when you last saw her." He told Carter what had happened to Petra. When both their tales of woe were done, Sebastian paced the cell trying to figure a way out, but it appeared hopeless. He prayed to Illya to send some help to Petra and to watch over Bree wherever she was. The hours passed, and when the jailor visited them with food, he implored him to let him see the mayor, to no avail. Both Carter and he thought up ways of escape, but none could work without the guards unlocking at least one of their cages.

Time moved on, and he imagined Petra moving ever closer to Jilrir. He sank into despair, poor sweet Petra a toy of Commech scum. How could Maine have considered Fenris, that odious pile of shit, suitable for his daughter? He was not even a lord or even a gentleman.

Something hard hit the back of his shoulder, and he spun about. A rock the size of his fist had come through the small window. At first, he thought it was prison hecklers out to bait the condemned, but he noticed a piece of paper wrapped around it. He pulled it off and saw a neat, educated script in pencil. "Sebastian, if this is the right cell, throw the rock back with no note, love B."

"Breanna Maine, what the bodragel are you up to?" He sighed wearily.

Breanna could not help but wonder how this oddball group would achieve a jailbreak. Her confidence marginally increased when she saw the arsenal they stored in an old pine wardrobe. Knives, swords, bows, maces, and axes. "Pick something." Kitty said, grinning at the wide-eyed girl who looked on in awe, "You have a pretty neat sword there, Bree, but a girl's got to have a backup weapon." Bree grinned. She may be odd, but she was starting to like the red-headed gang leader. She reached in and picked up a small, single-handed axe. It was lighter than it appeared and was not designed as a weapon, but it could certainly kill. She slipped the handle into the back of her belt, "Let me be honest," Kitty said, in all seriousness, as she pulled out a crossbow, "This ain't going to be a cake walk, ya know."

"It never is." Breanna shrugged.

"No serious and all that." Kitty looked at her with grim determination. "It will be kill or be killed."

"Yes, I get it." Breanna nodded. "These men are not what I believed them to be. My father would not have condoned this."

Kitty grinned again and shut the cupboard, "Sure, sweetheart."

"My father was many things, but he would not have allowed this."

Kitty shrugged, "The way I look at it is this. Either your dad was pretty ignorant for not knowing what was going on here, or you're pretty ignorant for thinking he did not know. Which do you think is more likely?"

Breanna did not like the logic in that. Was it that her father knew and did not care, or did he know and approve? She had devoted a lot of time thinking about how he never really knew her, but she never considered she probably did not know him. "I am never going back to that life, Kitty. It is my past now. We will get Sebastian out, but I am not going with him when we do. I would like to stay here with you guys."

Kitty laughed. "No, you don't. Sure, you do not want to return to that gilded cage, but I saw your reaction when I mentioned the Preacher's name. You love the guy."

"Ew, no." Breanna was aghast at such an idea.

"I didn't say 'in' love, you dummy." Kitty laughed, punching her in the shoulder. "But he is like family to you."

"Yeah, he is, but he is going to ditch me in Aranar and go his own sweet way. I am not going back to being Lady Breanna." She said firmly. She had never even considered the idea of ditching the family until now, but why should she go to Aranar to be married off and live a life she did not want?

"Of course he is, silly." Kitty chuckled. "'E is a Preacher. "'E 'as to spread her word. If you want to escape your destiny, then why not help him do that?"

"He won't let me."

"Did they teach you nuffing in that big 'ouse? If you becomes a priestess, then you lose all those fancy hoity-toity titles of yours." Kate shook her head.

"Me?" Breanna laughed so hard she snorted.

Kitty was not smiling, "Why not? All you do is ask Father 'Awk to give you a chance at the Choosing?"

"Choosing?"

"Yeah, you and 'im sit down and pray to Illya, and if she wants you, you will become a Feffer. You then get to choose 'im as your mentor. He can't refuse unless he already has a student."

"It's an interesting thought, but really it is not for me. Anyway he has Rachael." Before Kitty could reply, Breanna raised a hand. "We best get going."

Kitty shrugged and led her out of the cellar.

CHAPTER TWELVE

The First Battle of Nethili

War isn't fun. Sure, my father and Bree found joy in battle, but for the likes of Rachael and me, it was nothing more than a lot of pain, terror and suffering," – Memoir of a Marran Priestess by Emma Roark-Maine

It was mid-morning, and Breanna wished they could be doing this at night. She joined Fatboy on the roof of the building opposite the jail, where he lay face down watching it. She joined him, and he glanced at her with a grin. "Hey, me-lady."

She elbowed him hard. "You can cut that out, Fredegar," she said, but in the spirit of the joke.

"Fredegar?" He laughed as she studied the front of the jail.

"So that front entrance is the only way in or out?" Breanna asked, returning her attention to the job at hand.

"Yes."

"And the cells are around the back?"

"Yes, but I don't know yet which the Preacher and your guard is in."

"Well, we have no more time to wait. I'm going to try something." Before Fatboy could protest, she climbed down the drainpipe, but as she jumped the last two feet, she felt a twinge of pain in the ankle she thought Midge had healed. She limped across the street and around to the back. Grabbing up a rock, she felt in her pockets for a pencil, then pulled a flyer from the community notice board on the side of the jail. She wrote out, "Sebastian, if this is the right cell, throw the rock back with no note, love B." She then wrapped it around the rock and threw it high into the air and through one of the small grilled windows. She was most impressed with herself as she made it on the first try. She then sat down with her back to the wall and waited. A minute later, it came flying back out. She grinned and leapt up. The pain in her ankle worsened. She hop-skipped back to where Fatboy had to help her back onto the roof. "I thought Midge had fixed this thing," she said, rubbing her ankle as she sat down.

"No, it was only pain relief. It's probably wearing off. Here, let me help." He sat cross-legged in front of her, placed her foot on his lap, and unfastened the laces of her boot. He pulled it off, and she sighed in relief. She looked at him and those large, brown, intelligent eyes. He rubbed her foot gently, and she could not help but enjoy it.

"Looks like you's is out of this fight, Bree," Kitty said as she climbed up to join them.

"Shit, no," Breanna cursed, pulling her foot away from Fatboy and flushing slightly.

"You can't fight like that, lass," Fatboy said with concern.

"Not face to face, maybe, but ..." She eyed Kitty's crossbow.

"You wants Marie?" Kitty looked horrified.

Breanna raised her eyebrows. "You named your crossbow?"

"Hey, time's up," Fatboy said, staring across the street. Breanna looked to see Midge sitting on the roof of the jail next to the peacefully smoking chimney. Happily, as if playing with building blocks, she pulled slates off the roof and placed them on top of it.

"No time to argue, Kitty." Breanna put out her hand. With great reluctance, the girl handed her the crossbow.

"I guess I am going in your place," Kitty said as Breanna drew her sword and handed it to her.

Breanna grinned. "Good luck." Kitty rolled her eyes and headed off down the roof.

Pulling the drawstring of the crossbow back and locking it in place was harder than she had imagined, but it was not long before she slipped the quarrel into place and took aim at the jail's front door. Her finger hovered over the trigger, and her heart began to pound. She cursed as her hands began to shake. No, this was no slingshot at a guard's rear end. This was life and death. She was about to kill again, but the difference was that this time, she *planned* to kill.

Three guards burst through the door, coughing and spluttering. One came out into the street, and Bree tracked him with the small sight on her weapon. She fired. The quarrel penetrated the side of his head, and he was already dead as he spun a full circle and fell. All concerns left the Fourth Lady of Jilrir as the thrill of the kill pulsed through her bloodstream. She did not later recall reloading, but she did recall her second target staring at the dead man like a startled deer unable to move. He did, however, move when Breanna fired again. He flew back against the wall and slid down, crying out as he clutched at his chest and the quarrel that had sunk so deep only its blood-spattered feathers still showed. The third target was gone before she could reload. He had run back into the smoke-filled jail. Breanna saw Kitty and Hank run across the street with weapons drawn and brightly colored handkerchiefs tied around their faces.

Trying to look inconspicuous was frankly impossible. Four women dressed in shabby yet high-class attire along-side a green-eyed barefoot Marran priestess certainly stood out as they walked into Nethili. They quickly found themselves closely watched by the citizenry and perfunctory guards dressed in shabby, mismatched uniforms and looking more like highwaymen than security.

Rachael stayed close to Rebecca, who found it almost impossible not to walk like she owned the place. Although Jenri certainly sounded upmarket, she wasn't quite as bad as the Maines, whose dialects simply reeked of old money. So, talking was left to the Illyan Esselar. She asked a trader for directions to McCaffery and Main Streets. The response was suspicion, and the trader looked at each of the women in turn but still gave them directions. As they walked away, Jenri glanced back at him and saw him approaching a guard and pointing in their direction. "Looks like we just may have some trouble," she said softly to the First Lady, who followed the direction the Esselar nodded and saw two guards now following.

"Nothing is ever simple." Rebecca sighed.

"Should we run?" Rachael asked nervously as she also looked back.

"No." Her sister shook her head. "That would give them no alternative but to stop us. Let them follow, and hopefully, we will get to Braithwaite before anything happens."

Jenri dropped back to the rear of the group, casually resting her hands on the grips of her blades, and although she appeared to be sauntering along, she was alert for trouble.

Trouble did come, but in a way, none of them expected. McCaffery Street turned out to be a long, winding alley, and as they made their way down it, they passed two young men smoking pipes. They smiled at the ladies, bidding them a good day, and one even doffed his hat to them. However, as Rebecca's group moved away from them and the following guards stepped past them, Jenri looked back and was startled to see the two men drop their pipes and swiftly swing garrotes over their pursuer's heads. There was a short struggle, and by then, everyone was looking on in horror as the two guards tried to get their attackers off, but in less than a minute, both were dead and were being dragged into a doorway.

"I was getting concerned. You are late, milady." Logan had stepped out of a door ahead of them as they were looking back.

"Well, I am here now," Rebecca responded a little terse-ly. She did not recall setting a specific time. The two men who had dispatched the two guards now joined them. "Where are the rest of your people?" She asked, concerned.

"They are coming in from all sides," he advised her. "Don't worry, they know what they are doing." She was not convinced but was not about to argue as he took them down a back alleyway. There, a small rocket awaited, and striking a match, he lit it. After a few seconds, it took off into the sky and exploded with multiple colors. The Nethili uprising had begun.

Sebastian smelled the smoke before he saw it seeping un-der the door to the cell block. "Carter, I think we have a problem."

Carter looked around and saw it, too, "Oh, that is just not on. I would much prefer the noose to being cooked."

"I think we are in the middle of a jailbreak, my friend. Lie face down. It will give us more time until the smoke fills the..." he did not finish, for the door burst open, and a choking guard burst in, falling to his knees. Unfettered, the smoke rolled in.

"Unlock us, you idiot, before we all die," Carter shouted but was ignored.

The guard got up and made to close the door, but a tall, skinny girl with red hair and a bandit-style face mask stepped in with a drawn blade. The guard staggered back, trying to free his weapon from its scabbard. He may have made it had he not stepped within reach of the Preacher, who grabbed him through the bars and pinned him while their mysterious benefactor ran him through the heart five or six times until Sebastian cried stop. A stocky young man appeared and unlocked Carter's cell as the Preacher dropped the corpse. The girl dragged it to one side, away from the cell door. "Who are you?" Sebastian asked.

"Oh dear, no time for that, love," the girl, who was clearly in charge, stated. "I'm 'ere wiv Bree."

"Where is she?" He asked as the boy unlocked his cell.

"Well, if you is patient, I will take you to 'er," the girl said casually and headed back out. Both he and Carter retrieved their weapons. As they exited through the front door, Bree was standing there looking at him, open-mouthed at his facial cuts, bruises, and swollen eyes. "I'm none too keen on the new look, Sebastian."

Sebastian did not know whether to hug her or box her ears for taking such a risk. "You have a lot of explaining to do, young lady. However, first, I have an appointment with Mayor Fenris."

Bree grinned. Some major arse kicking was on the horizon, and she was loving every second of it.

Rachael could not help but find the crimson streak of smoke that trailed up and across the sky over Nethili to be incredibly beautiful. However, the irony that it was a signal for killing to begin did not escape her. She sighed softly and looked back to her sister, who was still talking to Logan.

"All across Nethili, my men are taking out the guard posts, milady. The mayor will be panicking and will send most of the men from his house to find out what is happening and put a stop to it. Now, my two lads here, and I will go ahead to the house and dispatch whoever is left. I want you to follow, but stay back."

"I can help you," Jenri said confidently.

Logan was startled by the offer at first, but then he just smiled. "I think it's best if you stay back with the ladies."

Jenri narrowed her eyes at him. "You don't think I can do it, do you?"

Logan shrugged. "Well, it's not my place to say that, Esselar, and I certainly did not."

"But you are certainly thinking it, aren't you?" She growled. However, Logan simply smiled again and turned away, summoning his men forward as they stepped out into Main Street. "Why that condescending little shit. Why are all the good-looking guys so annoying?"

"Oh, you think he's good-looking, do you, mistress?" Rachael giggled.

Jenri shot Rachael a cold yet embarrassed look. "Shut up, Rachael."

"Yes, mistress," Rachael replied, trying but failing not to laugh.

"Come on," said Rebecca, who was not at all amused as she headed out into the street. "We may have to stay back, but we can't lose sight of them."

The Main Street of Nethili was deserted, and all were silent except for distant shouts and cries of pain. It was not a large town, and the wind carried the voices in their direction. Logan and his men were some distance ahead, walking at a brisk pace. Rebecca sped up with Jenri at her side. Behind them came Rachael and Keri. Devin lagged far behind, not wanting to be part of any possible altercations.

Rebecca had been to Nethili before. Although it had been some years, the buildings were still familiar, and she knew exactly where the mayor's house and offices were. Looking ahead, she saw two guards outside who stiffened as they watched Logan and his men approach. Suddenly, Jenri cried out, "Everybody down," as she pushed Rebecca to the ground. She then broke into a run towards the three men, continually looking up at the roof across the street where several shadowy figures were aiming their crossbows at them. They had been hard to spot, cloaked in colors similar to that of the tiled roof, and it was only when they had moved to fire that she spotted them. She knew she could not save all of them and had to make a split-second decision before she leapt up and landed on the back of Logan.

As he went down with her on top of him, bolts flew over their heads. It did not help his two companions, however, who both cried out as they were struck. One was killed instantly, but the other lay writhing in pain. "Stay down, Mr. Braithwaite. I will deal with this." Jenri was up on her feet and racing across the street, zig-zagging to make the aim of their attackers impossible. By the time Logan even lifted his head again, she was scaling the sheer wall, and she was no longer in the line of sight of the men overhead. He watched the figures searching frantically and trying to peer down the wall, but Jenri was pressed hard against it underneath the ornate overhang and remained completely invisible to the enemy. Suddenly, she took a jump backward and caught the lip of the rim. With an ability that left Logan open-mouthed, she pulled up hard and momentarily appeared to take flight, landing on the roof and killing two of the men with her blades before she even set foot upon it.

Logan quickly came back to his senses and looked up at the two guards who were no longer paying him attention and were also staring in disbelief at the woman in the red cloak killing their comrades without abandon. Logan quickly got to his feet and started to run at them, but he could not resist glancing up to see his Esselar running across the rooftops in tandem with him. As he drew his blade, the two men turned to see him. Blades drawn, they came at him. Logan was a good fighter, but he was not the best, and he momentarily thought this might be his last fight. However, just as his sword clashed against the nearest opponent, Jenri took a flying leap from the roof and landed halfway across the street, her blades in her hands as she ran towards him. This distraction almost cost him his life, but at the last second, he parried what was almost a killing blow to his neck.

The priestess engaged the second opponent, her arms moving faster than he had ever seen. With two quick slashes across the chest, she stepped in, headbutted him, and thrust a blade into his stomach. Logan continued to parry, but not for much longer, as Jenri stepped up and stabbed the man in the back.

Her blades were back in their sheaths before he hit the ground. "Glad of my generous offer now, Mr. Braithwaite?" she said sarcastically, stepping past him. He found words could not come, and he turned to look to see his charges walking up.

Jenri bent down over the injured man and placed a hand on his stomach. She closed it around the shaft of the bolt. "What's your name, friend?" she said softly.

He looked up at her with eyes of pure agony and muttered, "They call me Lynk, milady."

"Well, Lynk, I can't lie to you. This is going to hurt like hell, but don't worry, everything's going to be okay." As she said that, she tightened the grip around the bolt, and terror appeared in his eyes. She pulled it out, and he cried out before passing out from the pain. She looked up at everyone standing around watching her. "Don't you have anything better to be doing? I thought you were supposed to take the house." She directed this at Logan, who simply nodded. She then turned back to the man and placed her hand up over the wound. "It's not that bad. It's just that a stomach is probably the most painful wound to receive. I'll see to it that he's okay. You go sort out that mayor." Logan nodded again, but she wasn't looking at him as she began the prayer of healing. He stepped up to the door with Rebecca at his side, but he held it back from entering and stepping through it himself. Rebecca allowed herself a little smile. She had taken Nethili with so few casualties and so few men.

CHAPTER THIRTEEN

Taking Nethili

"The rivalry between Logan and my father was born out of male pride. Most of us found it quite amusing but for me anyone who upset father upset me." Memoir of a Marran Priestess by Emma Roark-Maine

The armed group marching down the high street looked formidable despite its odd makeup. In front, with Breanna Maine on one side and Carter Monroe on the other, Sebastian Hawk took the lead, grim-faced and blade drawn. Just behind him, with blade also drawn, was Katherine Longfellow, flanked by Hank on the left and Fatboy on the right. Behind them, skipping along quite merrily, came Midge just as if they were off to an afternoon picnic. Those who saw them along the way jumped aside or ran in, slamming their doors.

Sebastian was surprised to see no guards outside the mayor's residence this time. He raised a hand to stop the group and looked around suspiciously. "Something is not right here." He muttered, then signaled Carter to flank the other side of the open doorway. Carter moved into position, and then Sebastian moved closer to the doorway and listened. There was silence, and he stepped slowly around into the room. The foyer was vacant, but he heard voices from the mayor's office.

Slowly, he crept towards it. Suddenly, from the corner of his eye, he saw a figure rushing toward him. He spun his sword towards it. There was a scream, a high-pitched female scream, and a cry of "No, Sebastian!" from Breanna behind him. His blade stopped a hair's breadth from removing Rachael Maine's head as it was blocked by another sword, Sebastian instinctively pushed it up and out of the way as he turned on its wielder. A tall man with a long black beard stared death at him as Sebastian pushed the sword away, stepped up to him, and slammed his forehead into his face. He barely heard Breanna's cries as he swept his ankle around the back of his opponent's and brought him down onto the ground. The man stared up at him as if accepting his fate. "Slay the fair Feffer, and you will be forever cursed." The black-haired man cried. Sebastian hesitated from plunging his sword into the man's throat, and he could finally hear Breanna's voice and feel her hands tugging at his arms. He turned back to face them, and seeing Rachael, he realized what he had almost done.

She stood, hands up to her mouth, shoulders tensed, and eyes closed tightly shut. Time seemed to freeze as no one moved. The shock of what he almost did caused him to throw his sword to the ground. He grabbed her and pulled her to him, knocking her spectacles askew as he checked her neck for injury, then pulling her tightly to himself, "Oh sweet Illya, forgive me. Rachael, forgive me." He kissed the top of her head.

"I will if you let me go. I can't breathe." She laughed but was still visibly shaking.

He released her but held her shoulders and looked down at her. "Easy, Logan." He heard Breanna say behind him. "This is the Sebastian I told you about."

Sebastian turned to see Logan approaching him, weapon drawn but looking thoroughly confused. "This vagabond is a priest? Do you jest with me, child?"

Sebastian tensed and looked back at him. "I am indeed, and I owe you the life of my Feffer and my soul that would be cursed even more."

Logan picked up Sebastian's sword and returned it to him, and both of them sheathed their weapons at the same time. "You have me at a disadvantage, Sir," Sebastian said, still with a lack of trust in his voice.

"I am Logan Braithwaite, former Captain of the Guard and the newly in the service of her ladyship, The Honorable Rebecca Maine," Logan replied. "Forgive my caution, Josser, but I do not understand. If Her Holiness Rachael is indeed your Feffer, why did you try to strike her down? I am oathbound to protect her as I am any who bear the name of Maine, whatever their position within that house now is."

This indeed annoyed the preacher. The implied moral superiority to his own position was challenging. "Only a fool can see that that was not my intent, and it was a blunder on my part that I must now carry to my grave among my many mistakes within my life." He took a step towards him, and both glared at each other. "But who are you exactly? A stranger who comes into the lives of those under my protection."

"I am someone who *did* protect them while you were left on the floor of the city jail." Logan snarled.

Breanna stepped between them and started to sniff the air, and both the men looked at her questioningly. She shrugged and looked at each of them in turn. "Oh, don't mind me, gentlemen," she said cheerfully. "I'm just smelling the macho bullshit around here."

Sebastian grinned first. "One day, my dear Breanna, they will speak of your wisdom." She blushed at those words and stepped back to Rachael. The preacher looked at Logan, gave a long sigh, and then smiled as he proffered his hand. Logan remained cautious for a moment, and then the tension relaxed in his shoulders, and he took the hand. "Welcome to Nethili, Josser."

Sebastian turned back to Rachael, "What are you doing here, Feffer."

"Becks brought us here," she replied like it was just a day out in the country. "but please tell me, master, why have we lost our bond? I have been trying to communicate with you for such a long time?"

"Our bond is still growing, little one. Heightened emotion restricts it, but in time, that will lessen. These last twenty-eight hours have been exceptionally stressful for both of us, and that is why it has been difficult. Where is Rebecca?"

"She is in the mayor's office." She pointed to the door.

Sebastian turned to Breanna, "Bree, get her out of here."

"Sebastian, wait," Rachael started to say, but Breanna pulled her out of the front door while Sebastian kicked open the office door.

He stepped in with Logan close on his heels. The startled Rebecca, seated behind the mayor's desk, looked up at him. "Oh my, you look a complete mess, Sebastian," she said, referring to his bruised and battered face.

He ignored the comment, going straight to his primary concern. "Where are Keri and Emma?"

"They are quite safe. We left Emma back at the camp with Portkind. Jenri and Keri are headed out there now to bring them to us."

"Portkind and safe in the same sentence is rather an oxymoron."

Rebecca smiled at that. "I assure you they are safe, Sebastian."

The preacher looked around the room and then back at her. "Where is Fenris?"

"We cannot find him. He's either hiding or gone on the run," Rebecca replied.

"Forgive my interceding most gracious lady," Logan said, stepping up to the desk and giving her a bow. Rebecca tried not to laugh as Sebastian pulled a face at what he considered fawning at Logan's expense. "My men hold all the known and unknown exits to this town, and if the mayor ventured onto the streets, he would have been spotted. We are not permitting anyone to enter or leave Nethili without your authority."

Sebastian stepped up beside him, a look of deep concern on his face. "He has Petra. I do not know what he has done with her, although he did state he was going to take her back to Jilrir and hand her over to Crotoc."

"We are doing everything we can, Sebastian. Logan has his men searching for them both of them right now." Rebecca replied

"Clearly, it is not enough," said Sebastian sharply. He felt his way into Rachael's mind and asked her to send Breanna and the red-haired girl into the office, and moments later, they both hurried in. At the sight of her sister, Rebecca jumped up and ran around the desk, grabbing her younger sister and pulling her tight. "You had me so scared, you little brat," she said, but her tone was caring and did not match her harsh words. Briana made to return the hug, but Sebastian stopped her.

"Yes, well, we will have time for family reunions later when the entire family is together," he turned to the red-headed girl. "Do you have time to tell me your name now, young lady?" he asked her, but there was no reproach in his voice, and he said it teasingly.

The redheaded girl grinned. "Lady indeed. Oh my Josser, aren't you quite the charmer." The preacher found himself flushing at those words, giving Breanna a good chuckle. "I'd be called Kaferine Longfellow, but everyone round here calls me Kitty. You can call me Kitty if you have a liking for it, Josser."

Sebastian could not help but smile. "Indeed, I do have a liking for it, Kitty, but right now, I need some help from your little gang out there."

Kitty frowned at him. "That little gang is the Rowe Street Posse, and if you be willing, I ask you to show them some proper respect."

Sebastian took an instant liking to this little working-class version of Breanna. Usually, he would take her comment as cheeky, but he smiled and said, "Of course,

Miss Kitty, you are quite right. But I ask you now to search this house and the surrounding houses for any sign of the mayor. Would you recognize him?"

"Oh, trust me, Josser, anyone living in Nethili would recognize that fat git."

Sebastian chuckled. "Well, move fast, Miss Kitty. He has the Lady Petra Maine in his possession, and we want her back unharmed."

Kitty pondered this and said, "does you want the mayor back un'armed?" she asked casually.

"Let's just say I want him alive and able to talk. As long as he can do that, I don't care how he comes back."

A wide grin crossed Kitty's face as she said, "By your will, Josser," surprising him with her knowledge of Illyan phraseology. She turned to leave, but as Breanna started to follow her, Rebecca stopped her. "Where do you think you're going, Breanna?"

The young Maine looked back at her sister with a wide smile. "Following the jossers orders, milady. I am, after all, a member of the Row Street Posse."

Kitty grinned and slapped her on the shoulder. "That you be, that you be." Before anyone could say anything more, the two disappeared out of the room.

Sebastian stared after his young ward and could not have been prouder. Not for the first time, he wished she would one day find her way to Illya's door. He turned back to Rebecca, who did not look quite as impressed by the statement her sister had made but thought it best to change the subject quickly. "so you now have control of the town." he said. "What are your intentions."

Rebecca sighed and returned to her seat behind the desk. "As of yet, I do not know. What is your counsel, Sebastian?"

"As soon as we have Petra, gather the provisions that we require. Gear up for cold weather and press on to the mountains and Aranar beyond."

Rebecca nodded. "That is probably the wisest move."

"Forgive my intrusion on this conversation, honorable lady." Logan interrupted them currently. "I did not just go through fire and hell for you to abandon us. My men put you in place as the new leader of our town, and yet you intend to abandon us immediately?" Although his words were polite, his tone was incredulous, and he let out a dispirited sigh.

Rebecca looked a little embarrassed, and Sebastian waited for her to make it clear to the man that she had no choice but to leave.

There was a long silence as she looked at each of the men, in turn, both glaring at her to take their side. Eventually, her eyes remained upon the preacher, and knowing his reaction, she tensed as she said, "he has a point, Sebastian."

"So do the tips of the swords and spears of the Commech who will be coming here," he growled.

"But how long will that be before that happens, Sebastian? Do we not have time to organize an orderly evacuation of the town before they get here."

"They could be on their way here by now, for all I know. No, I do not believe you have the time."

"Forgive my disagreeing with His Holiness," Logan said directly to Rebecca. "But he is wrong. The mayor struck a deal with the Commech before Jilrir even fell. They consider this town already subjugated under their rule through that odious pile of filth. No doubt they will learn of his demise from power eventually, but I believe we have some days before that will happen, and even then, it would take several days for them to march here. "

"I will not permit them to remain. As the guardian, I forbid it." Sebastian said firmly.

This only Rebecca dig her heels. "Do forgive me, Sebastian, but I think Arden himself said that your guardianship does not exceed the needs of the state," she said, referring to the chief justice who had been slain in a warehouse back in Jilrir.

Sebastian tried to fight the anger welling up within him, but he was unable to, and he snapped aggressively. "Oh, come now, Rebecca, you know full well the House of Maine is dead. The Commech now control this state, as you call it ."

Rebecca sighed, and with her anger spent, she sat back. "You are very dear to me, Sebastian, but my love of Ithia and The House of Maine here exceeds whatever I think of you. So I will give you a choice. You can turn around and walk out that door while you remain in our hearts and considered as dear as family. Or you can accept that the House of Maine is still the rightful ruler of this province. Then, of course, your guardianship as laid down by the Baron remains intact."

Sebastian pondered calling her bluff. He did not believe she would let Rachael go so easily. However, Rebecca was stubborn, and there was always that possibility. "Very well, we will stay, but understand I will judge each day as it comes, and when I instruct you to leave, you will do so without argument."

"Will you make an oath that you will only do that when the absolute need arises and an immediate threat is real?"

Sebastian hesitated before raising three fingers to his brow and saying, "By Illyas's will."

"So we got a job, see." Kitty Longfellow looked quite proud as she stood upon the steps of the mayor's house, walking up and down with her hands behind her back as she addressed the Row Street Posse that stood before her. "Mr. Sebastian, the Illyan preacher, has given us a task. We got to find the freak. I want yous all to spread out and pick an 'ouse down this street and search it."

"But there might be people in those 'ouses, Kitty," one said with a questioning frown.

"You 'ave the aufority of the Honorable Lady Rebecca Maine." She once again over-emphasized the H in honorable. "You goes into them there 'ouses and search, and you don't go letting anyone stop you."

The posse looked at each other in turn. They had done many things in service with Kitty, but this seems a lot to ask. Sure, they had broken into houses and stolen things, but that was to survive. They had only done that when they were assured that no one was at home, but now she was asking them to walk brazenly up to the front doors and force their way in. Breanna saw the looks on their faces and took a step towards them. "I know you're uncomfortable with this, but remember, all these houses down this road are frequented by those who work for the mayor. In doing so, they are all traitors serving as enemies of the state."

No one present, including Kitty, knew what frequented meant, but they got the idea. Slowly, they came around, nodded, and started to pair up.

"You want to come with me?" Fred said to Breanna with a smile. The young man smiled back and was about to say yes before Kitty stepped between them. "You keep your head in the game, Fatboy. I want you to concentrate on finding the bloody mayor and not whatever you might find in Breanna's underpants."

Fred instantly colored up, but not as much as Breanna at her side. "By Marran's girdle, will you shut up," she hissed at her red-haired companion. But the damage was done, and Fred was already sauntering off with Mitch.

"I was just looking out for you." Kitty shrugged as she led Bree down the steps. "That boy 'as it bad for you, and I don't want him getting 'urt when you turn 'im down."

Breanna said nothing. Her feelings for Fred were confusing, and she wasn't even sure what she was supposedly going to turn him down about. She had absolutely no concept of dating. Maines simply married who they were told to.

CHAPTER FOURTEEN

The Hunt for Fenris

*"I never got to meet Kalvin Fenris, the odious
Mayor of Nethili, but by stories I have heard
from my mother, he was clearly at home being
a stooge of the Commech." Memoir of a Marran Priestess by Emma Roark-Maine*

The first and only house that Fred and Midge ex-
plored was fortunately empty, but they were quite
thorough and spent a good thirty minutes looking in clos-
ets, under beds, and every nook and cranny they could
find. Fred found it comfortable to talk to Midge. Since
she could never repeat anything he said, it was like having
someone with whom he could share anything but not
spread it to others.

As he stepped back into the hallway at the end of the
search and as Midge joined him, he looked at her and,

summoning courage, asked her, "So do you fink Bree n me have any chance together?" Midge responded with a frown, clearly not sure what he was referring to. "Do you think she might want to be my girlfriend?" to his embarrassment, Midge laughed soundlessly and shook her head. She pushed her nose into the air and walked around in a monk imitation of the upper classes. "You're prolly right. But she seems alright when you gets to talk to 'er. She's got a voice like a toff, but she don't talk like a toff, do you know what I mean?"

Midge smiled back at him more kindly this time, and she nodded. Fred smiled back as he went to the door and opened it.

The others started to come out of the houses they had been searching, and Kitty was very irritated that no one had found anything. She kept interrogating everyone about how they did the searches and if they were certain they checked everything, and when everyone claimed they did, she sighed. "Well, I guess we better go and report to the josser." She led the way, heading back to the mayor's house.

Midge and Fred were at the back, and he was busy staring at the back of Breanna's head and had eyes for nothing else. Midge happened to glance over the street, and she saw something very odd. The streets were deserted. It was a matter of law for everyone to get off the street when there was any form of altercation or challenge to the mayor, as there had been several times over the years. No one was supposed to be out, yet over the street, she saw an old lady bent over with a shawl about her and a scarf covering her head and obscuring her face. She tugged at Fred's sleeve. "Hmm?" he said, barely audibly unable to escape whatever dream or fantasy he was having about the Lady of Jilrir ahead of them. She pulled harder as the old lady turned into an alleyway, and by the time Fred turned round and followed to where she was pointing, there was no one there. "What is it?" he asked.

Midge glared at him irritably for the stupid question she clearly couldn't answer.

Gripping his sleeve, she stepped out into the road and tried to pull him towards the other side. "Okay, okay, hold on." He turned and called up to Kitty. "Hey, Midge has seen something. We're just going to go over there and check it out."

Kitty stopped and looked back at him. "What is it?"

"Well, if she could answer that, I wouldn't need to go and look, would I?" he said quite aggressively. He was still quite mad at Kitty for embarrassing him in front of Breanna.

"You watched that mouth, Fatboy. I ain't your prairie wife, and you can't go talking to me 'ow you want."

Midge tugged harder. He turned without another word to Kitty, which seemed only to infuriate her even more. He headed across the road with his silent partner.

They entered the alleyway and looked up ahead at the back of the old lady walking casually up the street. Fred sighed and looked at Midge. "Oh, come on, sweetheart. Is that what you want me to look at, an old lady out for a walk."

Midge glared up at him, shaking her head and tapping the side of it with her finger repeatedly to indicate he was being stupid. She then did a big curve over her stomach.

"Okay, so she's a fat old lady. What's your point? "

Midge rolled her eyes and pulled a coin out of her pocket, waving it at him. She then curved her stomach again and pointed at the old lady before tossing the coin away and shrugging. Fred clearly didn't get it and stared blankly at her as she picked up the coin again and slipped it back into her pocket.

She placed her hands in her hair and ruffled it in a gesture they had come to know meant Kitty. She turned away and started to head back out of the alleyway, but Fred stopped her. "No, no, come on, it won't hurt us to go up and talk to her."

For that, he got a smile and a pat on the arm before grabbing it and pulling him along to catch up with the old lady before she turned out of the alley.

"Excuse me!" Fred called out to her as they got closer. At first, he thought she had not heard her, but he noticed her speeding up. His suspicions were now aroused. However, it could be simply that the old lady didn't want to meet a teenage boy on the dark streets at dusk. She had no idea what his intentions were or how honorable or dishonorable he could possibly be. "Excuse me." He said again as he caught up with her, with Midge just a step behind, holding his hand.

"Oh, you be leaving me alone, sonny," the old lady said, and a cold chill ran down his spine. He grabbed her by the shawl, spun her around, and pushed her against the wall. Although the man had tried to sound like an old woman, he had completely failed, and as Fred pulled away the scarf, he immediately found himself looking into the face of the terrified mayor. However, it was not for long, for under the shawl, the deposed leader clutched a small lead pipe, and it was suddenly whacked upon Fred's head. He went down to the ground and almost took Midge with him, whose hand he still held, but he snatched it away in time and ran.

She had to get to Kitty, and not for the first time, she cursed that she was unable to call for help. She did not look back, but she heard feet running behind her. For a moment, she was about to look back, thinking it may be Fred having recovered, but then her ears picked up the sound of labored breaths of a man who was overweight and probably never run anywhere in many a year. As she got to the corner of the alley, she saw the Rowe Street posse going back into the mayor's house. Kitty and Breanna stood aside, watching them go in and clearly waiting for them to return. However, they were both in conversation and not looking in her direction. Despite the differences in their relative health, she was small, and he could still outrun her. Even though it was futile, she tried to call out to Kitty, but again, as always, only air came out. She felt the man's hand grab at her collar. She ducked down and tried to roll away, aware that he had a weapon. She managed to slip out of his grip and jumping up to her feet, she turned to the window in the house nearby and, grabbing up a small pot plant that sat by the door, threw it at the glass, which shattered into a thousand pieces just as the lead pipe struck her in the back. She momentarily saw stars and went down, but she was not out. Despite the pain, she managed to smile as she heard Kitty and Breanna's cries, their voices getting closer. She just managed to look up to see the heels of the mayor disappear back into the alley. Both of them wanted to stop to help her, but she just looked up at them and waved her hand in the direction he had run, indicating that she was fine.

Kitty was way ahead of the young Maine. Whilst Breanna had maintained a level of fitness, it was nothing compared to the girl who had lived on the streets by her wits and abilities. It was not long before Kitty grabbed the back of the mayor's hair and pulled him back. He tried to turn and wave his makeshift weapon at her, but she placed her heel around his ankle and let gravity bring him down to the ground. Bree was now at her side puffing and panting and resting her hands upon her knees as she looked down at the man who stared up at her in fear. "Is that him?"

"Aye, that's the freak, all right." By this time, other members of the Rowe Street Posse who had heard their leader's cries were coming down the alley. Sebastian and Logan closely followed them. As the mayor tried to get up, Kitty placed a foot on his chest and pressed down hard, keeping him in place. She smiled up at the Preacher. "Here you go, Josser. One fat bastard, as promised. I am sorry I couldn't gift wrap him for you."

Sebastian grinned at her as he and Logan bent down to lift him to his feet. Kitty stepped back, her face beaming with pride.

The two men frogmarched him back to the house. Kitty was helping Fred along, who, it turned out, was not as hurt as Midge had feared, but he had a nasty bruise and cut upon his face. Midge was already up, and although her back would hurt for several days, she couldn't complain.

The mayor was pushed into Rebecca's office and forced into a seat. "Milady, I beseech you." he cried as he saw the first lady watching curiously. "Why do you permit this ruffian to manhandle me? I have done nothing wrong."

Kitty, who had been by the doorway, stepped forward, her sword raised. "You is referring to a priest of Illya. Choose your next words carefully."

"You!" Fenris spluttered, then turned to Rebecca, "Katherine Longfellow is on our most wanted list. She is a renegade and criminal of the lowest order."

"You spineless whelp." Sebastian turned to Kitty, "How old are you, girl?"

"Fourteen, Sir."

He looked back at Fenris. "Wage war on only women and children, eh Fenris? Why not come outside and face me instead."

"Milady, are you going to permit this?" Fenris expostulated.

"Why are you wearing a dress, Mr. Fenris?" she asked softly.

"I had no idea what was going on, and I feared for my life and had no idea you had come to save us."

"Where is my sister, Mr. Fenris? Where is the second lady of Jilrir."

He looked as if the question was bizarre to him. "I know not, my lady." He then pointed up at Sebastian. "The last time I saw her was with this ruffian here."

"Sebastian was in your jail, Mr. Mayor." Breanna snarled.

"Lady Rebecca, are you going to believe that ragamuffin and that vagabond over me, a loyal retainer to the House of Maine?" Fenris laughed incredulously.

Rebecca narrowed her eyes at him, "That 'ragamuffin' is Lady Breanna Maine, and the 'vagabond' is her guardian Kirkman Sebastian Hawk."

The man looked back at Breanna. Her hair was matted, her face was grubby and stained, and she looked a far cry from the portrait of her hanging in the hallway.

He could find no more argument, and he sat there mutely, refusing to answer any more of Rebecca's questions. This did not seem to bother her, which fazed him more than anything. She simply looked up at Sebastian and nodded.

The Preacher lifted the man off his feet in a second and slammed him into the wall. The only thing holding him there was a Preacher's hand about his throat.

"Did you send her to Jilrir?" He spat into his face. Fenris blustered, so Sebastian pulled him forward and slammed him back against the wall again, but much harder this time, and his glasses fell to the ground. They bounced to just in front of Carter, who slowly lowered his boot down on them until he heard a satisfying crunch.

"She left as soon as you were locked up." He stammered, rubbing a small scratch on his face. "She has gone in my carriage with my guard."

Sebastian dropped him and took a step back. "I swear by all the Gods that if she is harmed in any way, I will be back and will hang you in the public square myself. If you value what is left of your squalid little life, and trust me, your time is short, get me two of the fastest horses you have in this village."

"The man is lying," came a growl, and Sebastian and Rebecca turned to look at Logan, who stood there shaking his head. "For some time now, my men have been monitoring who goes in and out of this town. It has been at least three days since any cart has gone out of Nethili, and no woman has been seen riding pillion to any of the guards."

Sebastian snorted. "And it is not possible that your men could make a mistake, of course," he said somewhat patronizingly.

Logan stared at him for a long moment. He was clearly offended by the sarcasm in the Preacher's tone. He would not tolerate it from any man who wasn't a priest of his church. "They cannot afford to make mistakes, Josser. I humbly assure you that I speak the truth." There was nothing humble in his tone. He turned to look at the mayor and pointed at his terrified face. "This man lies like the rat he is. The Lady Petra has not left this town, and by the will of Illyia, I state that my words are the truth." He placed three fingers upon his brow. For someone not of the clergy, this was merely a token of sincerity rather than an oath as it would be taken for Sebastian and Jenri. However, it was sufficient for the Preacher, and he had to curb his dislike for the man and accept what he said.

"How did you think you would get away with it?" Sebastian stepped back towards the mayor, fighting to keep his voice level.

"I...I don't know what you are talking about." He blustered as Carter and the Preacher closed in upon him. He looked to Rebecca imploringly. "I beseech you, my lady. Do not let them treat me in this way. I have been a loyal retainer to your father for many years. Surely, that must stand for something even in these days."

Rebecca glared contemptuously at the man and then seemed to relax, suddenly looking quite calm, and she glanced away as if she did not care what he had to say. "I am a considerate woman, Mr. Fenris, but where my family is concerned, I honestly care about nothing less." She looked up at the young red-headed girl she had only just met and considered her carefully with pursed lips before she spoke. "I am giving the mayor just two minutes to answer Sebastian." She paused and looked at the mayor, then back to the girl who watched the First Lady with curiosity, wondering where she was going with this. "After that, would you be willing to remove his fingernails … slowly."

A huge grin crossed Kitty's face. "I'd be honored to, me lady." She gave a little curtsy and turned that grin towards the mayor as she slipped a knife out of her belt and started twirling it in her hand. Even Breanna looks startled by her sister's instruction. It had been a long time since the Maines had ordered a prisoner to be tortured. It was not that she had a particular problem with it. It was simply unexpected.

"She never left the village; she is still here, isn't she?" Sebastian growled

"Look, I am the mayor, and you can't…"

"Did you think we would give her up for dead and go our merry way while you kept her? Or did you hope I would perish in the hands of you Commech friends?"

"S… she has g… gone to Jilrir, I tell you." He looked rapidly between Rebecca, Carter, and Sebastian in turn. Panic and fear made him almost ghost white as he wrung his hands.

"Where is she?" Sebastian repeated as calmly as he could maintain.

"I told you…she has…gone to Jilrir."

"I am very tired and very hungry, Mr. Mayor. My patience is wearing very thin. Where is she?" He glanced to Kitty, then back to Fenris. "I could leave you alone with Miss Longfellow while I search." Kitty grinned cruelly at Fenris and licked her upper lip provocatively.

"In my room, two houses down," he bleated, trying to push himself through the back of the chair.

"He's lying again," said Breanna indignantly. "The Posse searched all these houses, and we found nothing."

Sebastian sighed, turned away from the man, and nodded to Kitty. Her grin widened even more as she stepped over to the man with her knife in hand. "There is a secret cabinet at the back of one of the wardrobes," the mayor cried out. "She is in there. "

The Preacher leaned into him and hissed softly. "If you are lying to me again, I will have Kitty here slowly remove your organs, but not enough to kill you. She will leave your tongue intact."

Sebastian turned away. "Kitty, if this man tries to leave, kill him, but do it slowly."

"You gots it yer 'olyness."

CHAPTER FIFTEEN

Justice is Served

"My father wanted me to follow in his footsteps and follow the way of Illya's justice, but my heart belonged to Marran. I hope he would not have been too disappointed." – Memoir of a Marran Priestess by Emma Roark-Maine

Sebastian grabbed an aged servant by the collar and forced him to show him to the mayor's house. Rebecca had now caught up with him. Going up to the bedroom, he found the room was empty. Seeing four large wardrobes, he entered one, and Rebecca went to another. They banged on the rear of each, but when there was no response, they moved on.

When he stood there growing frustrated after none of them showed any signs of having a secret door or anyone behind it, he turned to Rebecca and cried, "I do not know what that little bastard is hoping to achieve. He clearly lied again." But as he spoke, he heard a muffled cry coming from one of the wardrobes. Stepping in, he searched around again as a thumping came from the back of the wall. Finally, he shouted, "Stand back!" and with a hefty kick, the panel splintered and burst through. Petra stood there gagged and bound, her face bloodied and bruised and her clothes torn. Her wide blue eyes looked into his with terrified relief. With her ankles tired, he had to lift her, carry her out, and sit her on the edge of the bed while Rebecca fussed around her. He removed the gag and pulled a handkerchief out of her mouth gently.

She was dressed in an inappropriate low-cut white lace dress, which there was no way the Petra he knew would have been wearing by choice. The dress was torn, and as he pulled out his knife and cut her bonds, she held the ripped parts together at her breast with her arms. She was shaking convulsively, and tears streaked her bruised and swollen face. Blood was dried under her lower lip, where it was split.

Rebecca sat next to her. "Oh, sweet Marran, what happened?"

"He called me a whore and tried to rape me." She looked up at her sister. "But I didn't let him. Honestly, I didn't." She looked imploringly at her sister. Sebastian fought back his tears of anger. If she were not intact, rightly or wrongly, society would consider her even more tainted and unfit for her position. Sebastian was aware of the injustice of it all, and it was one of the many aspects of society that the Goddess of justice stood against.

"It's alright. You're safe now." Rebecca knelt at her sister's side, taking her in her arms and pulling her towards her chest. As Sebastian cut her bonds, his mind was numb with a wave of anger so great that he could not think to speak as he looked at this scene. "He had me brought here and told me to put this on." They could barely make out her choked words between the breathless sobs. "I said no, and he said it would go worse for Sebastian if I did not do what he said. He even said that if I tried to escape or call out, he would kill you." she looked up at the Preacher.

"Is that why you did not make yourself known when these rooms were searched?"

She nodded. Unbeknownst to any of them, the room had been searched by Midge, who, unlike Fred, did not call out her name for obvious reasons. "I heard people out there, but I didn't know who it was. Are you telling me that it was someone looking for me?"

It was Sebastian's turn to nod. "It's a long story, and I will explain it to you in due course. Please go on telling us what you endured."

"Well, I sat alone for hours, then he came back and said he wanted what he should have gotten on our wedding night. I slapped him, and he punched me and kept on hitting me when I went down. He climbed on top of me, tearing my clothes. Then that guard, Jack, came and told him that you were here. He got scared but said if I shouted out, he would do for all of us and blame Sebastian. I'm sorry."

Tears were in Rebecca's eyes as she stroked Petra's hair and whispered, "Shhh, it is not your fault, little sister. You did nothing wrong."

Sebastian was torn. His soul screamed out at him to pick her up and take her far away and keep her safe, but anger, blood-red hatred, and desire for vengeance also filled him, although outside, he appeared calm, too calm. "Rebecca." he said softly, and both women looked toward me. "You heard my oath?"

"Yes." She replied gently, nodding.

"I have to keep it." He said determinedly.

"I know." She said. She, too, now had cold hatred in her eyes for what had been done to her sister.

"You are not going to argue with me or try to stop me?" No one could stop him, no one. He merely wanted and needed her to say it.

"Sebastian, I will even help you if you need it," she said. Her voice was calm like his as she gave him approval for the task that needed no explanation.

He simply nodded and turned away. "What's he going to do?" He heard Petra anxiously ask her sister.

"What he always does, sweet Petra," He heard Rebecca reply as she comforted her sister, "His duty."

Sebastian headed calmly down the stairs and entered the office. Fenris was visibly shaking. Kitty still had a knife at his pudgy neck, and Bree was sitting in the chair opposite him with her boots on his table and crossbow on her lap. Carter leaned casually against a credenza. "Do you recall my words, my oath?" Sebastian looked ahead, not meeting his eyes. Not of guilt for what he was about to do but with the knowledge that if he looked at him, he would not contain himself and would have slain him then and there. No, he wanted this by the book. It may be illegal for the state to execute without trial, but it was not for an Illyan

Priest. Although it had been hundreds of years since an Illyan Priest had done so.

"What do you mean?" He whined.

He looked to Kitty, then Bree. "Give us the room, ladies."

They looked disappointed but immediately obeyed. He waited until Bree closed the door behind him. "I said I would kill you if she were harmed."

"Y..you wouldn't." Sebastian saw tears well up in his eyes, and he sank from the chair and onto his knees, hands together, pleading for his life.

"That's the reason, isn't it? The reason you lied. You hurt her, and you knew we, her family, would avenge that crime." Sebastian looked down at the pathetic man with loathing and contempt, "but what if it worked, Fenris? What if we believed she was in the hands of the Commech and left with only our grief? You could not simply let her walk out of here." The Preacher was now shaking with rage. "Would you have killed her yourself, Fenris? Or would you have let one of your boot boys do it?" He thought of Marion, Petra's real mother, and her fate at the baron's cruel hands. "Would you have taken her down the river and drowned her?"

He had not intended that this comment was any more than that, a comment. Every hair on his body stood on end as the mayor replied, "But how did you know...." He placed a hand on a chair to stop his legs from giving way.

Fenris, seeing the complete and utter shock on the Preacher's face, closed his eyes, realizing he had not known.

"Oh, sweet Illya, it was you?" The words from Sebastian's mouth were barely audible. Things were becoming clear, painfully violently clear. "That is why the baron was going to let you marry Petra. It did not make sense. He gave you this town when she refused and turned a blind eye to your activities. He knew you knew his secret. You were that guard."

"Nonsense." He shrieked. "I don't...."

Rage boiled over. Sebastian grabbed the man's hair and yanked his head back. He leaned over him, looking down at his face, which spasmed with fear and pain. He scrabbled at the Preacher's hand to no avail. "Did she scream, Fenris?" Sebastian shouted into his face. "Did she cry out for mercy? Did she beg for her life?"

"You don't understand." He pleaded desperately. "The Baron made..."

Sebastian was not about to listen to excuses, "Say her name," he growled

"W..what?"

The Preacher pulled down on his hair, and the mayor's knees gave way, but he was not going to let go, and he went down on his knees with him. "Say it."

"M... Marion." He bleated.

"Her full name," Sebastian shouted, pulling back hard on his hair again.

"Marion DePengarthy," he cried out, and the anger was released from the Priest, who rose to his feet.

He turned away and lowered his head, and in a soft, almost melodic, he said, "Repent your sins and renounce evil, Fenris." These were the words used when ministering to the condemned.

"For Goddess' sake. For Illya's sake, Josser, stop this." Fenris pleaded.

"How dare you call on the purest of the pure with your black heart filled with odious slime." Sebastian sneered, dragging him to his feet. He called in the others, "Carter, take this man to the market square." He then pulled open the door. "Kitty, find some rope. Do you know how to make a noose?" She nodded with a grin at Fenris, "Good, don't make the slipknot too loose. This is not going to be quick. Bree," he looked at her as she looked back at him with her large brown eyes. They gave him hope that not all in this world was evil. His voice softened, "I know you and Petra are not close, but right now, she needs you, all of you."

"She is my sister, Sebastian," Breanna rolled her eyes, "I love her, and I will go to her because I want to, not because you tell me." She left the Preacher grinning after her.

Carter dragged Fenris to his feet and pushed him out as Kitty trotted off humming merrily. Carter was deaf to Fenris's wailing sobs. As they made their way down the street, they drew the attention of those they passed, and soon a crowd began to follow them. As they began to realize the reign of the mayor was over, they began to cheer and spit at him and curse his name. They found a tree near the marketplace and had many offers of rope from stallholders. However, he waited patiently for Kitty as Fenris tried to plead. When Kitty arrived, he tied it around Fenris's neck himself as Carter tossed the other end over a branch. The Preacher and Kitty held him up as Carter bound his hands behind his back.

Then he was ready.

Sebastian lowered his head and prayed silently. He asked for a sign from the Goddess that his actions were unjust, but nothing changed his mind. A soft, gentle song brought the crowd to silence as he opened his eyes. The Lament of Illya, one of her most famed psalms, was carried through the air. He looked in surprise at Kitty Longfellow, who spoke like a sailor yet sang like an angel. As her song ended, Sebastian took the end of the rope in his own hands and slowly hauled him from the ground. Fenris gurgled and hissed, his feet kicking and struggling as Sebastian tied the rope off on a nearby stall, and an almighty cheer went up. He then turned away and did not look back. He looked at the crowd and held his head high.

"Kalvin Fenris dies today by my hand and does so in the name of The House of Maine. Anyone who tries to release him before he dies will suffer the same fate. Nethili is now under the rule of Lady Rebecca. She frees you today, and you owe allegiance to her and only her. We are at war, my people, and we can brook no insurgency. There is no help coming, and the fate of Jilrir will be the fate of this town. Prepare yourselves as you will." He stepped through the hushed crowd with Kitty and Carter falling in behind him. A cheer went up, but his thoughts were of a young actress sixteen years ago.

Sebastian turned to Kitty, "Do you have a playhouse in this town?"

"No, Sir." She replied, a little surprised. "Closed down years ago."

"But the building? It still stands, I presume?"

She frowned, clearly thinking it was a little odd. "Yes, Sir, it stands. It's over on Duke Street a good 'alf mile up the road." She gave him the directions.

"There is something I must do. Can you tell the others that I will be some while?"

They parted company, and the Preacher found Duke Street with the boarded-up playhouse. He was not entirely sure why he had wanted to come here. He felt a bond with Marion, and being in a playhouse would bring him closer to the actress who had died so prematurely. He pulled off some slats and climbed through a window. It was pitch black. He struck a match and saw he was at the back of a stone-seated amphitheater that encircled a high stage. It showed no signs of age, and only the boarded windows indicated that it was not in use. He suddenly cried out, startled more than hurt as the match burned my fingers, and it fell to the floor, extinguishing itself.

"Oi, who's out there." The room was suddenly lit in a reddish-orange hue as an old man appeared from a side door. He was bent over but held his lantern high over his head. "Ain't nuffing to steal here." He called out, peering into the shadows where Sebastian stood.

"I do not want to steal, my friend," He said, stepping out into his light with palms raised to show he bore no weapon. "I just wanted to see the playhouse."

"Bit late fer sightseeing." The bent old man said suspiciously, squinting at him.

"I am sorry. Are you the owner?"

"No, Sir, I be Jenks, the caretaker." He replied.

"Caretaker? But I thought this place closed years ago?" The Preacher asked, surprised.

"Aye, eleven years ago, but I get paid by a trust, and I'm not going till I become worm food." He said defensively. "But you can look about if ya don't touch anyfing and then go the way you came."

Sebastian turned to go, but a thought occurred to him. "Have you been here long?"

"Sixty-two years, man and boy," he replied. "Why?"

"Have you heard of an actress from Jilrir called Marion Depengarthy?"

He rubbed his stubbled chin as he thought. "It's funny, but that name rings a bell, but I can't put a face to it." Then he looked at the Preacher. "Why?"

"I think a friend of mine was related to her." He answered truthfully, for how was he to know his friend was The Second Lady of Jilrir? "I was hoping I could find out if she ever performed here."

"I dunno, but I got all the old programs down in da basement if you want to look, but I warn ya, will take yer some time. Gotta lotta them."

Sebastian realized it was a long shot, but since few actors ever stayed still and toured the land, it might be possible that she had performed in Nethili, and his heart began to pound. The old man led him down to a dark cellar filled with old boxes. After he lit a second lamp, he left him to browse. Fortunately, the boxes were dated, and he bypassed any that were less than seventeen years old. As the hours passed, he began to look through a twenty-year-old box of faded programs. His heart leaped as he finally saw the name on a cast list. "Marion Depengarthy as the Maid" in a play called "Queen of Hearts." It was a small part, so no engraving of her appeared on the front, unlike the stars. Another hour went by, and he found more mentions of her, but he was praying now. He wanted to see her. He needed to see her. He felt she was a part of his life now.

Then, near dawn, he was about to give up. The weariness of two sleepless nights and a beating were catching up. He pulled out of a program from just seventeen years before. The writing was stylized in the way theatricals so loved and read. "Back by Public Demand...Miss Marion Depengarthy in The Sailor's Wife by Ilick Stemp. Sebastian fell to his knees, unable to stand. His hands were shaking, and every hair stood up on its end as his blood ran cold. For looking up at him in that dark, dingy cellar with sparkling eyes and a captivating smile was the image of Petra Maine.

Sebastian felt tears in his eyes, and his hands shook uncontrollably as Petra's mother stood in portrait before him. It took a while to speak. "You have a beautiful daughter with a good heart." He told her, "I promise you, I will keep her safe from this day on. I love her so very much, and I will one day tell her of you when she knows peace again. I am sure she would love you as much as I am sure you loved her. You can rest now, sweet Marion. Those who hurt you are paying for their sin. Your daughter will be safe. May Illya's blessings go with you." He kissed the forehead of the picture, then, folding the program carefully so that he would not crease the picture, he placed it in his inside cloak pocket. He would hide it and one day give it to Petra. She had gone through too much to know the truth that her mother was not her mother and was just a woman who was paid by the man who had her real mother slain.

He headed for the door, but just as he turned the handle to head back upstairs, he heard a voice. It was gentle and distant and bore a hint of joy. It was almost ethereal, one could say. It only said two words. "Thank you." He did not feel fear. Instead, he felt a warm, loving, and kind presence. He simply smiled back into the empty room. He could not explain how Marion had heard him, and she was finally at peace.

Chapter Sixteen

The Council of Lady Rebecca

"The Illyan concept of justice is something I have never been able to understand. Even if I had not followed Marran's path I doubt i would have followed my father's desire for me to be one with Illya." – Memoir of a Marran Priestess by Emma Roark-Maine

Rebecca was late for the meeting she had arranged, but none of the town officials had a mind to complain, especially as Logan's militia surrounded them in the general assembly room of the Town Hall. The facts were simple. She did not know who she could trust and who was loyal to Fenris and potentially the Commech.

However, she equally could not remove everyone from office without drastically slowing down her transition of power to herself. Anyone fired would need replacing. As she entered, everyone rose from their seats, but that was not an indicator of favor as everyone rose for the baron's daughters and would have done the same for Bree or Alannah. Amongst the town officials were Carter, seated in the rear, and Jenri, leaning against the wall with her arms folded.

"Gentleman," Rebecca said firmly as she took her seat in the mayor's chair, "We need a smooth transition of authority."

"Who is to be the new mayor?" interrupted a stern-looking man of senior years.

"I am," she replied curtly.

"With all due respect, milady, this is unconstitutional. No woman has ever ruled a town or city or region in the history of the kingdom."

Rebecca sat back in her chair, "And who exactly are you?"

"I am Henry Arkwright of the Treasury Department."

"Well, Henry Arkwright of the Treasury Department, there is a first time for everything,"

"Milady, unless you are going to enforce your authority at the point of Captain Logan's sword, you will have a hard time getting the people to listen to a woman."

Rebecca glared at him but finally said, "Portkind."

"Yes, milady?" The officious bureaucrat perked up.

"You are the new mayor of Nethili."

"Indeed, Milady." He said. He was many things, and stupid was not one of them, and he knew full well that he was now mayor in name only.

She looked back at the protestor. "Satisfied?"

"Milady, you intend him to be a puppet." Arkwright stood up, "The House of Maine is dead. It died with its last son. I do not recognize your authority here."

Rebecca fixed her eyes upon him and pondered whether her next move would either stamp her authority or lose control entirely. "I am the senior surviving member of the House of Maine. If I want you to dance, you will dance. Now, you have challenged my authority several times. You compel me to set an example."

"Example?"

"We are at war, and you have now refused to recognize my authority several times." She looked to her new captain of the guard. "Logan," The bearded officer stood to attention at the mention of his name. "Have Henry Arkwright of the Treasury Department out back and hang him."

"On what charge, milady?" Logan asked casually.

Rebecca's eyes narrowed. "Are you questioning me too?"

"Not at all, Milady. Just have to fill in the legal paperwork requirement."

"I see," Rebecca looked to Jenri, "You're an expert in justice, Esselar. What do you think Captain Logan should put in his paperwork?

Jenri shrugged. "Anything you like, we are at war. Normal law does not apply. However, whatever you decide now, it will establish a precedent that people will not ignore."

Rebecca nodded, "Make it so, Captain Logan."

"Wait! What? Milady, you don't have the authority." Arkwright protested. "Fine! I withdraw my objections."

Rebecca sat back in her chair. Seeing that she did not respond to his Arkwright's, Logan pointed to two guards and nodded to the door. They grabbed the man who was screaming and protesting.

"Hold up." Jenri stood upright. Rebecca looked at her, thinking she was now about to intervene. Even Arkwright looked desperately at her. "If I may be so bold to recommend. A private hanging serves little purpose. Take him to the market square and hang him next to the mayor. Do it slowly for all to see."

Terrified, Arkwright tried to fall to his knees, begging Rebecca. However, she nodded to Logan, indicating he should follow the Illyan's recommendation.

Henry Arkwright of the Treasury Department was dragged outside. It was an extreme move, but she knew the Commech would be coming, and she had no time to win hearts and minds. Every official had participated in the former mayor's crimes, whether actively or passively, and she was not going to lose sleep over them.

"Any other complaints, gentleman? No? Good. Let me make myself clear: war is coming to Nethili, and I shall brook no abstention or opposition. You are all guilty of crimes against the people of this town and under sentence of death. However, I am postponing that sentence. Work with me on helping evacuate this town, and you may get a pardon. Oppose me, and you will join Henry Arkwright of the Treasury Department. As Illyan Esselar, I will be appointing Jenri O'Fere as Chief Justice pro tem. If she agrees." She looked to Jenri, who nodded, "Captain Logan, you are responsible for civil order. Lieutenant Carter, I am promoting you to captain with immediate effect. You are responsible for protecting us from the enemy. Watch out for signs of advancement and eliminate any scouts in the area. You may need to coordinate with Logan on this. Also, my people need paying. They cannot eat on loyalty alone. Portkind, see to it that they all get sufficient purse for their needs. This time tomorrow, I want to see the first plans for an orderly evacuation of the town. That is all for now, gentleman. I will be announcing further postings throughout the day. You are dismissed."

As the door opened, she saw through the reception hall and the Preacher sitting himself down on the steps outside the open front door.

As if a spell was lifted, Sebastian started to feel every ache, pain, and bruise he had endured the past twenty-six hours. He sunk on the step outside as if doing this final task had taken the last of his energy. He reached for his pipe but found it in not two but three broken parts. He lowered his head and closed his eyes.

He knew it was Rebecca who came and sat beside him. He could smell her favorite scent. That meant she had not only had a bath but also established herself enough that whims like scent were catered for.

"How is Petra?" He asked wearily.

"She will be fine; she is sleeping now." She advised him.

"She's tougher than she looks," he said calmly. "However, I think I should go help heal those bruises."

"She is in discomfort but not pain. Let her sleep." Rebecca smiled, taking his hand in hers. "I do not think you are up to it. You look exhausted."

"And then some." He agreed with a smile. Then, he turned to a more serious matter. "You surprised me back there."

"Really?" Rebecca tilted her head questioningly at him. "How so?"

"That treasurer. You ordered his death so casually."

Rebecca sighed, "Oh, it wasn't easy, Sebastian. You can trust me on that. But most of these men served under Fenris, and although I am loathed to admit it, I cannot replace them. I cannot trust them to serve out of loyalty, so they must be compelled to work out of fear." She paused and glanced back into the doorway behind her. "Jenri does not have a problem with it."

"Ah, but Jenri has a heart filled with vengeance to right the wrongs brought down upon her sisters in Heron Bay. She is pledged to slaughter the Commech and those who support them. If she had her way, they would all be hanged."

Rebecca frowned. "Did I do right in choosing her as my chief justice if she cannot see any mercy?"

"There is no mercy in justice, milady. There is only right and wrong, and killing those supporting a war against Illya is just. The Esselar has both my absolute faith and my absolute loyalty."

"She is barely older than your daughter."

Sebastian laughed. "She is the same age as you. You question whether I should bend the knee to her but would gladly see me bend the knee to you."

There was a pause, and his smile faded as she looked at him most seriously. Then softly, she said, "I would consider it the greatest honor to be your liege and accept your service."

There was a long, uncomfortable silence during which Rebecca wished she could take back those words. Sebastian looked away down the street and rubbed his hands together as he pondered. He then looked back at her. "You are both a fine woman and an honorable leader, milady. My respect for you is more than you probably realize. If I were not a priest and were assured you would retain your authority, I would be equally honored to bend my knee and bow my head, pledging myself to you. But you will no doubt be wed once more, and any service I gave to you would pass to your husband as he assumes your authority."

"Well, technically, you are still considered to be in service of the First Lady." She chuckled.

"Actually, it is to the office of the First Lady."

Rebecca laughed. "Is there any difference?"

"Most certainly, milady. You are not the First Lady anymore. Until it is ruled otherwise, you are the Baroness of Ithia. The First Lady is now Petra, but only if her legitimacy is recognized. If not, it is Breanna."

Her lack of reaction told him she was already aware of this, but she simply leaned back on her hands, closed her eyes, and lifted her head to enjoy the noon sun. "I would pay all the sivs in Ithia to watch you bend the knee to Lady Breanna Maine," she smirked and heard the Preacher chuckle.

"Don't dismiss young Bree out of hand. She may not have Rachael's mind or your civil leadership ability, but from what Emma told me, she took charge on that Last Day in Jilrir. She will never sit in an office willingly like you, but she has great potential."

"Oh, now you choose to offend, Mr. Sebastian." She said lightly, not sounding remotely offended. "I do not dismiss any of my sisters. We will all have a role to play when The House of Maine rises once again." But her heart fell as she heard the soft sigh come from the Preacher and realized he truly had no faith in this ever happening.

After a while, he said, "I have only seen Rachael and Bree. I assume everyone else is here?"

"Yes, all the houses along this street are Maine property. Everyone has a place to stay awhile."

"Emma?"

"She stays in the big house here with us."

"Us?" Sebastian raised an eyebrow.

Rebecca blushed and, looking back at him, said, "I mean, I thought, well, you know, you should stay here."

"Sure, but I want a room with Emma, though. No one is safe until all of Fenris' cronies are identified." He started to get up, "We need to...."

"Stop." Rebecca placed a hand on his shoulder and made him sit back down. "You need to go get some sleep. You can deal with the world's problems tomorrow."

Sebastian nodded, "I suppose you are right. I'll go up in a bit."

Rebecca got up. "If you need anything, anything at all, let me know."

He hesitated then, with determination, said, "Rebecca, I don't want to be difficult, but I plan to sit out the politics and other shenanigans. I want to devote my time to Emma and to train Rachael."

She smiled down at him, "You got it, Sebastian."

"Oh, and if you could find me a pipe, I'd appreciate it."

Rebecca chuckled, "I'll get right on that." She laughed at the humility of such a suggestion.

He thought she was trying to be funny, but Midge and Kitty appeared with a pipe and a pouch of very fine tobacco a few minutes later. "Why, thank you, ladies," he said warmly as he filled the pipe. "Why don't you sit with me a bit so I can get to know you better."

"If it's pleasing to you, guv." Kitty sat down on the steps next to him, and Midge sat on the street cross-legged and looking up at him, elbow on knee and chin in the palm of her hand.

"And what is your name?" The little girl made no sign of replying.

"She cants talks nothing, guv. We call her Midge, and she seems to like it."

"Do me a favor, Kitty?"

"Anyfing you likes, guv."

"Call me Sebastian."

Kitty looked horrified and shook her head, "That wouldn't be proper like, begging your pardon, guv. I was raised to have proper manners in dealings with clergy."

He looked at Midge. "She always like this?"

Midge grinned and shrugged, then nodded. "Why, Midge, you cheeky lil bugger." She immediately covered her own mouth and flushed pink, "Forgiving me language."

Sebastian chuckled, "I hear worse from Breanna."

Kitty looked horrified. "If that be the case, you should puts her over your knee n tans her hide with your belt."

Sebastian laughed at the idea but returned his attention to Midge. "How long has she been like this? Unable to talk, that is."

"Ever since I knows her, guv. She was like it when she joined the posse two year ago. Can you fix 'er gov? I knows Illyan priests does that sort of fing."

"Sadly not. Whatever injury caused that has healed, I have nothing to work with."

Midge smiled and shrugged.

Kitty looked disappointed but also shrugged, "Oh, wells, was just a thought."

"It is a shame she never learned to sign." Sebastian sighed.

At that, Midge lifted her head with a frown and sat up. She studied him for a while. She concentrated as if trying to remember something. She then raised her hands and gesticulated at him. He laughed and slapped his knee. "Yes, Midge, I do understand you." Midge laughed soundlessly and stood up excitedly.

"Yous understanding that to be words?" Kitty's eyes opened wide.

"Yes, it's called signing. Deaf and mute people can learn it. Clerics in my church have to learn it."

Midge signed more, and the Preacher translated for Kitty. "Her name is Siobhan but she likes Midge." Tears came from Midge's eyes, and she threw herself into Sebastian's arms but jumped back when he groaned in pain.

"I woulds not believes it if you told me. Look, there you go, yous got me all a crying too." Kitty dabbed the tears from her eyes as Midge hugged her, too.

"Not adopting more waifs and strays, are you, Sebastian?" he looked up to see Jenri coming out of the house.

"No, mistress, not this time," he laughed. "But come meet my new friends. This is Siobhan, and this is Kitty. Ladies, this is my friend and mistress, Jenri."

"Mistress?" Kitty queried. "But yous a preacher yous don't...." she stopped and stared at Jenri, "Unless you is...."

Sebastian was amused at her expression, "Jenri is the Esselar of the Illyan church."

Kitty flushed bright pink and leapt to her feet, bowing and curtsying. "Oh my life, humble greetings me, lady ma'am. I is so sorry I is not dressed proper like... stand up Midge stand up for 'er ladyship."

"Relax." Jenri said, bemused, "Are you one with Illya?"

"Oh, yes Miss, oh most certainly I is so. Born and raised. I was dedicated as a babe in arms in the chapel right 'ere in Nefli. Me Ma raised me proper in worshipin' Illya, if you please. Like, before she died, that is. Tis why we all gots so mad when we done 'erd they was gonna 'ang the preacher."

"That is just fantastic, my dear." Jenri beamed at her.

"You honor me, miss. If there is anyfing I can be doing for yous, please lets me know."

"Well now, Kitty, do you keep up your studies?" Jenri asked.

"Studies miss?" Kitty frowned, not liking this turn.

"You know, do you study your scripture?"

Kitty looked very embarrassed as she slowly replied, "I can't, Miss. The likes of us don't read."

"Well, we have to rectify that." Jenri smiled sweetly. "If you're willing to learn, that is?"

"If that's what you be wanting." Kitty said but sounded very unsure, "We is honored that you would think of us."

"Well, on that note," Sebastian said, getting like an elderly man, "I'm exhausted. I will leave you lovely ladies to sort out those details. I really must be getting these tired old bones to my bed," and he headed into the building.

Jenri took his place next to Kitty, who still looked up at her in awe. "You seem very dedicated to Illya's service. Have you ever considered a vocation in the church?"

Kitty balked, "The likes of me? Oh, Illya wouldn't want me. I ain't no educated lady. I ain't got no class or nothing. Illya only wants proper brought up people like what you is."

"Who in the land told you that?" Jenri responded with incredulity.

"Well, it's just a fact, innit. I have never met no priestess who talks like what I does and can't read like."

"Really? And how many priestesses have you met exactly?"

"Well, to be honest, there was Sister Tate, but she took a dirt nap an awfully long time ago. Then there is you, and there is Mr. Sebastian."

Jenri leaned in conspiratorially and said with a grin, "Well, keep this to yourself, but I have it on good authority that Brother Sebastian could not read before he became a priest. There is certainly nothing stopping you from pursuing a place as a feffer in the Illyan church. You certainly appear to have the heart for it."

Kitty looked at her companion. "Did you hear that, Midge? The likes of yous and me could be preachers." Midge responded with a noncommittal smile and a thumbs up, clearly uninterested in such a course of action.

"Give it some thought and prayer," Jenri suggested. "However, in the meantime, we need to get you two reading and writing. I will arrange for Rachael to meet you in the morning."

"Glory be, fings are changing around 'ere." Kitty laughed.

CHAPTER SEVENTEEN

Judgements

"All the signs were there for the growing tension between Sebastian and Rebecca... Her determination to restore her House and his determination to keep them all alive." – Memoir of a Marran Priestess by Emma Roark-Maine

Over the next two days, the Maine family took over the entire row of houses on either side of the mayor's residence. Of course, Rebecca remained in the mayor's house, and Sebastian resided with her, taking the rooms with young Emma. Both Devon and Alana stayed with them, too. Alana was in a room next to Sebastian, and Devin was in a room next to Rebecca. Petra took a room on the top floor and was not seen for several days.

Although there are still some tensions between them, neither Jenny nor Kerry argued when they were allocated the house next door. However, Carter protested when he was moved in on the opposite side with Portkind and Daniel. Not that he had a problem with Daniel. However, His complaints were only to Sebastian, and he would never dare challenge the instructions of her ladyship Rebecca.

When it came to Breanna, things were not quite so simple. She wanted to move in with Kitty and some of the Posse.

Rebecca hadn't even remotely considered that the gang of street urchins would reside like retainers to the House of Maine, and she suddenly didn't think it appropriate that her younger sister continue to associate with them.

"I understand what they did for us, but it's not like you can bring them home with you." They were alone in Rebecca's office with the door closed.

"But we're not exactly home, are we, Rebecca." Breanna said to her irritably, "Home is down south where some Commech barbarian is probably taking a shit on your portrait."

Her use of profanity did not exactly endear Rebecca to the concept of her sister continuing to hang out with the Rowe Street Posse. "They certainly appear not to be a very good influence on you." Rebecca frowned.

"Oh, come on, Rebecca, stop being such a snob." Breanna had always held her own with Rebecca but never quite this firmly. The Row Street Posse is more honorable than half the retainers you had back in Jilrir. They may not be educated, but you will never find a more upstanding and loyal group of individuals in the whole of this province or beyond, for that matter."

"All the same, Breanna, there are certain social expectations of you, and what you do reflects upon me." Rebecca insisted.

Breanna snorted, "Fine! Send them back to the gutters, hiding away like they did under your predecessor here. However, I will go with them. Anyway, who are you to tell me what to do? You are not my guardian. Sebastian is."

"This falls under the best interests of the state, young lady, and you will do what I tell you. Until the king says otherwise, I am the Baroness, and it is my duty to ensure the best interests of the House are maintained. You will move into this house and share with Petra."

Breanna glared at her, "Well, make sure it's a room with one of those secret compartments to lock me in. Because I'm telling you right now, Rebecca, I am not doing it."

They both shared the stubbornness of the Maine women, and the Baroness was not about to back down. "If that is necessary, then I will." She said, standing up.

However, Breanna was staring at something in the corner of the room. Two swords in fine scabbards rested against the wall. Bree narrowed her eyes and looked back at her sister. "I think one of those is mine." She nodded to the blades.

Rebecca turned to look at where Bree indicated. "I'll return it when you deserve it," she said aggressively, but Bree just stepped around and grabbed the sword Rebecca had kept under her cloak since she had liberated it from Ronan back in Jilrir.

Rebecca moved to stop her, but Breanna spun about to face her. "Don't touch me, Rebecca. I'm taking what's mine."

The Baroness stepped back, fearing her sister was about to strike her.

There was a long pause before Breanna replied, "I'm not going to hit you, Rebecca. By Marran's girdle, you really don't know me, do you." Bree sighed, and her shoulders slumped. "Go stick your head up the arse of a bodragel, Rebecca." And with that, Breanna turned on her heel and pulled open the door. As she strode out, Rebecca considered calling a guard to have her dragged back in, but that would certainly not look good in front of the staff. Instead, she sat back down and pondered how she could get through to the girl. She knew it was not entirely the fault of her time with this Row Street Posse. Breanna had always been quite the handful. However, there was one person she knew who *could* get through to her.

Sebastian and Emma were eating lunch together in his room when the Baroness knocked at his door. They were enjoying their time together, and the young girl was so happy to be reunited with the Preacher. She told him all about her time with that annoying Mr. Portkind, who wouldn't let her go and play with Daniel, and spoke about their situation like it far exceeded anything her father and the others had gone through. Emma was quite put out when they were interrupted. However, she politely got up and opened the door. It was not that Sebastian expected her to do these sorts of tasks, but he had simply given up trying to stop her because service was what came naturally to her, and she seemed most frustrated if he ever tried to stop her.

"Hello, milady." Emma gave a curtsey as Sebastian finished his mouthful of food and dropped his napkin on the table, waving her in. He saw from her face that she was not in a pleasant mood.

It did not make *his* mood better when she simply ignored Emma and stepped in. "You really need to do something about Breanna," Rebecca said haughtily.

Sebastian inwardly rolled his eyes but didn't actually show any reaction as Rebecca stepped over to him and sat down in Emma's seat. "She seems to be doing fine by herself, but what is your problem with her now," he said wearily.

"She wants to reside with those filthy little lower-class street urchins. I need you to change your mind." Rebecca insisted.

Sebastian immediately saw Emma tense this description, and his mood darkened even more. "You mean the children that saved her life? And mine, for that matter?"

Rebecca frowned. "I understand what they did for us, Sebastian, and they will be duly rewarded. However, I have no intention of moving them in like they were family. And I'm certainly not going to let my sister live in some cellar with them.

"You now sound like Ronan or your father. I thought much more of you, Rebecca."

"I have no idea what you mean." The Baroness flushed.

Sebastian looked over to Emma, who was still standing by the door. He beckoned her over, and she duly came. She stood by his chair, and he slipped his arm around her waist before looking back at their guest. "Perhaps you can explain to me and my daughter where you think these lower-class people belong." Emma turned her gaze upon the Baroness and waited.

Rebecca looked a little flustered and realized the point the Preacher was making. "Emma is different," she said weekly. It had only been in return for saving Lady Rachael that she had agreed to turn over the indentured servant to Sebastian. She had certainly not approved of his adoption of her, and had it not been for that incident on the road to Ternal, she would have probably declined it. She was too wrapped up in her issues with her brother and her hopes that Sebastian would assist in removing him from office to be that concerned about it.

"Oh really?" Sebastian raised an eyebrow. "Perhaps you could elaborate on that?"

Now, the Baroness turned crimson and felt a deep resentment for Sebastian putting her in this position. She glared at him. "What would you have me say, Sebastian?"

"You consider me a member of the House of Maine, and whilst I question whether that entity still exists, if I am a member of the House, then so is my daughter. Who is by your standard a filthy little street urchin of the lower classes."

Emma shot her father a reproachful look. She didn't know what street urchin meant, but filthy? The girl was fastidious about her cleanliness even more than he was. However, he gave her a gentle squeeze of reassurance that she accepted that he meant no offense to her.

"What would you have me do, Sebastian?"

"I don't know, Rebecca." The Preacher sighed. "As for Breanna. The more you push, the more she will pull. As for the Row Street Posse. Why don't you throw a purse of money at Katherine Longfellow's feet? After all, that is what the Baron did to me for saving your sister. Why should Kitty be treated differently now you are Baroness?" Now, this really hit Rebecca. She had come to rely on the Preacher and wondered if she had now pushed him too far. The one thing Sebastian put before anyone else was the girl that stood at his side. Before she could say anything, he said. "I think we are going to move out of here, Rebecca."

She narrowed her eyes at him. "Why?"

"Somewhere where my daughter is respected as the lady that she is now. Possibly, I will move us into that cellar with Breanna and the Rowe Street Posse. Who knows."

That stubborn streak once more ran through the Baroness, and although she would almost instantly regret saying it, she did not retract it before she left. "That is up to you, Sebastian."

As the door closed behind her, Emma turned to look at him with concern. "I'm not wanted here," she said softly.

Sebastian led her around to the front of his chair and pulled her onto his lap, where she sat and snuggled against his shoulder. "Oh, my dear sweet child. Do not take the games that adults play to heart. Rebecca is under a lot of stress right now, and she says things she possibly doesn't mean." He knew in his heart that she meant every word, but he simply did not want to increase the discomfort his daughter already felt around the Maines.

Rebecca's anger diminished once she returned to her office, and closing the door, she paced up and down for a while before making a decision. He swung over the door and called for Portkind. He came hurrying in, and she simply said to him. "Find me that Kitty whatshername. I want to speak with her." he nodded and scuttled off.

About fifteen minutes later, the red-headed, freckle-faced girl was knocking at her office door with Breanna close behind her. Rebecca did not address Kitty at first, who had curtsied and waited patiently as the Baroness addressed her sister. "I want to see Kitty alone, Breanna. You can wait outside."

Breanna fixed her gaze upon her sister, saying quite family, "I'm really not going to let you give her a hard time, Rebecca. I will stay here for my friend close both."

"And since when did you have the authority to dictate to me, Breanna Maine?" Rebecca raised her voice. "You will get out, and you will get out now, or I will have you dragged out by the guard."

But Breanna stood there resolutely folding her arms and indicatingclearly that she was going nowhere. However, Kitty rested a hand on her shoulder and said, "It's OK, Bree. I'm sure me'lady just wants a quiet word in me ear like. You can waits outside."

Not taking her glare from her sister nor changing her expression, Breanna finally turned around, strode out the door, and slammed it hard behind her. Rebecca returned to her seat behind her desk, indicating to her visitor to take a seat. Uneasily, the leader of the Row Street Posse sat down as she tried to work out what the Baroness possibly wanted. "I want to thank you for what you have done." Rebecca began. "Without you, I think Sebastian would now be dead, and possibly Breanna, too. I intend to reward you in coin. I just wanted to know what it is you plan to do now that you no longer have to hide."

Kitty shrugged. "We ain't got no plans, me'lady. Honestly, we ain't 'ad time to think of it."

"It would appear my sister wishes to remain with you. I want to be completely upfront that I don't approve of that." She studied the kid's face for her reaction to her words, but her response surprised her.

"I don't blames you for that, me'lady." Kitty shrugged. "Bree is a nob. She'll always be a nob, and I understand you don't want 'er to be mixing with the likes of us. I got to admit I like Bree, and I'll miss 'er, but I get your point."

Rebecca had not expected this, and her estimation of the young girl increased. "I'm glad you see it my way. Perhaps you can explain this to Breanna."

"If that is your wish, but I don't see what difference it will make. Breanna knows her own mind, and I ain't gonna change it."

"Where do you plan to stay now? You don't have to hide in that cellar of yours."

"That cellar is the only home I know, and it does at a pinch."

Rebecca sighed. She was thinking of an alternative, but she wasn't sure whether it was a wise one. However, her priority was to keep her sister at her side and under her control. "How many are there of you in this posse?"

"Twelve, me'lady."

"How about you come and work for me?"

Kitty frowned. "Doing what exactly, me'lady? We ain't exactly cooks and cleaners, you know."

"I realize that. However, Braithwaite is taking over as the new captain of my guard, and I'm sure he could put your skills to some use."

Kitty clearly liked that idea grin widely. "I'd be honored, me'lady. I can't speak for the others. Some of them do 'ave families they may want to go home to now, but for me, I think I would like that."

Rebecca permitted her a smile. "In that case, you can take the house at the end of the street and move out of that cellar."

Kitty got up, looking as happy as could be. "That's mighty fine of you, me'lady." But then she hesitated. "Does you still wants me to 'ave that talk with Bree?"

Rebecca shrugged, and with a faint disingenuous smile, she said. "just tell us she can move in with you."

Petra Maine had stayed in her room for several days. She had hoped Sebastian would have come to see her, but he hadn't, and that did nothing to raise her sunken spirits. Her room was at the front of the house, and she had had the servants move her armchair to the side of the window and spent her time watching people come and go. She kept hoping Sebastian would look up and see her as he came back and forth, but he never did. On the odd occasion she saw him leave or return with Rachael, she felt a pang of jealousy.

She was watching him leave one morning and was startled when her door was flung open, and Rebecca came in, "Enough is enough, Petra. You cannot sit in here all day, every day."

"Why not? Am I not safer in here?" She replied curtly.

"Get over yourself. You got beat up, not raped and murdered."

"Bitch." The word came out before her brain connected to her mouth.

However, Rebecca surprisingly smiled. "That appears to be the pet name for me these days. But come on. I need your help."

Petra frowned. "What can I do?" She said with incredulity.

"Well," Rebecca started with a modicum of embarrassment in her voice, "it would appear I had the town quartermaster hanged the other day."

"Well, things like that happen, don't they?" Petra stated, nonplussed.

Rebecca grinned and shrugged, "Anyway, I need some to conduct an inventory of supplies for the evacuation. I would like you to take over as quartermaster, or rather quartermistress."

Petra raised both eyebrows, "I cannot read nor write."

"No problem, I'll assign a scribe to do that for you."

"Why not just have them do the job?"

"Two reasons: first, you need to get off your behind and stop moping, and secondly, and more importantly, I only trust my own people." She sighed, "I need you to help me, Petra."

Petra could not help but grin from ear to ear. No one had ever needed her for anything before. "In that case, Lady Rebecca, I am honored to be at your service," and she stood up and gave a neat curtsy.

⸻

Jenri arrived at the jailhouse in the late afternoon and found Logan busy interviewing new guards for the militia. She was surprised at first by how old they were but then realized that most of the young men had been conscripted for the defense of Jilrir, never to return.

The moment she entered, he rose to his feet and bowed his head, "Milady!"

She smiled at him but rather abruptly said, "Let's deal with these prisoners then, shall we?"

He nodded and led her to the back room where Sebastian had recently been imprisoned. The two jail cells were packed with men who were standing almost shoulder to shoulder. They looked weary and dejected, and the smell caused the high priestess to cover her nose. They had been there several days, awaiting her arrival. She looked at each of them, at least as many as she could, making sure they made eye contact.

"All I need to know is when you want to begin the trials, milady," Logan stated.

Jenri pondered a moment, looking the men over one last time. Then she shook her head slowly, "That's not going to be necessary."

Logan looked at her quizzically, "Milady?"

Jenri turned away from them and looked up at the captain. "They chose to work with the mayor, knowing he chose to side with the Commech—the same people who destroyed our temple in Heron Bay and killed twenty-two of my sisters. We are at war, captain. Normal rules of justice do not apply."

Logan nodded. "Very well, what is your wish, Madam Justice?"

Again, the Esselar pondered, "How many are here?"

"Thirty-three," he replied.

Jenri smiled ruefully, "Here is my ruling. Have them choose among themselves twenty-two of their number and have them hanged. Of the remaining number, have them stripped of all they possess and banished them from the town. They can be reminders for people of the price of betraying the Lady Rebecca." She looked up at Logan, "Make sure it is clear it is the betrayal of Lady Rebecca, not the House of Maine. We need everyone to understand who is in charge."

Logan smiled. "You are most merciful, milady. I would not spare even one of them fools. But that is why you are high priestess, and your wisdom is greater than mine." He bowed low again and led her back into his office. She chose to wait outside in the street to avoid the smell while he drew up the paperwork, then she went back inside and signed off on the judgments. As she headed back out to the old chapel, she raised her eyes to the sky, "Let them never forget you, Kara Adair."

CHAPTER EIGHTEEN

Destiny Rising

"There was an age difference of six years, and whilst that was quite substantial when I was nine, and Kerianna was fifteen, it was nothing once we were both adults. She was more a sister to me than many bonded by blood, and ultimately, we became bonded in the sisterhood of the Marran faith." – Memoir of a Marran Priestess by Emma Roark-Maine

Had there been any onlookers, it could be considered that Jenri had made her judgment easily. She considered her final decision to be just, but it had not been done without considerable thought. She did not exactly feel guilty about her decision, but the taking of a life did not ever sit well with her. As she left the jail, she headed up to the Old Chapel, which was set up for the generic use of all faiths. It sat a little way out of town and would afford her some privacy. At least, that was her plan.

As Jenri knelt before the small altar with her head bowed deep in prayer, she barely heard the footsteps behind her. However, her survival instincts quickly kicked in as they grew closer, and she hardly finished her prayer before turning around and getting to her feet. Keri stood there looking a little uncomfortable. Despite their brief truce in which Jenri assisted Kerianna back in the forest, the differences between them still remained strong ever since the incident at Boddington's Farm. They had rarely conversed and had gone out of their way to avoid each other's company.

"I'm sorry, sister. I didn't mean to interrupt you," Keri said softly.

"It is of no matter, sister," Jenri replied coldly. "I had almost finished. I will give you privacy." She then made a step past the Marran but suddenly stopped as she noticed something around Keri's feet. At least a dozen field mice were running around her.

"Please don't go. It is you that I wish to see."

Jenri sighed and placed her hands on her hips while looking away from her. "To be quite honest, Keri, I don't think we have much to talk about."

"Please, Jenri, hear me out." Keri took a seat in one of the pews, and the little gang of field mice followed her. Jenri remained standing and stared at her one-time companion. Keri glanced down at the little creatures excitedly hopping around and occasionally running over her bare feet. "It started when I got up this morning. The moment I stepped out of the house, little creatures started coming over to me and following me around. I have noted that for several days, animals have been coming out of the fields and forests and watching me."

"Well, you *are* a Marran," Jenri shrugged disinterestedly. "You have empathy with these animals, but you speak like this isn't normal."

"It isn't." Keri reached down and held out a hand, and one of the little creatures happily ran onto it. She ran the back of her small finger over its neck, stroking it gently. It just sat there contentedly twitching. "Of course, if I were to reach out, they would come to me, but I have not done that."

Jenri's animosity started to morph into curiosity, and she relaxed somewhat as she stared at the little creatures and then back up at Keri. "Well, you look like you have an answer to this issue, but clearly one that you're not happy with, or at least you have doubts."

Keri paused, and slowly placing the mouse back onto the ground, she sat back and sighed. "It is stated in the Book of Marran that the beasts of the fields will pay homage to a priestess when she is elevated to a certain position. However, it makes no sense that it is happening to me."

"Oh, quit with the cryptic stuff Keri." Jenri actually smiled, and she took a seat on an opposite pew in fear of stepping on one of the little creatures. "What position are we talking about?"

Keri looked up at her but seemed unable to find her voice until she looked away again. "It happens when a new Esselar of the church is called."

Although a little startled, Jenri quickly thought about herself and her sudden rise to office. "Considering what I went through, it's clearly possible that you have been called to the highest role yourself."

Keri shook her head, "There is a very big difference between you and me. I am not the last of the Marrans. There are our churches all over the land, and whilst our numbers are insignificant compared to what they were before the war, there are still hundreds of us out there. I am not the only choice." At those last words, she stopped herself and flushed slightly. "Not that I'm saying…"

Jenri laughed. "Oh, you do not offend me, Keri, as I think the same thing. I am only Esselar because there is no alternative." But as she thought about it, her face became grim once more. "I have been thinking about our situation a lot, especially in relation to spiritual matters. Everything that is going on is not as we expected. None of this is normal."

"Has anything else happened to make you think this way other than your elevation?" Keri asked softly.

"Well, little things have happened. Insignificant that I wonder if I'm just imagining it." "

"Now it's you who is being cryptic." Keri chuckled. "Would you have a care to share?"

Jenri pondered this a moment before saying, "Well, to take one example." She hesitated for a moment before continuing. "Back in Jilrir. That day, Petra was attacked. Do you remember it?"

Keri chuckled slightly, "I hardly think I'm going to forget that day in a hurry."

"When Petra was lying there wounded, the first thing I wanted to do was get everyone out of the way. However, young Emma was holding on tightly to her hand, and it was as if I had a voice telling me to leave her there. Petra's healing was much faster than I understood it to be, and I have a feeling it wasn't me who healed her."

"You think it was Emma?" Keri raised a surprised eyebrow.

Jenri chuckled, "I know it sounds foolish, and whilst I'm not absolutely certain, I do feel that is the case."

Keri frowned. "But my dear sister, that is impossible. Emma is not even a Feffer. And her life force is too young and fragile to impart upon another."

"I understand all that. Like I said, it's probably my imagination, but my Goddess keeps telling me that it is not. I feel that we are being set up as a game of the gods, and Illya is setting up her pieces to her greatest advantage."

"I am not Illyan," stated Keri.

"No, but Illyans and Marrans have historically worked closely together. But it's not just Emma. There is also Rachael, who until recently had no teachings of the Illyan faith yet now seems to be an expert on everything about it."

"She is a highly intelligent girl who reads a lot. It's quite possible that she studied the book of Ilya before you met her." Keri suggested.

"I thought that too, but she didn't. She rejected religion in favor of science and did little studies on the matter. That, too, makes it very strange. She converted to the Illyan faith and became a Feffer in just a couple of weeks. The whole thing is quite bizarre."

"We are indeed living in strange times. " Keri sighed. "There is another concern I have regarding Emma. She has expressed a desire to follow the faith of Marran."

Jenri laughed at that. "Well, good luck telling Sebastian that."

"Would he be really so mad?" Keri asked despondently.

Again, Jenri pondered her answer before saying, "Oh, he'll certainly be mad. He can barely control that temper of his. However, he will accept it if that is truly the direction she wants to go in. However, she is still young, and it will be some years before she can follow her own beliefs. So I would not worry about it yet."

"I do not want to upset him. I want to get close to him, but I do not know how."

Jenri chuckled. "Talk to him, sister. He really isn't as fierce and scary as he makes out."

Sebastian, true to his word, stayed out of all the 'political shenanigans' as he put it. He avoided almost everyone and spent nearly all his time with Emma. However, one morning, he dressed quietly so as not to wake his daughter and slipped out the door. He wanted some time alone. Sinking his hands into his pockets, he decided he would simply enjoy a nice walk in the morning sun.

"Sebastian." Keri came down the steps behind him and joined him. She was in new clothes of Marran green, a short dress with matching stockings that looked odd on her otherwise bare feet.

"Ahh, Keri," Sebastian said, smiling. "I hope you are enjoying the rest. I have to go into town and sort out some provisions," he lied, not really understanding why he felt a need to avoid his daughter.

She smiled as her eyes met his, and he looked away, hoping to make it appear casual. "May I speak with you?" She asked with just a hint of desperation in her voice.

"Well, I do have a lot on this morning. Perhaps we can meet up later," he said evasively.

"Why are you avoiding me?" She blurted out. Her voice was suddenly sorrowful and full of hurt.

"I...I'm not." He replied, flustered, and looked down, deciding to straighten some gravel with his boot. He did not know what to say to the fifteen-year-old woman he learned was his blood daughter.

"Please do not lie to me, for that is unfair," She looked so hurt now that a pang of guilt stabbed at him. "You are my father, but even if you do not want to be part of my life as a parent, you are still my brother in fellowship."

Sebastian grinned. "You are right. I have been what Bree would delightfully call 'an arsehole,' let us take a walk together." Placing an arm around her shoulders, they walked down the old streets, not caring which way they went.

"What worries you? What makes you avoid me?" She asked with genuine concern.

Sebastian pondered this and replied, "Selfishness, I guess. You remind me so much of your mother. When I look at you, I remember my failure fifteen years ago."

"Please do not take this the wrong way, but that is somewhat of a relief," she responded initially causing him concern. "I thought you resented me for being your daughter."

"Kerianna Hawk, you are a part of me. The better part of me." he smiled. "Please forgive me, and let us start again." She embraced him, and both felt the sting of tears. She held him close, then he took her hand in his, and they headed away from all their troubles. They spent that morning alone, talking about their faith and sharing prayers, and it felt good, and he felt a new surge of pride in his eldest yet newest daughter.

"You seem to be spending a lot of time with young Daniel," Sebastian commented as they walked back to the house at noon.

"He is very clever; I am teaching him to read and about the wisdom of Marran."

"Is he a potential Feffer?"

"Oh, he is far too young to even think of that, but I do hope so." She admitted, "What about my little sister?"

"Emma? Well, yes, I hope she will become a Priestess one day, but I shall not pressure her."

"She thinks the world of you, you know." She laughed, "I am kind of jealous that she gets to do the things I didn't."

"I would have been there for you if I only knew. Maybe not at first, but at least as soon as you were old enough to know what a father is."

"I understand... well, actually, I don't get the whole pretending to be dead thing... but I understand you would have been there had you known."

"Come stay in my rooms with Emma and me. Let's be a family for once."

Keri laughed, "I'd like that, but why not come stay with me? I have taken over a whole house at the end of the row. There will be much more room."

"That sounds like a plan." He paused, unsure how she would react to his next statement, "I really should bring Rachael with me."

Keri laughed. "Relax, Sebastian. I may be jealous of your wards, but I am still rational about it all. Of course, your Feffer goes where you go."

That day, he, Rachael, and Emma moved out of the mayor's house and set up a temporary home with his eldest daughter. Over the next few days, he only saw Rebecca in passing as she organized the town's affairs. The evacuation was her prime concern, and she constantly met with advisors to discuss the distribution of provisions, transportation, and the like. Sebastian kept out of the way but one day was catching up on the news in the mayor's house and hesitated in the hallway, looking at the portraits of the family. It was Petra's portrait that drew his attention the most. The artist had captured the spirit in her eyes as well as the beauty. Her smile beamed down at him, and he saw her with her hair tied up in a bun for the first time. She wore a high lace collar and looked regal and elegant yet still vibrant.

"The real thing is much more interesting, trust me." He turned to see Petra in the doorway. She looked cheerful but tired. The bruising on her face had started to fade. He felt a little guilty at not having fixed that. It was the first time he had seen her since liberating her from her prison.

"Hey, Petra." He smiled, scratching off the thin scab that formed on a small cut on his hand and went to her. "How are you?"

"Tired, Rebecca has had me working with clerks all morning doing an inventory of supplies in the village.

Incredibly dull." She said, but he realized she loved every minute of it. "However, she has given me the afternoon off. I was about to take a nap when I saw you through the door from across the hall." Her smile faded as she asked, "What have I done to upset you?"

Sebastian frowned, genuinely confused by the question. "Nothing. What makes you think I'm upset?"

"You seem to have been avoiding me since we arrived in town."

"To be honest, I have been avoiding everyone," he said, then added, "Are you too tired to eat?" He asked as he reached up to the bruising on her face. She did not resist.

"Actually, I am rather hungry." As he dropped his hand, she reached up to touch where the swelling and discoloration had vanished. "That is some gift," she said, amazed.

"I was about to go grab some lunch. Care to join me?" He invited her with a smile.

Being slow on the uptake, Petra replied, "Becks is having sandwiches brought in from the kitchens. We can join her if you..." She stopped and looked at him, for his head was slowly shaking back and forth. Her eyes widened, as did her smile. "Or we could just find somewhere a little less hectic?"

"I think we should raid the kitchen larder to find somewhere where no one will bother us with inventories."

A little while later, they were seated upon the edge of the stable hay loft with a plate of bread, cheese, and cold ham. As they ate their feast, they engaged in idle chat, but as they finished, he lay back on his side and rested his head in his palm. She was sitting up but leaning back on her palms. As the sunlight poured in through the hay loft's high doorway, it shone upon her. Her hair glistened and left a glow around her face. Her small, upturned nose looked sweeter as she squinted slightly in the sunlight, causing little wrinkles along the bridge. "Looking out there, you would think everything in the world is fine," she said. "No one would believe that soon this place will be gone too." She looked over her shoulder at him. "Is there really any hope, Sebastian?"

"There is always hope," he replied. "If it is Illya's will, we will make it."

"I do not mean just us. I mean everybody. There is a war, and we're losing," she sighed.

"Hey," he said, sitting up and placing an arm around her shoulder. "Do not despair."

She looked at him. "It is not that, Sebastian. I do not despair; I feel guilty because I feel truly alive for the first time in my life."

"It's fine, little one," he whispered, "Be glad you are alive." He looked into those deep blue eyes and fought the urge to kiss her; it was what he knew she wanted, and she would give herself to him without reservation. Did his oath of celibacy still stand? His oath of nonviolence was long gone, after all. His feelings for her, however, were nothing like he had known with any woman since his wife. The usually assured preacher felt so conflicted. Maybe it was alright? Maybe it was meant to be? No! He wanted her so much but felt sure they had no future together. As she raised an eyebrow at him, he realized he had been silently staring at her. Before he could say anything, she launched herself at him, her arms about his neck, and as he fell back, she pressed her lips to his. As her warm body landed on him, he felt his heart pound and his loins stir. Her hands ran through his hair, and for a moment, he forgot all his worries. His loins screamed at him to take this all the way. It felt like she would, but if he truly cared for her, he would not dishonor her as he had so many women in his past. She seemed to feel this too as she eventually rolled off of him, and both stared up at the roof of the barn, breathing deep, frustrated breaths.

"That was close," came Rachael in his mind. Nothing kills one's ardor faster than the realization his sixteen-year-old Feffer was aware of his activity, and with her sister no less. He sat up and pushed Rachael out of his head, telling her irritably, "This is why we don't bond across genders."

CHAPTER NINETEEN

Dancing with Fatboy

"Oh, to dance by the light of the moons. My greatest joy. My greatest comfort." – Memoir of a Marran Priestess by Emma Roark-Maine

Lady Breanna Marie Maine found the dull monotony reminiscent of life in Jilrir had begun to set in. She had taken the house at the end of the street, and the Row Street Posse came with her as agreed. Unlike the others, she had dispensed with servants, and for all intents and purposes, they had been left alone. While the Posse enjoyed their new luxurious surroundings, Breanna became more restless and touchier as each day passed.

"You need to chill a bit." Kitty Longfellow told her one morning when Breanna was in a particularly foul mood. "I 'ear you 'ave been promoted?" she grinned.

Breanna was seated at the kitchen table toying with the porridge Midge had made her, "Promoted?" she looked up at Kitty bewildered.

"Your sister Rachael's abdication. I 'ear she is a Priestess now, not a Maine."

Breanna scowled. "She is no longer a member of the House of Maine, but she is still a member of *the family* of Maine. She is still and always will be my sister."

"Sorry," Kitty said gruffly. "What's got up your arse? I fought you would be proud of 'er. I would give my right arm to be a Priestess of Illya."

Breanna felt a wave of guilt, "I don't know what is wrong with me. I *am* proud of her. I always have been, but I believe I'm a bit jealous."

Kitty sighed. "Then go see the 'igh Priestess Jenri and see that she tests you."

"No, you dumb arse." Breanna frowned. "I have not, and never will have, any desire to take holy orders." Though she was not sure that was true, it was more like she doubted her ability than her desire. "It is true I now worship Illya where before I worshiped little more than hope but to do all that praying, chanting, and feeling sorry for people. Well, that's not for me. What I mean is Rachael has escaped the politics and bodragel shit. In doing so, she has moved me up the damn ladder. I have her title now. Third Lady of Jilrir."

"Oh, will you, for the love of pie, stop with all that self-pity." Kitty slammed the palm of her hand down on the table, startling her. "You complain because you is wealfy and 'ave influence. You, missy, are a spoiled brat who finks of little other than what you want. You is in a position to do good in this dark and terrifying land, yet you devote your time wiv pointless bellyaching." Kitty glared at Bree, who sat staring dumbstruck. Kitty did not back down. "I met your sister the other day, the sexy blond one with the tight arse."

"Petra."

"Oh, so that's Petra." Kitty pondered, then came back to her point, "Do you know that even though she cannot read or write, she is up in that 'ouse sorting out rationing for the evacuation? Midge 'as a job running messages all over town for Me'lady Rebecca and Mayor Portkind, and you are sitting on your backside spoutin' bodragel shit."

Breanna broke into a wide grin, "You fancy my sister?"

Kitty flushed, "I never said that, did I?"

"Hey, I have no problem with you preferring girls." Bree shrugged.

"Of course, you don't. So do you, after all." Kitty chuckled.

It was Bree's turn to flush, "I so do not. What makes you think that?"

"The way you reacted to Fatboy on the building that day, you looked most uncomfortable."

"That, my friend, is because I do not have much experience with boys." She flushed deeper.

"Oh, and there was me finking that you and I might...." Kitty said disappointedly.

"Not going to happen, not now, not ever." Bree shook her head vigorously.

"And you like Fatboy?"

"Well, I admit he is attractive and kind," Bree said uneasily.

"Aye, well, that he is, for a boy at least." Kitty shrugged. "'e will be delighted to 'ear about this."

"Well, he won't." Breanna stared daggers threateningly at her.

"Oh, of course not. Illya forbid that I should interfere." Kitty put her hand on her heart and grinned.

"I think we need to take time out to celebrate." The suggestion seemed to come randomly from Rebecca one morning at breakfast.

"Celebrate what exactly?" responded Petra derisively.

Rebecca just smiled at her and shrugged. "I don't know. And to be honest, I don't care. I just think a lot of good has come out of everything that has happened. We have clearly proved that despite being 'stupid women,' we have been able to run Ithia quite effectively.

Petra wanted to say that taking care of Nethili could hardly be considered the same as running Ithia, but her sister was in such a positive mood she didn't want to spoil it. "I'm sure we can arrange something. What did you have in mind?" the golden-haired sister said.

"Oh, I don't know. As long as there's music and dancing, I will leave everything to you and Mr. Portkind."

Oliver Portkind did not look very impressed by this idea, nor did the Lady Petra. She did not want to spend even more time with the annoying little man who spent more time staring at her chest or her legs than discussing work whenever they had to get together. She had considered bringing up the issue with Rebecca, but she knew her response to such behavior would be incredibly extreme. Mr .Portkind wasn't really a bad guy. He was just a bit weaselly.

However, she was saved by Rebecca having a change of heart. "Actually, get Breanna, Rachael, and Alannah to help you out. Let's make it a family affair."

"I'm sure we can organize things." Petra agreed, although she was not about to include Allannah.

"One last thing," Rebecca said softly to her sister. "I reluctantly need to invite that Row Street mob. Petra, could you do something to smarten them up? At the very least, obscure the smell."

Breanna Maine was surprised when, late afternoon, Emma and Daniel turned up at her door. Apparently, they wanted to go over to the fields and had no one to take them. Although Breanna did not really want to go, the two young people made her feel sufficiently guilty that she went to head out with them. She asked Kitty if she would join them, and she was surprised when her new friend declined.

Little did she realize that just five minutes after she left, Petra had turned up at the door. She had arranged to take the Row Street Posse out to get them appropriate clothing for a high-class baronial celebration. Kitty had somehow neglected to tell Bree! The truth was she was a little uncomfortable with the whole idea.

It was not cheap to outfit seven young people at the finest tailors in Nethili. The tailor was a short, fat, round man who appeared to look down his nose at the vagabond Posse with that common speech and strange concepts of manners. However, with Petra dressed in a style that made her appear quite affluent, he was more than willing to take her purse. Fortunately, Rebecca had been quite generous with the stipends she paid out from the Nethili treasury to everyone in the company.

Everyone except for the Lady of Jilrir laughed when Kitty came out dressed in a fine lacey frock that would have made Alannah jealous. "I knows. I knows. I looks silly," she said sadly.

"Just ignore them," said Petra. "You look positively beautiful, and it will be perfect for the party."

Kitty positively beamed at the compliment from the blond-haired beauty.

Midge went next and went for a style a little less lacy but with more bows. She beamed proudly and did a twirl for all to see. Unlike Kitty, she ignored the jeers and comments and walked around the store with her nose in the air, imitating a lady of refinement.

Then, one by one, it was the boy's turn to dress up in fine tunics with ties and ruffled shirts. As each finished, they took the tied-up packages outside to wait.

Finally, only Fatboy remained. He looked quite smart in the new outfit, but Petra could not help but notice something concerned him. "What is the matter?" she asked.

"There's somefing bovvering me about tonight," he said quietly, looking around to make sure the rest of the Posse could not hear him.

"Go on, you can tell me," Petra said gently in a conspiratorial whisper.

"Will I 'ave to dance?" He asked nervously.

"No, you won't *have* to. Are you taking a partner?"

Fatboy flushed slightly, "No, but I was 'oping to ask someone there to be my girl."

"Oh really?" Petra tried to hide her amusement at this young love. "Anyone I know?"

"Yes," he swallowed hard, and looking down at his shiny new shoes, he mumbled, "I really like your sister, Lady Breanna."

Petra was surprised by this. She had assumed that he was talking about Kitty, and she was not sure how to respond. "Oh well, umm, in that case, then, absolutely, you will have to dance. To be honest, at the party, that's probably the only way you're going to get her alone to talk to her."

"I don't know 'ow to dance. I mean, it's not for the likes of us, is it?"

Nor is Breanna, thought Petra with amusement, but she said, "Well, you have a few hours to learn."

"I don't 'ave no one to teach me."

Petra smiled. "You do now. Come over to my house when you get back, and I'll show you some basic moves."

Fatboy beamed happily as he headed to the door. He stopped before he went outside and turned back to her. "We don't need to tell anyone about this, do we now, miss?"

Petra smiled. She was hardly going to let Sebastian know she was helping a backstreet boy pursue one of his noble young wards. "We shall just keep this our little secret."

***

Petra had completely forgotten her arrangement with Fatboy and was busily putting away her own purchases. She had become quite conflicted about her return to Nethili. She had never wanted to go and live in the Great House in Jilrir and had longed to return to the town she called home. Now she was here, it just wasn't the same. She realized it was not Jilrir that she hated. Free from the terrorization of Ronan Maine, life wasn't exactly that bad. She enjoyed working for Rebecca even though it was just logistics, such as working out what provisions and supplies could be ready for an evacuation of the people. She even found learning to read was not the trial she once considered it to be. She was never going to be into book learning like Rachael, but she now saw a value in it. Maybe life as a Maine was not so bad after all. As she hung up the last item in the closet, something she could have got a servant to do, she pondered the future. The confidence of Rebecca was quite infectious. Maybe if the House of Maine prevailed, it might not be too bad going back to Jilrir one day.

Then there was Sebastian. Tall, handsome, rugged veteran of the holy wars. A man who made her feel special but who also ran hot and cold. She had never been a particularly religious person, and she was not sure that she could become so. His closeness to Rachael also bothered her. Whilst they were both kind and caring to each other, she had never been particularly close to her sister. It had not bothered her at first when she learned Rachael had become some sort of apprentice to him, but it started to when she learned that she could have chosen Jenri as her mistress. Why would she have chosen Sebastian unless she had some other interest in him? She never really believed that men and women could simply be friends. It just didn't seem natural to her.

She was deep in these thoughts when the knock at her door came. She was already opening it when she realized she was expecting him.

Fatboy stood, looking nervous, and for the first time, she saw him looking shiny and clean like a new button. He certainly washed up well, and she could not deny he was an attractive lad only a year younger than herself. However, for Petra, he was a little too attractive for her tastes. She preferred the more rough and ready dominant type. Harrison Feyer had originally seemed like that, but eventually, he began to fawn over her and cater to her whims rather than be a man who knew what he wanted. Since Jilrir, she had come to realize that her attraction to him had soon waned and that she truly saw him only as the hope of escape from that city.

"'Ello, me'lady," Fatboy said, shuffling his feet. "Is you still willing to show me how to dance?"

Petra smiled and stood back from the door. "Of course, come on in."

He entered the room nervously, and she was surprised he looked uncomfortable when she shut the door. "What's wrong?

"Well, I..." He hesitated, looking at time uneasily and then at the door and shrugged. "I was raised it was not proper to go into a lady's room when no one else was there."

Petra chuckled. "Well, I can hardly teach you to dance and keep it secret if I had a chaperone here."

"You 'as a good point, me'lady ."

She was about to tell him not to call her my lady, but it only then occurred to her that she liked it after all. "Unfortunately, I have no musicians here. And with our limited time, I can probably only teach you one dance. Do you prefer something jaunty or something a little more romantic."

She chuckled inwardly when he blushed lightly. "Well, if you'd be willing, I want to do a dance that shows lady Breanna what I thinks of her. "

"Well, okay, let's see." She took his left hand into her right and held it up. She took a step closer to him, but he instinctively took a step back. She chuckled at this. "Come now, you could hardly dance with Breanna from that distance." She stepped in again, and this time, he did not resist, but he looked at the ceiling uncomfortably. She then took his right hand with her left and felt him tense as she placed it around her waist. He colored even more. "Relax," she said soothingly. "This is the one time where touching a lady is perfectly acceptable. No one is going to think anything bad of you for doing it ."

He appeared to relax slightly, but Petra still felt the tension in his body as she placed her hand on his shoulder. "So, in an actual dance, we will be standing much closer, but I want you to be able to look down and see my feet."

Over the next few minutes, she instructed him on the movements in between humming a popular ballad. He seemed to take to it quite easily, and after about twenty minutes, she instructed him to look up at her and pulled him in. He let out a startled breath, looking terrified as their faces came closer together, and they looked into each other's eyes. She tried not to laugh and increase his discomfort, but it was she who would become uncomfortable when, a few minutes after moving around the room, he said, "You is so bootiful." in a soft and loving tone. She instantly let go of him and took a step back, her eyes wide.

"Oh, I'm sorry, but that is so not appropriate," she chided.

Fatboy looked mortified. "Oh, by Maran's beard, I'm so sorry. I was thinking about what I wanted to say to Breanna, and it just came out."

Petra looked unsure and narrowed her eyes. "Oh, it is Breanna that you think is beautiful, not me?"

"Well, Me'lady," he said awkwardly. "You is indeed incredibly bootiful, but if you forgives me, there is something about Breanna no woman can match."

Petra found this so unbelievably sweet that she immediately forgot her concern. "Well, there are some things you should know about Breanna. If you get too mushy with her, you will just make her uncomfortable. You should also be aware, as I am sure you are, that she is a Lady of Jilrir and a member of the House of Maine. One cannot simply just date a member of my family. Breanna knows her own mind, but ultimately, you need both the approval of Lady Rebecca and her guardian."

Fatboy frowned. He found the Lady Rebecca most intimidating, and this was the first he heard that Breanna had a guardian. "Who is that?"

Petra smiled again and said, "That would be Sebastian, and trust me, he is *very* protective of my sisters." And added as an afterthought for her own benefit, "And me, for that matter."

"Does that mean I need to be asking them their permission to be taken out, Me'lady Breanna?"

"Well, proper royal etiquette would be that you first seek her approval to ask them. I do warn you that my sister is quite stubborn and will probably not see your need to seek permission to court her. However, for your own safety, if you value your life, I would clear it with Sebastian." She did not have the heart to tell him that Sebastian would probably not agree. Whilst he stood up for the common man, he still believed in the class system as it was presently constituted, and knowing him as she did, he would be very particular and protective of his young ward. "Well, I think I have told you enough to be going on with. At least you will get through one dance with her if, of course, she accepts."

"You fink she might turn me down?" he looked positively mortified at the prospect.

"To be perfectly honest, I have no idea. Bree and I do not talk very often, and when we have done, she has not mentioned you. So I really cannot advise you on what she thinks about you, but it will certainly be a lack of courtesy for her to decline your offer of a dance in public."

"Well, fank you, me'lady. I really appreciate you 'elping me out, like." He did not look very confident and was most troubled. Petra could not help but chuckle as she closed the door, but it did not last long. She looked at the clock on the wall and realized she was late for going to help Rachael.

CHAPTER TWENTY

The Posse and the Posh

"They still say that one can never rise from the lower classes and all should know their place. All I can say to that is look at me. I may not be of the blood, but I am now family to the Maines, as are several members of that exclusive club known as the Row Street Posse."
– Memoir of a Marran Priestess by Emma Roark-Maine

Rachael took over the hall of the house, and with the help of servants, she decorated it in the red and gold colors of the House of Maine. She had found items stored for such an occasion should the first family ever be in Nethili as they found themselves now. She was a little frustrated that Petra was not there to help as promised but was relieved when she finally turned up almost two hours late. However, when Petra told her in hushed, conspiratorial tones what she had been doing and the crush the boy had on Bree, Rachael was delighted,

Rachael and Petra never really spent much time together, and it was interesting how much they enjoyed each other's company. However, it would constantly grate on Rachael whenever Petra joked about her being part of the priesthood.

"Petra, I really need to ask you. Do you have a problem with me being a priestess?" Rachael eventually had to say.

Petra seemed surprised at the question. "Why would you think that?"

"You always seem to be ribbing me about being a member of the order. Is there something bothering you about what I do?"

"I really don't know what you mean. I'm just messing with you," Petra stated defensively. "If that's what you want to do, that's fine by me." She turned away to straighten a tablecloth. "I just find it curious why you would want to spend *so* much time with Sebastian."

"Well, I don't really spend much time with him. I should be spending much more, in fact. We're supposed to be studying together, but with everything going on, he never has the time."

"Why did you choose Sebastian to be your mentor?" Petra was trying to sound casual as if it was just general conversation, but she failed. "Surely it would be more suitable to bond with Jenri?"

The realization came to Rachael. "I see. It is not that you object to me being a priestess. It is that you do not like me being with Sebastian."

Petra flushed pink, "I really don't know what you're talking about, Rachael Maine."

Rachael sighed softly. "Petra, my interest in Sebastian is purely platonic. I have no interest in him beyond that of a friend and mentor. I am not rival for his affections."

Petra could not look her sister in the eyes, "I still do not know what you are talking about. It's not my business if you are or you are not interested in him," she said snippily, now folding napkins hurriedly.

"He tries to hide his feelings for you from me," Rachael lowered her voice. "However, sometimes they come through, and that first night in Boddington's, I was aware he kissed you."

Petra looked at her and tossed the napkin she had been folding onto the table. "You say he has feelings for me. Are you sure?"

Rachael smiled as she pushed her glasses up her nose. "There is no doubt about it, Pet. But he is also confused. He is concerned about your heritage, your place in the House of Maine, and, of course, your age."

Petra sighed and was quite frustrated when she said, "Well, the age thing is just stupid. Most women marry older, established men, and he is half the age of the old farts our father had lined up for us." Getting more irritated as she thought about it. "He must surely know that I have no interest in titles, position, or any of the responsibilities of being the second lady of Jilrir.

"Therein lies the problem. Sebastian is a monarchist, and he takes our positions a lot more seriously than we do. He is torn between what he perceives as his duty and his feelings for us."

This infuriated Petra all the more. "He had no problem taking you out of the royal line."

"He did not take me out of it. Illya did. Sebastian did not even have a say. He did not even want me as his Feffer."

Petra bit her lip and stared up at the ceiling with a sigh. Her shoulders then slumped, and she looked down at the ground. Then, looking up at Rachael, she said faintly, "I love him so much it hurts."

"I know, Pet, I know." Rachael softly replied.

The celebration was an even smaller affair than Breanna's coming-of-age celebrations a few weeks before. It was mostly family and members of the senior household, but notable figures from within the community were also invited. And, of course, the dressed-up remnants of the Row Street Posse.

Despite having told Sebastian that she would be there to welcome the guests, Rebecca was late as usual. Rachael wore a short red dress that came just above the knee with matching red shoes. Unusual for her, it had a slight heel, albeit a thick one. The color had been chosen to reflect her faith, and the Preacher found the outfit quite daring for the modest young feffer. He could not help but feel a little guilt that he never did replace those glasses, which, as she entered, she pushed up her nose again. "You are looking quite radiant, my young feffer." He smiled at her and gave her a quick hug.

"To be quite honest, master, I feel absolutely slutty," she laughed with a mixture of amusement and embarrassment. "I just thought I would change it up a bit, but I honestly wish I hadn't now."

"Do not worry yourself, my dear. You look positively beautiful."

She smiled. Sebastian could be so charming, and she felt sure what he said wasn't true. She was quite aware that she was plain in comparison to her sisters, having taken more after her father where they took after their mother. It was not that she was self-deprecating, for she didn't really care about appearances. However, she smiled up at her Master, gave him a very neat curtsy, and thanked him. He held out his arm to her, and she took it. He led her over to the bar, where he got them both a glass of wine. When he turned back towards the door, he saw that Breanna and Kitty had arrived together, with Midge tagging along behind them, as was often the case. He was most surprised to see Kitty, who had probably washed for the first time in years. Someone had worked on her mop of red hair and straightened it out so that she had a long ponytail that hung fashionably over her shoulder and down over her breast. She had clearly gone out of her way to make an attempt to fit in with what she called the nobs. Sebastian could not help but smile when his eyes alighted upon Breanna, who had clearly gone out so far away not to fit in as a nob. Wholly inappropriately, she was dressed in black leather pants and a matching tunic. It was of a fine cut and no doubt expensive but was certainly not appropriate for a lady to wear to a dance. As a traditionalist, Sebastian would usually be most put out by this from a young ward, but he had come to accept this was simply Breanna Maine. The pair were talking to each other in hushed whispers and did not pay any heed to him or Rachael, apparently unaware they were even there.

If Breanna's appearance had startled him, that was nothing compared to the sudden arrival of Alannah Maine. Whilst she was still in a fine dress. It was not her typical hardcore, massively expensive frock that she would wear just once and cast aside. She did, however, have a lady in waiting at her side, unlike anyone else. Sebastian was not sure if this was her typical need to show her position, but it was not unreasonable for a twelve-year-old noble to have an escort. However, the biggest surprise was yet to come. The moment she saw him, she radiated a smile and ran up to him and gave him the biggest hug ever. "Oh, it's so good that we get a chance to forget about the troubles for just one night," she positively gushed as he uncomfortably returned her embrace. He could not help but grin at the wide-eyed look of surprise from his Feffer, who stood behind her sister pushing her glasses up her nose.

"Indeed, it is, my lady," Sebastian replied to the young girl as she let go of him and promptly held onto his hand. "You are looking exceptionally nice tonight," he told her.

"Oh, this little thing," she said. "I thought it important that I did not go too extravagant with the purse strings with the House of Maine currently having a lot to contend with."

He barely heard her, distracted by Lady Devin coming in. She glanced over at him but immediately turned to talk to Breanna.

He was surprised when he saw Jenri and Keri enter. He made to let go of Alannah's hand and go to his mistress, but the little girl clearly had no intention of leaving his side. So, with the twelve-year-old in tow and Rachael following behind, he walked over to them. Keri was dressed in formal dress robes of the Maran church, although instead of coming down to the ground, they hung just below the knee, and he was surprised to see her wearing soft shoes similar to that of a ballerina. He glanced down at them and then looked up at her questioningly. "I know, I know! They are positively hideous, Sebastian." She chuckled. "But I am hoping someone actually asks me to dance for once, and my fear of someone stepping on my toes is rather extreme."

"You so remind me of your mother," he said softly, finally managing to release his hand from the young Maine at his side and hug his daughter.

"To be honest, I cannot think of a greater compliment, father. Thank you." Keri beamed.

The Preacher turned his attention to his mistress, "How are you doing? I was not sure if you were going to attend this event?"

"Oh, somebody has to keep an eye on you, Sebastian." Jenri grinned. "Who knows what trouble you would get into without me?" She, too, had not gone to a great deal of trouble and pretty much wore the garb she usually did, with the only change being she had swapped out her cape for a longer cloak.

Sebastian summoned over servants and ordered more drinks. He turned to ask Alannah what she wanted, but she had disappeared. He looked around the room but could not see her and then immediately put her from his mind.

Then, the rest of the Posse arrived.

All had bathed and wore the outfits they had purchased with Petra but still looked completely out of place, looking shifty and uncomfortable. They all made a beeline for Kitty, who appeared like a refined lady surrounded by would-be suitors for her attention. He could not help but smile with amusement until he noticed a good-looking young man who did not seem to be able to take his eyes off Breanna. His own eyes narrowed as he pondered what that might mean and made a mental note to keep an eye on this young man.

It was only then that he became aware that Petra had not yet arrived. Considering his feelings for her, he was concerned that he had not thought about her before. He was so looking forward to the possibility of getting another dance with her. When the music started up, and she still had not arrived, his concern grew. However, he was immediately distracted when one of the Posse came up to Keri, gave a very deep bow, and said, "Wanna dance, Missy?" He felt a little annoyed at the way he had addressed the Marran priestess, but Keri just grinned at him and, giving Hank a very neat curtsy, she replied, "Why, Sir, I would be most delighted." She held out her arm to him, and he stared at it, wondering what he was supposed to do. Sebastian rolled his eyes, took the boy's arm, and placed it in Keri's, Who let him onto the dance floor rather than the other way around. This seemed to be the catalyst for the boys with a posse to make a beeline for any unattached woman. Jenri headed off to the dance floor with Chip, and even Rachael accepted the invite from a little lad half her age. Sebastian could not help but smile as he watched the ragamuffin gang dancing with the elite of the House of Maine and the churches of Illya and Marran. He made to take a seat at one of the tables but felt someone tugging the back of his cloak. He turned and looked down. Stephanie made some of her rapid hand movements, which he followed closely. "I know it's not appropriate for a girl to ask a man, but since no one has asked me to dance, I have little choice." Her hands told him.

"You are certainly correct in that it is wholly inappropriate for you to ask me to dance," he admonished but with a huge grin on his face. He then took a deep bow. "Miss Stephanie, if your card is not full, would you give me the gracious honor of joining me on the dance floor?"

She giggled soundlessly at that, and he held out his arm to her, and she joined him in the first dance of the evening. About halfway through, he noticed Rebecca had arrived with Petra and his young daughter. Petra was looking over at Stephanie and him with a frown. At the same time, Rebecca was engaged in a conversation with Kitty, who seemed to want to curtsy every time she spoke, only stopping when the first lady appeared to ask her to. he saw Oliver Portkind walk up to Rebecca and say something with a gracious bow. Momentarily, she looked startled, and when she took his arm and came out onto the dance floor, Sebastian realized what he had just asked her. He wanted the dance to end quickly so that he could go and greet Petra, but he was not about to offend the young Midge, who moved around the room with him, looking most happy.

However, his mood was most sullen when he saw Logan Brathwaite come in and immediately ask Petra to dance. It looked at first as if she was about to say no, but after over at the Preacher, she smiled at Logan and took his arm. Sebastian's stomach turned over. He felt sick, praying to

Illya that Petra would not fall for this man. He truly had nothing to fear, but jealousy is an insane bitch.

Breanna Maine stood to one side, watching the goings on. However, her attention was concentrated in her peripheral vision, where Fatboy stood two tables away, watching her nervously. She had declined several offers of a dance, waiting patiently for him to make his move. However, he didn't, and she was most irritated when the band came to the end of the romantic ballad. The dancing figures began to separate for a lively jig. This was not something Sebastian was about to do, and to her horror, she saw the Preacher walking over to her. "Oh no, not now, Sebastian." She glanced over at Fatboy, who, seeing him coming, appeared to deflate and turn away. Sebastian's smile disappeared when he saw the angry glare on her face. "Yes, what is it?" she asked him snippily. She looked over to see Fatboy now talking to Kitty.

"What's the matter?" The Preacher asked her.

Breanna sighed, "Oh, nothing. I was just hoping..." Her voice drifted off as she looked over at Fatboy once more, and Sebastian followed her gaze.

"Ah, I see." His sense of protection came to the fore, and he was about to give her a lecture on the dangers of amorous boys. However, someone suddenly pulled roughly at his arm, and as he spun around, he saw Rebecca smiling up at him with a desperate look on her face. "I think it's time for that dance I promised you, Sebastian," she said both pleasantly yet with force.

The Preacher frowned, for he knew of no such promise. However, when he saw Portkind looking most put out on the dance floor, standing alone, he realized what she was doing.

It was a fast dance with the group moving in unison, swapping partners, and spinning each other around, and although he knew how to do it, he still felt so foolish. As the music came to an end, Rebecca stepped up to him. "Oh, thank you, Sebastian," Rebecca said with a sigh. "While I have respect for Portkind's skills, I don't think I can stand an evening of him staring at my cleavage."

At those words, it was automatic for the Preacher to look down. He had not really noticed that the fashionable dress was cut quite low, exposing her undeniably pleasant bosom. Realizing what he was doing, he flushed slightly, but Rebecca just rolled her eyes.

"Men are bastards." Both of them turned and saw Kitty Longfellow watching them. She was shaking her head disparagingly at the Preacher. "If you be forgiving me for saying so, Josser."

"Go away, Kitty," Sebastian said pleasantly but firmly, and she simply shrugged and strolled off to talk to Breanna.

"She is certainly quite the character." Chuckled Rebecca.

"Indeed, she is," Sebastian commented with a smile. "However, she is clearly a natural leader, and you could do worse not to give her some position of authority within the house."

"Maybe in time, but don't you think she is a little too young and immature right now."

"She is the same age as Bree and a couple of years younger than Petra, who, despite being just as uneducated and lacking maturity, is one of your most important officials these days."

Rebecca's eyes widened as she looked over his shoulder, and a chill ran through his body as he heard a gasp. Turning, he saw that Petra had been coming over to him and heard every word he had just said. "So, the truth comes out." She said curtly, with her eyes filled with hurt. He took a step towards her and was about to say something, but she simply turned away and strode off.

"Oh, well done, Sebastian," Rebecca said sarcastically and headed after her sister.

CHAPTER TWENTY-ONE

A Night to Remember

"They say the gods work in mysterious ways, and for the most part, as a priestess, I accept that but I will forever question Illya's timing for what happened that night." Memoir of a Marran Priestess by Emma Rourke-Maine

He pondered following Petra but held back, not wishing to engage in a drama. Instead, he headed to the bar to order a stronger drink, where he found Portkind drowning his sorrows. "oh, there is nothing worse than unrequited love, Oliver," he said, unusually sympathetic towards the man.

Of course, Portkind's next words completely destroyed any concern he may have had. "I have no idea what you are talking about, Major Hawk," he said surprisingly aggressively, considering since that time in Jilrir, he had felt intimidated by the preacher. However, the use of that military title just irked Sebastian considerably.

He took his drink and turned away from the man looking out at the assembled company. Once more, his eyes alighted on Breanna and the young man who appeared to be edging his way closer and closer to her as she continually denied others' requests to dance. He noticed her furtively glancing at him every so often, but the boy was oblivious to her mutual interest.

He was distracted by the arrival of Carter, whom he had hardly spent any time with since the night of their jailbreak. The man had been on duty and missed most of the start of the evening. He was dressed relatively respectively, having been compelled to change quickly if he were to spend any time at the celebrations. Both he and Sebastian headed toward each other, but Rebecca suddenly grabbed his friend, and Sebastian noticed that Portkind had left his side and was heading toward her. He was sure the weaselly clerk muttered some profanity before returning once more to the bar as Carter and the Baroness began to dance. When he looked back at Breanna and her would-be sweetheart, he saw the boy had finally walked up to her, and Breanna had that huge silly grin on her face that had made her so endearing to the preacher. He decided he would not interfere and let her have this moment, but he couldn't watch and instead headed out the door to take a walk and clear his head.

"Excuse me, Miss Bree." Fatboy could not hide the nervousness bordering on fear in his voice, and Breanna could not help but find it quite endearing. But then she found nearly everything Fatboy did to be endearing. He was so good-looking and so sweet and so, so, so...... *everything!*

She did not reply but simply waited for him to continue. "If you be willing." his voice faltered as he became lost for words. "I mean." Again, he hesitated, and Breanna waited patiently. "I understand if you don't want to." Breanna's patience started to wane. "I mean, you don't have to."

"Oh, for fucks sake, Fred, are you gonna ask me to dance, or are you not?" she snapped irritably and loud enough to turn some reproachful heads around her.

Fatboy instantly coughed it up. "Wanna dance?"

Breanna's irritation instantly vanished, and she giggled at the simplicity of how he asked her. She gave him an eloquent curtsy and said in her most ladylike voice, "Why thank you, Fredegar, I am most honored that you asked me. I will most certainly join you in a dance." She grabbed him by the sleeve and pulled him onto the dance floor. His mind went back to what Petra had shown him, and obviously, he placed his hand around her waist and took her hand, remaining as far away from her as possible. Breanna scowled at him and shook her head disbelievingly, pulling him against her body and bringing surprised looks from those watching them. Once more, Fatboy looked uncomfortable, but as he looked into her large brown eyes, a smile crossed his face. "You is so bootiful, Anna."

It was her turn to blush as they moved around the floor together, and she felt her heart beat faster as he kept his eyes so lovingly upon hers.

She did not see Rachael grinning inanely at her from the other side of the room. She was so happy for her sister. She could not help but wonder about herself and why she had so little interest in romance. Sure, it was nice to dance with someone now and then, but she really did not see herself ever being involved with anyone. Her father and Ronan tried several times to arrange marriages for her, but the idea of having to share her life and cater to another, taking her away from her studies, was abhorrent. She had often wondered if she was normal, for she did not even have the carnal desires that most people seem to be obsessed with. She did not find herself attracted to men and had once considered whether she may be attracted to women, but they did not do anything for her either.

No, she was quite content to remain single, and now she was free of the traditions of her family. That was how her life's path was going to take her. This did not stop her from feeling absolute joy for the happiness she could now see on her sister's face. She had not spent time with Breanna lately, for she seemed to spend most of her time with those Row Street lot. However, Breanna was closest in her heart than anyone else, and she knew her sister felt the same. Despite their many differences, the bond of sisterhood ran deep.

***

Sebastian did not go far. He walked up and down the street outside where the party was held with his pipe lit in one hand and his other sunk deep into his pocket. He did not see Petra come out and look up and down the dark street. The door guard pointed out where she was, and she slowly came down the steps and walked towards him. He was staring at the ground, trying not to think of that boy from the gutter and his possible intentions with Breanna.

"What does it take to get your attention, Sebastian Hawk?" he looked up to see the golden-haired beauty standing with her hands on her hips, glaring at him.

"You only need to say my name, Petra, and I will come running," he said softly.

This was not the response she was expecting. She had assumed he would get all defensive again. Her anger faltered, and she stood there momentarily, confused and unsure of what to say. She eventually sighed, let her hands fall by her side, and stared away deep in thought, looking down the street before looking back at him. "Sebastian, I'm growing tired of all this. This hot and cold you are towards me makes me feel cheap. Either you want me, or you don't. It is time to make up your mind."

He stepped up towards her and made to take her hand, but she didn't let him. No, Sebastian, not until we have sorted this out. I am no one's plaything and no one's whim. Either commit to me or walk away. Either way, I want to know tonight right now."

Sebastian sighed. "If only it were that simple, my dearest Petra, if only it were that simple."

"Oh, by Maran's girdle, it *is* that simple." Sebastian had seen her get angry before, but she had never shouted this loudly at him, and her voice carried down the street. The guard at the door, who had been leaning against it with his arms folded, now stood upright and was watching them.

"Petra, you have to understand there are things to play that we have no control of," Sebastian stated with growing irritability. "You have clearly embraced your place in the House of Maine, and that conflicts with my position in the church."

"You are just making excuses, Sebastian." Petra snapped back apparently not caring who heard her. "You are just as entrenched in the House of Maine as I am, and you *know* the king will not recognize my legitimacy. Once we arrive in Aranar, I will be a commoner just like you, and you know it."

Sebastian looked over her shoulder, noticing the guard was now walking towards them. "Please lower your voice. You're causing a scene." He did not see the slap coming, but he felt it for sure. There was certainly some strength behind those soft, well-manicured hands.

"Is there a problem here, ma'am?" The guard clearly knew Petra, but he didn't know the preacher who so rarely ventured into Rebecca's seat of government.

"There is no problem here. Please go back to your post," Sebastian said aggressively.

The man fixed his gaze on the preacher. "I was asking the lady, Sir," he said threateningly as he placed his hand upon his sword hilt. It was a move intended to intimidate more than threaten, for Sebastian was unarmed, and drawing a blade would be unnecessary. "Please step away from her."

Of course, Sebastian's pride and ego did not permit him to obey the command, causing the guard to step even closer and insert himself between Petra and him.

"Everything is fine, Samuel. Kirkman Hawk and I were just having a disagreement, but I can assure you he is quite harmless." And then added as an afterthought, "Well, at least to me, he is."

The attitude of the guard swiftly changed, for although he had never met him, he had heard the name. "My apologies, Kirkman. I hope you understand I was following my duty."

Now that was something Sebastian could respect, and he nodded to him. "No apology necessary. I commend your diligence in the protection of her ladyship."

The guard nodded at that, and still looking a little uncomfortable, he glanced at Petra before returning to his post.

Sebastian looked back at her and went to take her hand again, and this time, she let him. Their anger was spent. "Listen to me, Petra, no, just hear me, really listen to me." He waited for her to acknowledge this, but she simply lifted her eyes from the ground and looked upon him again. "There's nothing more than I want than to be with you other than my continued service for Illya. I care greatly for you, but I struggle to see a future where we can be as one." She went to speak again, but he just squeezed her hand and said, "Please let me finish. I cannot promise you now or anything for the future. My duty now is to protect you and see that you survive this war, whether it is with me or without. "

"Call me stupid, Sebastian," she said softly. "But I can't see a future without you in it or any point in surviving this war to live out any sort of life where you are not part of it. Yes, I have come to care about the House of Maine and the family, and I did not realize how much I love them until now, but that is insignificant to how I feel about you. It hurts too much in here," she tapped her chest. "However, I am left with no choice but to accept your decision on this matter." She sighed and forced a smile upon her face. However, there is an issue that you need to address."

"Indeed, and what is that, my lady?" He asked with some concern, although realizing what she was about to say was not very serious.

"You have permitted Breanna to upstage me with her young beau. She gets a dance, and I have not yet had the delight of your company in that manner." Sebastian was amused by the formality with which he spoke, acting like the proper Lady of Jilrir that she was supposed to be.

He grinned at her. "Well, I must certainly rectify that abominable situation." He bowed low. "Would the most honorable Lady of Jilrir demean herself sufficiently to dance with a pathetic wretch like myself?"

Petra looked down her nose at him with a grin, and in her best Rebecca-like posh voice, she said, "Oh, I will consider it. I cannot promise more than that young man." Turning on her heel, she headed back to the house with a highly amused preacher following at her heels like an errand boy.

When they returned to the party, the music had ceased, and food was being served. Sebastian looked apologetically at Petra, who rolled her eyes and shook her head with a grin before leading them over to the table where Rachael, Breanna, and Emma sat.

Fatboy stood nearby, looking over at her like a lovesick puppy. "Oh, my dear Bree." Rachael was reprimanding her. "You just left him standing there like a lemon the moment that dance finished."

Sebastian and Petra took a seat beside them. "Well, it was kind of awkward," Breanna responded. "He is so nervous, but he doesn't even say anything without stammering. He doesn't seem to know what he's doing."

Rachael chuckled. "Oh, come off it, Breanna. We all saw the way you were looking at him. You have it bad."

"All right, I'll admit he is cute, and yes, I like him."

Sebastian remained quiet, and Petra had a little smile as she noticed the concern in his eyes as he listened to her sister. He blocked out further conversation regarding the romantic adventures of his young ward. He had other things on his mind as he pondered his conversation with

Petra. When the conversation moved on to idle chat, he ate silently as Petra joined in the conversation with the others.

When the music started again, Sebastian stood and turned to face Petra.

"Lady Petra Maine, I ask again if you would do me the honor of giving me this dance."

Her thin lips curled into a slight smile. The soft, slow music started up as he led her to the middle of the floor. His knees went weak as he looked down into those deep blue eyes, and his heart pounded into his ears. It was a slow tune, and he had no choice but to hold one hand and place the other about her slender waist. Slowly, they moved in time to the music, and when their eyes met, it was as if they had become locked together. They both forgot their audience. Her eyes lit up with joy at the attention he showed her. In turn, all he wanted to do was kiss her. They moved around the floor in a fluid movement until, finally, the music ended.

They did not hear the gasps of the others as he pulled her to him and, leaning into her, their lips met. Once more, the world spun around with no one else in it.

"Rachael?" Bree stared, her jaw hanging loose as she whispered.

"Hmm?" Rachael responded with amusement.

"Am I high?"

"Nope," Rachael replied with a grin. "At least not that I'm aware of."

"So," Breanna hesitated, rubbed her eyes, and looked once more at the couple on the dance floor. "So I am seeing that Sebastian is snogging Petra?"

"Yup." Rachael giggled.

"I am really not imagining it?"

"Nope," Rachael replied as she pushed her glasses off her nose and popped a piece of bread into her mouth while sitting back casually as if what her master was doing was perfectly normal.

"Wow, Sebastian," Breanna gasped. "Let the poor girl up for air."

When Sebastian finally released Petra, she looked around at the wide-eyed stares aimed at her. She smiled, blushed, and briskly headed out the door.

Emma walked up to Sebastian in determined strides. Stopping in front of him, she placed her hands firmly on her hips and said angrily, "Don't fink I am gonnabe calling Lady Petra, Mom." she said, turning on her heel, and she ran out.

Rachael could not help but be incredibly amused by the startled look on Sebastian's face as he started to head toward the door.

She went to get up to follow them to make sure Petra was alright, but a soft gasp of pain from Breanna made her turn back to look at her sister.

The young Maine was clutching at her stomach with an intense look of discomfort. Rachael sat back down and looked at her with concern. "Are you okay? What's wrong?" she said, slipping her arm around her sister's shoulder. "It's just a cramp. Feels like I've got the menses coming on."

"Are you sure? Rachael found, "It isn't your usual time of the month."

Breanna looked up at her frowning through the discomfort. "Since when have you kept track of it?"

Rachael laughed, "Well, you usually come on about a week before me, and I'm not due for another couple of weeks."

"Rachael. You know I love you more than anything in this world, but you are *sooo* fucking weird." The pain seemed to ease, and Breanna sat upright again. "I don't even pay attention to when my cycle is on the way, and you're keeping track of it?"

Rachael flushed lightly and shrugged. "Well, I'm not exactly keeping track of it, Bree. It's just that I remember things more than you do. Do you want to go home?"

"No, it's passing. I'm okay now. I just have these butterflies in my stomach now." Breanna was startled when Rachael went positively rigid and stared at her. Slowly the young feather felt her jaw drop as she stared at her sister. Stomach cramps followed by butterflies? This was all a little too familiar.

CHAPTER TWENTY-TWO

A Church Restored

While my father would be thoroughly appalled at me, I can only describe the Calling as a sensation far exceeding the best sex you ever had—an orgasmic wonder beyond imagination." – Memoir of a Marran Priestess by Emma Roark-Maine

Breanna frowned at her sister's reaction. "What the hell is the matter with you?" she asked but got no reply. Rachael suddenly stood up on her feet and looked around for Sebastian, but he had gone out. She saw Jenri across the room looking around frantically, and as she moved, she appeared to be drunk. Something impossible for the Elessar no matter how much alcohol she could consume.

"Rachael, what is going on?" Bree asked her urgently. "You are scaring the shit out of me."

Rachael looked at her wide-eyed, and Breanna started to see tears running down her face, and with a mixture of both shock and joy as she struggled to speak. "I think it's happening. I prayed for this every day since I became a priestess, and I really believe it's happening."

Fear and confusion crossed Breanna's face, and she found herself unsteady as she tried to stand up. In a split second, Fatboy was at her side, holding her up. Rachael looked up again, hoping to draw Jenri's attention, but she saw the Esselar crouched down with someone else who was sitting up on the floor. Rachael closed her eyes and opened her mind. She called out to Sebastian, "You have to come back. You have to come back now! Please!"

"I have felt it, Feffer. I am on my way." Sebastian rushed back in with Petra and Emma at his heels. He, too, was looking around the room urgently.

"Sebastian over here," Rachael called out but saw that Jenri was also waving fervently at him to come over. But at her shout, the Esselar looked over to them, and her eyes widened at the sight of Breanna being held up by the boy from the Row Street Posse. As the Esselar got to her feet, Rachael did not think her eyes could open even wider, but they did as she saw the red-headed form of Katherine Longfellow holding on to her belly. "By all that's holy," she murmured.

Sebastian was now at their table, and with Fatboy still holding on to her, he took Breanna's hands into his and looked at her intently. Rachael saw he, too, had a tear in his eye. Then, a huge drunken grin appeared on his face. "Breanna Marie Maine, you are being called."

"I know. I know, I know, I *know*," she said, her words almost slurring.

Rachael looked on with a little concern creeping into her mind. Not wanting to scare her sister, he opened her mind to Sebastian once more. "This seems different to me. It's not the same as when I was called."

"That's because it *is* different, Rachael. You will see," he replied cryptically.

Breanna started to giggle drunkenly. "Do you accept?" he said softly, reaching up and stroking her cheek.

She nodded. "Like I would have a choice even if I didn't want to." she laughed.

Sebastian grinned. The little girl who always said she hated reading had clearly read the book of Illya, at least the parts related to the Calling. There was no choice when the goddess called one would follow. For she never called anyone who wasn't willing. "Can you walk?" he asked. Now that the music had stopped, everyone was looking at him or Jenri.

Breanna just laughed. "I can't move my legs. "

"That's okay." Said Sebastian, rising. He looked at Fatboy. "Thank you for your assistance, young man, but this is now a private matter."

The boy said nothing as he let go of Breanna. Sebastian lifted her in his arms, but as she lay her head against his shoulder, she whispered. "Please let him come. It will mean so much to me." Although reluctant, Sebastian could not refuse her request. It was her right to have whoever she chose with her, and he nodded to Fatboy. "Come on."

As he turned and headed to the door, Jenri joined him, and at her side, Logan was carrying Kitty in a similar manner. They both just looked at each other for a moment and made for the door. Had he not been going through the euphoria, he would probably have objected to Logan's presence, and as they stepped out into the night, he could barely hear Rebecca shouting at them, demanding what was going on.

Sebastian looked over at Logan and Kitty and whispered to Jenri. "Interesting choice."

"I cannot think of a finer recruit." Jenri grinned.

"I cannot deny that her heart is in the right place, but you are going to have trouble getting her to even talk like a person."

"Sebastian Hawk, you can be a complete snob, you know." The Esselar frowned teasingly.

"Indeed, I have been told more than once." He grinned.

Rebecca looked confused as she followed them out. "What is going on with Bree?"

"She's been called, Rebecca," Rachael told her.

She tried to place a reassuring hand on her arm, but she pulled back, "No. No, you are not taking another one," she said, running in front of Sebastian and trying to stop him.

"It's not our choice, Rebecca, it's Illya's will." He replied.

Rebecca screamed at him, "You can't have the entire family. What next, Alannah, as a warrior monk?" Alannah, who stood in the doorway watching with Devin, balked at the suggestion and backed out of sight nervously.

Breanna smiled at her sister as she clung to Sebastian's neck. "It's all right, Becks, I've been wanting this for some time. It's not like I'm going to make a good Lady of the Manor."

"But it's not fair." Tears welled up in Rebecca's eyes, not concerned, for once, in losing face amid her subordinates. "I'm losing all of you. How can I help restore this House when there will be no members of it?"

"I'm not leaving the family, Rebecca. Rachael and I will always be here for you. It's just that I now have a destiny that means something. Can you understand that?" Breanna slurred.

Rebecca sighed, "It's just all too much for me right now."

Sebastian smiled at her, "Come with us and take part in this. Watch and see what it means to her and Rachael." Reluctantly, she nodded.

Kitty Longfellow was looking dreadfully embarrassed, "I is sorry, honest, I ain't touch no drop of grog."

"It's fine, Kitty, you are not drunk," Jenri reassured her.

"Then's what's making me all squiffy in the 'ed like?"

Jenri grinned, "Well, I am going to ask you a very simple question, and you will know the answer yourself.... Are you ready?"

As if a part of her mind had been suddenly unlocked, she realized Illya's Calling. "Glory be Mistress Esselar, Ma'am, that I am. Though whys she calls the likes of me, only she can know."

"Don't do yourself down, Kitty. You showed true loyalty to Illya when you saved her son, Sebastian. For if I am not wrong, you did it in her name?"

"'Ow's you be knowing about that?" Kitty looked to Midge and Emma, who had followed them out. "You bin talking out of turn, missy?" She said to Midge, who raised an eyebrow at her, "Yeah, sorry, sis, heads all out of wallop right now."

Jenri laughed, "As Esselar, I get insights from Illya. I know things when I need to know them."

"Illya, praise be her name, like she talks to ya?"

"Not directly. I just simply know things when she needs me to know it."

"Well," Sebastian said, "Shall we get started?"

"Nuh-uh." Rachael shook her head, "We had to rush mine so my brother couldn't stop us, but we don't have to do that now. Can you do it properly?"

"Oh, so my Acceptance of you wasn't good enough." Jenri chided softly.

Rachael flushed, "Oh, I did not mean..."

"Do not tease my acolyte, please, Esselar," Sebastian laughed.

Jenri grinned, "Yes, Rachael, we will go down to the chapel and do it properly."

"Run along to the house and collect my copy of the book of Illya," Sebastian instructed his young feffer. "See if you can find a handbell. If not, take the dinner gong from the kitchen. We will meet you at the chapel."

Rachael nodded and headed off as fast as she could. Sebastian, Jenri, and the two potential Feffers started to walk down the street. Sebastian looked back to see Emma and Midge still standing on the steps with long faces, "Well, come on, if you are coming," and their frowns turned upside down as they ran up to join the party.

The two preachers hung back, talking privately. "You can only bond with one, and an unbonded acolyte cannot survive without it," Sebastian said in earnest.

Jenri shrugged, "If Illya did not have an answer for that, she would not have called both. We must simply trust our goddess."

"It's a big risk."

Jenri raised an eyebrow and studied him, "Trusting Illya is a big risk?"

"Well, no," Sebastian said with a rare experience of being flustered.

They reached the small chapel. Logan and Sebastian placed their charges down upon their feet, and following tradition, Breanna and Kitty went in first. They were looking at each other and giggling like little girls up to no good and enjoying every minute. Rebecca stopped at the doorway, her face sullen and deep in thought. Sebastian slipped her hand into hers and squeezed it reassuringly. "I promise you, Rebecca, everything is going to be alright."

Rebecca smiled at him faintly and nodded. He led her and Logan inside, and with Midge, Emma, and Fatboy, they took a seat in one of the rows of pews. Sebastian and Jenri joined Bree and Kitty at the altar. Sebastian moved to stand to one side, and the Esselar stood before them. Smiling, she reached out a hand to each of them. Rachael suddenly burst in through the door, panting like a dog back from the hunt. She held Sebastian's copy of the book and what looked like a small cowbell in her hands. She quickly composed herself and walked reverently up to the two clerics. Jenri looked over to where Midge and Emma sat. She winked at them and beckoned them to come up to the front. They looked at each other, then grinned widely, and leaving Rebecca, they went up to the altar. "Midge," Jenri had Rachael hand her the small bell. "When I begin, I want you to ring the bell once, and then I want you to continue to ring it on the count of five until I indicate for you to stop." Midge nodded eagerly at Jenri, who then took the book from Rachael and turned her attention to

Emma. "Emma, I want you to stand next to me and hold
the book in your upturned palm. I then want you to place
your left hand on top of it and keep it that way until we
have concluded."

"Yes, Ma'am," Emma said eagerly following the instructions.

Jenri then turned first to Bree and then to Kitty. "Come
closer, stand either side of me." Jenri then took Kitty's
hand in her left hand and Breanna's hand in her right,
"Katherine Longfellow, you seek to serve Illya, Goddess of
Justice?"

"If you please, Me'lady, I does want it so bad." Kitty
looked fit to burst with eagerness, her eyes wide as excitement filled her voice.

Jenri grinned and looked to Bree, "Breanna Marie
Maine, you seek to serve Illya, Goddess of Justice?"

"I do." Although her words were more formal than
those of her companion, the eagerness was just as potent.
Sebastian looked on with pride and joy. Callings were always an amazing experience, but it was even more special
when it was someone you cared about.

Jenri turned once more to Kitty, "Do you renounce all
your sins?"

"I does so, most certainly." And so, it went with both
Rachael and Sebastian trying not to laugh each time Kitty
answered in her back street Nethili way.

Finally, in all seriousness, Jenri bowed her head, "Illya,
my most gracious and just Goddess, Breanna Marie Maine
and Katherine Longfellow seek to enter your service as
Feffers. Guide on your will in this matter. Show us your acceptance or reject them should you find their souls wanting." Silence fell, and moments later, the trio of Esselar

and Feffers began to glow white. Smiles of the sheerest joy crossed their faces.

As the light faded, Sebastian turned to them, "Welcome, sisters."

Rachael could not hold back any longer, so she jumped up from her seat and raced to Breanna, throwing herself into her sister's arms. They hugged tightly before Rachael pulled Kitty into the hug. Rachael's eyes then met with Rebecca's, who was still seated at the back of the chapel. She released her sisters and went to sit at her side. She interlocked her fingers with Rebecca's, and seeing a tear run down her face, the young acolyte tried to think of something to say, but in the end, she just laid her head on Rebecca's shoulder.

Sebastian was looking at Jenri grimly for a sign of what to do next. It was time to bond, but with two new Feffers and only one free mentor, he was at a loss. He sighed as he saw her expression and that she, too, had no idea what to do.

It was Rachael who suddenly rocked her superior's world, "So, who is taking on two Feffers?" she looked to Sebastian and Jenri, each in turn.

Jenri sighed, "I had hoped at this point we would have a sign."

"A sign of what?" Rachael looked confused.

"We can each only have one apprentice," Sebastian advised her.

"Says who?" Rachael frowned.

"It is the way it is," Jenri said, assuming this was simply acolyte ignorance.

"Well, that's been the tradition for sure, but it isn't doctrine," Rachael said, confused. "It's just a way to avoid all the confusing voices in your head, but one of you has to deal with that. I can tell you straight there is not a single word in the book of Illya that states a cleric can only have one Feffer."

Jenri stared at her, "She is right." Her words were but a whisper.

She looked to Sebastian, whose brow was furrowed in deep thought. "Give us the room if you please, everyone. The Esselar and I need to talk."

Everyone filed out, and Jenri sighed. Sebastian made sure he had Rachael blocked from his thoughts before he sat down wearily on the front pew. "Unless you command me otherwise, you have to take them."

"I thought you would at least want Breanna?" Jenri said, leaning back on the altar and folding her arms.

"I didn't even want Rachael, but she gave me no choice." Sebastian sighed.

"Do you regret it? "

Sebastian smiled, "Surprisingly, I do not. Bonding with Rachael has brought a bright spark into my life I had never known before." He then grew grim. "However, that does not mean I am willing to take a gaggle of females into my head. It is hard enough having one female, but two ..."

"What is so wrong with having a female apprentice?" Jenri frowned.

"It can be extremely embarrassing. Rachael can become privy to aspects of a man that no lady should experience."

Jenri laughed. "Oh my, Sebastian, think of it this way: Rachael will have a unique understanding of men that most priestesses will never have."

"I'm hardly representative of my entire gender. However, this is not solving our problem."

"Bree might not give you the choice. You are no less close with her than you are with Rachael."

"Yes, but Bree will go with you if she sees no alternative."

"I am not so sure, but we can try."

They summoned the two new Feffers back in but asked the others to remain outside. Jenri made no mention of there being a choice. "You need to form a Bond; a priestess must oversee your studies and training. As the souls merge, you become one with that Priestess, and that bond cannot be broken other than in death, or the Feffer becomes ordained. When both of you choose, you can open your mind, understand each other's thoughts, and feel each other's feelings. You can even see and hear with each other's ears and eyes if both wish it. However, if one or the other feels strong pain or anguish or indeed great joy, it can find its way into the consciousness of the other without choosing and experiencing the same." With her grim warning made, she smiled at Breanna, "Look into my eyes. Try not to blink or look away." She guided her head to his until they were so close that their noses almost touched. She stared into those large, energetic brown eyes, and they stared back.

Jenri suddenly let go and jumped back as if punched. She sighed and looked at Sebastian, "You might be able to persuade her to agree, but you cannot persuade her about what she wants. Breanna does not want me as her mentor. She wants you."

CHAPTER TWENTY-THREE

The Great Divide

*"Separation of church and state has been the
way of things since the end of the holy wars
and the Treaty of Massir. However, as I waited with Midge outside of that chapel, I had
no concept that that was about to come crashing down." Memoir of Marran Priestess by
Emma Roark-Maine*

B ree looked embarrassed. "It's nothing against you,
Esselar," Bree said weakly. The euphoria of the Calling had faded. "It's not really possible to make yourself
want something that you don't really want."

Jenri smiled and placed a hand on her cheek. "It's all
right, Feffer. I am not offended."

Breanna looked at Sebastian apologetically. Although he
still did not like the idea, he knew he could not show this

to the young woman, who clearly still had doubts about her worthiness. The idea was as horrific as it had been with Rachael, but this time, he was not going to fight it.

Sebastian smiled at her and asked, "Do you know the bonding rite? "

Breanna's face fell as she shook her head, but Sebastian smiled at her, "Are you sure? Think about it."

A light seemed to come on in Breanna's eyes as, somehow, she did know the rite. Sebastian took her hands into his.

"Look into my eyes and try not to blink." He bent towards her so that their eyes were level. "I will be your mentor," He intoned solemnly.

"I will be your student," she replied, her voice shaking.

"I will be your guide." He squeezed her hands reassuringly.

"I will be your follower." She smiled back at him, relaxing.

"I will instruct you in all things."

"I will obey you in all things."

"We are one." They both said this final line of the rite together.

They stepped down from the altar hand in hand. <Oh my.> Came Rachael into his mind, <I can feel Breanna's presence.>

<Yes, we are bonded. You can share thoughts, too, but only through me. Now, hush, it's Kitty's turn>.

But as Jenri took Kitty's hands in hers, the same thing happened. The high priestess jerked back, another rejection. The Esselar looked a little annoyed this time. "Katherine, while I'm sure Sebastian is awesome in all things, he cannot bond with every acolyte."

"I don't gets it. I ain't choosing the Josser. I chooses you. I'd be honored to be the Esselar's Feffer."

"Then I do not know what's going on. It doesn't make sense." The High Priestess looked to Sebastian for answers. "She *has* to bond with someone. I know not why Illya is refusing this."

"Maybe she changed her mind," Kitty said nervously

Jenri reached up to stroke her cheek with the back of her finger, "That's not it at all, I assure you. If you are truly choosing me and not subconsciously choosing Sebastian, then the problem must lie with me."

"Nothing personal to Josser, but I don't know him half as well as Breanna, and I really don't want to bond with a bloke," Kitty said nervously.

The room around them suddenly began to shimmer like a heat haze in a desert. Jenri's face went impassive, and she stared off into space. Scared now, Kitty moved to stand behind Sebastian, and even Bree took two steps away from Jenri. Rachael suddenly ran in and up to them, "I am sorry, something compelled me to come back to you."

"It's fine," Sebastian said, and taking her hand, he pulled her close to him and Kitty,

"What's going on?" Bree said fearfully, convinced Illya had changed her mind.

Gradually, a smile returned to Jenri's face as the shimmering dissipated. She looked around at each in turn and reached out to them, "I have had a revelation. Illya has changed the rules. In this time of strife, we are not all able to choose our mentors. Kitty is to bond with Sebastian."

This time, Sebastian could not hide the shock on his face. "But seriously ...."

Jenri raised a hand to stop him. "It's not open for debate. Illya has made it clear that you are to bond with Kitty."

Kitty looked at Sebastian nervously. She could clearly see that he did not want to bond with her any more than she wanted to bond with him. Seeing this, he smiled at her, shaking his head. "Oh, don't worry, it is not you that I'm having a problem with. It is hard enough training Rachael, and taking it on two more Feffers was more than I bargained for."

"I get that. Perhaps I should wait until there's another Josser around."

"That isn't an option," Jenri said, "Once accepted, the acolyte needs to bond within days, or she will die."

"Kitty," Sebastian spoke softly. "I am sorry if my reaction has made you feel uncomfortable. I would be happy to bond with you."

"Kitty." Breanna stepped forward, smiling at her friend, and taking her hand, she pulled her towards Sebastian. "Trust me on this, he can be a bit of a grumpy wanker ..."

"Thanks," Sebastian muttered.

"But he's alright."

"Well, I can't say I likes it. Me being in some bloke's 'ed and some bloke being in mine. But if that's what Illya wants, then 'oo am I to argue."

Kitty sighed, and then she smiled and stepped up to him, and he took her hands in his. "OK, boss man, let's do this."

"Have you memorized the bonding rite?"

"I 'ave."

"I will be your mentor."

"I'll be ya student."

"I will be your guide."

"I will be ya followa."

"I will instruct you in all things."

"I will obeys ya in all fings."

"We are one." He said, but at the same time, she said, "We is one."

Sebastian felt her crawling fast around his mind <Slow down, Kitty, don't be scared, relax.> He would find it hard to differentiate the thoughts of the three different girls now circling around his mind. Bree and Kitty were nowhere near as calm and collected as Rachael. He had to verbally hush them so he could hear more from Jenri, "There is a new structure of just two orders. Sebastian, Rachael, and I are henceforth known as Teachers. It is our duty to study and spread the word and to administrate the church. This replaces the First and Second Orders. Next, the old third order is to be replaced, and they will not be Feffers like Rachael. It is not their place to study The Word but to defend the order and its interests. Illya has decreed the first of those will be Breanna and Katherine. Sheildmaidens of Illya."

Breanna laughed with delight and slapped Kitty on the back. However, Kitty looked concerned, "So's we ain't priestesses?" she asked dejectedly.

Jenri smiled, "Yes, you are. You are preordained and are priestesses right now." At those words, Kitty looked incredibly proud.

"So," Bree softly spoke, "I already outrank Rachael?" She grinned at her sister.

Jenri laughed, "In title only, you can't order her about."

Rachael rolled her eyes and shook her head at her sister, "Priorities, Bree, priorities."

"Come on, let's go see Rebecca before she busts a blood vessel." Bree then looked quickly to Jenri, "With your permission, Esselar."

"Go ahead," she chuckled. "Sebastian and I need to talk anyway."

They watched them depart the temple, and The Preacher and his mistress sat together on the front pew. They were both tired. This Calling had been exceptionally challenging. "So why did Illya stop you from taking an apprentice?"

"This is not going to be easy to tell you, but Illya has a different plan for me. I will not be traveling with you when you leave Nethili." Jenri paused, and she placed a hand on Sebastian's.

He grew concerned and turned in his seat to face her directly, "Why?"

She simply smiled, "I do not know. All I know is that Illya has a mission for me and a mission for you."

"And what pray tell is my mission?" Sebastian was growing irritated.

"You ought to follow your instincts and continue down the path you're planning. It will lead you to your true objective, which I cannot reveal."

"Yet you know it?'

"Part of it, yes, but I'm also not permitted to speak about it. I'm sorry, Sebastian. I know you don't like this cryptic stuff, but that is how the gods work, and who are we to question their wisdom." She reached over and kissed him softly on the cheek. "It does not matter what changes and what our roles are. I value your experience, and you are still as much a mentor to me as you are to Rachael. This is purely for survival, my brother. Illya has a plan, and in the fullness of time, it will be revealed to you."

The pair rose and headed out into the night. They initially walked in silence back towards their residences.

"So," Sebastian said at length, "Shieldmaidens huh?"

"Yes."

"What if they get married?"

"Huh?"

"Well, umm ... they won't be maidens."

"It's just a name, Sebastian." Jenri rolled her eyes, most amused by her prudish companion.

"Fair enough."

"I'm going to bed," She reached up and kissed him on his cheek again, then headed into the Mayor's House. Sebastian could hear the angry shouts coming from Rebecca's office as the front door opened.

No one had seen Devin leave the party with Alannah. They strolled along the dark streets unconcerned about their safety, "It appears another of your sisters has left the line of succession. With Breanna out of the way, you are now Jilrir's third lady. You are doing good to ingratiate yourself with Sebastian, but you need to do more," Annabelle Devin looked down at the young girl, "He does not trust easily, and therefore, you need to make sure that he does not have a single doubt about you."

"It is not easy, Auntie. He's quite the most contemptible, odious man that I have ever met. I am sure I can smell him on me."

"He is also the man who is keeping you alive until we reach the capital." Devin sighed, irritated by the girl's stupidity.

"I still do not see the point. Even with my father and brother dead and Rachael and Breanna joining that odious cult of his, I'm still fourth in line. It would take a small miracle to remove Rebecca, Petra, and the King's son from the succession."

"You lack vision, child. We will not be trusting to luck to ensure our mission is complete. Petra can be taken care of politically. She is, after all, just the baron's bastard. I highly doubt that the King will acknowledge her position."

"I should hope not. She is an unbelievable embarrassment to the entire family."

"Have a care, child. Have you not been watching your half-sister and Sebastian."

"As little as possible."

"Then you are a bigger fool than I thought you were. Something is going on between those two."

"Do you think he has designs on seeing her being in power in Aranar?" Allanah looked disgusted.

Devin sighed, "Don't be a complete idiot, Alannah Maine. They are romantically involved."

Alannah wrinkled her nose, "I don't know what grosses me out more, that she would be interested in that old man or that he would demean himself to fraternize with that half whore slut."

"Your hatred and contempt are commendable, young lady. However, you must curb it for now. Your dislike for your half-sister is almost legendary. If you are to ingratiate yourself with the odious Preacher, you must also ingratiate yourself with those he cares for. His first priorities are now on those foolish sisters of yours, Rachael and Breanna. As his apprentices, he would happily die for them.

"Really? As your apprentice, would you happily die for me?"

"Don't be ridiculous, child. I serve a different authority. Do not compare me to that Illyan scum."

"It is hardly fair," Alannah pouted.

"Don't you worry. By the time we are through, you have a nation willing to die at your feet."

"As it should be," Alannah said softly, knowing that her aunt would be the first with her head upon a pike for all the insults she had leveled at her.

"But do not get ahead of yourself, child. First, you must get to Aranar. In the meantime, you must win the hearts and minds of those in our party."

"I will try, Auntie."

"You will do better than try, girl. If you want to fail me, then I will look elsewhere for someone who can achieve our destiny."

"No, do not worry, Auntie. They won't know what hit them, and to be quite honest, I'm looking forward to it."

"I really don't think you're fully aware of the situation we now find ourselves in," Devin said in a most conspiratorial tone. "Rachael and Breanna have both removed themselves from the line of succession. Petra is a bastard and unlikely to be recognized. The only person standing in your way as head of the House of Maine is Rebecca. One of our goals is to keep an eye out for an opportunity to permanently remove her from the picture."

"Will you not be satisfied until you have recruited every single member of my family into your church?" Rebecca glared at Sebastian in livid anger.

"Why do you think that any of this is my master's fault?" Rachael said with some irritation.

Rebecca turned her wrath on her sister. "You can just be quiet. I'm talking to Sebastian. And stop calling him master."

Rachael took a step towards her sister and was about to respond when Sebastian placed a gentle hand on her shoulder. "I can justify myself, feffer," he said softly.

"Actually," Breanna put in. "I think this is more of a family matter than one of the church *master*." She was deliberately provocative when she said master and her eyes remained fixed on her eldest sister.

"Do we even have a family anymore?" Rebecca said, slapping her hand on her desk with irritation.

"That's entirely up to you, Rebecca." Breanna shrugged and continued curtly, "I think you're confused about the difference between the House of Maine and family."

"They are one and the same, Breanna," Rebecca responded with equal vehemence.

Breanna snorted, "With all due respect, my dear sister, they are not. One is a hereditary government organization, and the other is." Breanna's voice faulted as she realized she had not thought out clearly what she was saying. "Well, family is family."

"The House of Maine is bonded by blood." Rebecca would not give it up. "It has lost our father. It has lost our brother. Rachael has left it, and now you. That leaves me, Petra, and Alannah. And it is highly doubtful the King would recognize Petra."

"It is not the family that concerns you, Rebecca," Bree retorted. "It's the family name and all that honor bullshit that goes with it. The House of Maine is dead and good riddance."

The hand that slapped across Breanna's face stung her cheek only slightly; however, the fact that Rebecca had done it stung Breanna within.

Breanna slowly reached up to rub her face. "Fuck you," she said softly. "Fuck you. Fuck this family and fuck the House of Maine."

Rebecca clearly already regretted what she had just done even before Breanna strode from the room. Rachael glared at Rebecca but said nothing. She just shook her head despondently and turned to follow her sister out.

Tears began to well up in Rebecca's eyes, and she turned away from Sebastian in shame.

"Rebecca," he said softly, but she did not look back. "I understand how you feel. I really do. I would like to be able to say to you that this is not my will. In truth, it is the will of Ilya, but I would be lying if I did not say I was proud of both Rachael and Breanna for the decisions they have made." Rebecca did not respond and just stood, arms folded, resolute, and staring out of the window. "As you and Breanna are sisters, I'm going to let it pass that you struck her. I will not do so if it happens again."

Rebecca spun about, her eyes filled with resentment. "I once laughed at Ronan for saying I brought a serpent into the House of Maine, but it appears that he was right."

Sebastian did not reply straight away. He just stared at her for a moment or two before finally saying, "If your best argument is to quote your incompetent brother, then you really have no argument at all."

To Rebecca's embarrassment, the tears now flowed freely. "Do not speak ill of Ronan. I know what he was, but he is now dead. He was still my brother, and you did not have to watch him be killed."

Sebastian started at this and narrowed his eyes questioningly, "I thought it was you who killed Ronan. At least that was the plan."

"I could not do it. It was Annabel who actually stabbed him."

Sebastian did not know what to think of that, but he simply put it aside for later consideration. He knew that Annabelle Devon was only motivated by self-interest and certainly would not have put herself at risk of the hangman's noose for a member of the House of Maine unless it was going to benefit her considerably.

Sebastian sighed and tried to reach out a comforting hand to Rebecca. However, she stepped back out of his reach. "I trusted you, Sebastian. I trusted you to take care of my sisters."

"And that I am doing, Rebecca. It may not be in a way that you envisaged, but I am..." He stopped and corrected himself. "Illya is giving them a destiny that is so much better for them than the one dictated by the line of kings or the House of Maine."

"Sebastian, I will not let you break up my family. I am committed to the reformation of the House of Maine, and that cannot be done if the House does not have members. You were pledged to me long before you were pledged to your goddess, and I expect you to honor that ."

Never before had the Preacher seen such determination in those young eyes as she fixed him in her gaze. With equal determination, he glared back and, with a voice filled with incredulity, said, "Are you seriously asking me to put you before Illya?"

"I am simply asking you to honor the oath you made fifteen years ago. Breaking such an oath is considered to be treason."

Sebastian couldn't help but laugh mercilessly at that. "You forget the Treaty of Mercia sweeps away all of that. I am officially pardoned of all crimes against the state and released from all bonds in my role as a cleric."

To his surprise, Rebecca merely smirked. "Yes, I've been thinking about that treaty. Does it not say the churches shall not raise arms against the state."

"Only in self-defense, but what are you getting at?"

"Surely you cannot disagree that attacking the House of Maine nullifies that treaty," she said quite coldly.

"Of course, it would, but..." he stopped mid-sentence, his confusion turning to realization. "The Commech are signatories to the Treaty of Massir," he said despondently.

"Indeed they are, Sebastian." she gave him a vitriolic grin. "When they invaded Ithia, the treaty was effectively torn up."

Sebastian sighed "I cannot refute this and can only say I am pleased that Ronan did not realize this."

"My brother is no longer the head of the House of Maine by either proxy or right. I am the rightful heir of my father, and I say to you now that I expect your oath to be honored."

"Even if I was to consider that, my oath is to the First Lady of Jilrir, and if you are now claiming to be the Baroness, then the first lady is Petra if her legitimacy is confirmed," Sebastian growled.

Rebecca did not relent. "Until there is a ruling on that, you are beholden to me, and I'm telling you very clearly and plainly to release Rachael and Breanna from these holy orders that you have convinced them to participate in."

Now, Sebastian's patience failed. "Even if I were able to do that, I wouldn't. It is not my choice, nor is it now theirs."

"I am your mistress, Sebastian, and I command it," Rebecca shouted back.

"And I adamantly refused to do so. As I have said, I cannot even if I wanted to, which I don't."

"Then you leave me no choice, Sebastian." Rebecca's voice lowered, but the venom in her tone did not. "You are now guilty of treason. You are to leave the service of the House of Maine, and you are to leave Nethili. For your services to my family, you will be exempt from the death penalty for this crime. But you are outlawed and no longer subject to the protection of the state. You are stateless and without rights."

Sebastian laughed, but there was no humor in his voice. "If I am to leave, then both Rachael and Breanna are coming with me. Do you realize this?"

"I forbid it. You will leave, and you will leave them behind."

There was a long silence as the two incredibly large egos stared at each other across the desk before, in barely a whisper, Sebastian growled. "Over my dead body."

"If necessary, Sebastian," Rebecca replied with equal vehemence. But you will be out of this town before the sun sets, and you will not take my sisters with you even if I have to lock them up."

It was his turn to pause and lower his voice and temperament. "You have just declared war against a servant of Illya. You have not revived the House of Maine. You have ended it." With that, Sebastian turned away from her and strode from the room, trying to hold back his fury.

If Rebecca wanted to fight, he was going to give her one. Blood would run in the streets of Nethili before he ever gave up Rachael or Breanna.

Produced by Tairis Anders Media, LLC